Pra

THE
FAR SIDE
OF THE DOLLAR
and Ross Macdonald

* * *

"It was not just that Ross Macdonald
taught us how to write; he did something
much more, he taught us how to read,
and how to think about life, and maybe
in some small, but mattering way, how
to live.... I owe him."

—Robert B. Parker

* * *

"Ross Macdonald must be ranked high
amongst American thriller writers."

—*The Times Literary Supplement*
(London)

* * *

more....

"Reveals a disturbing segment of California coastal society. . . . As always, Mr. Macdonald's persons and environment enrich his schema."

—*Book Week*

* * *

"Macdonald should not be limited in audience to connoisseurs of mystery fiction. He is one of a handful of writers in the genre whose worth and quality surpass the limitations of the form."

—**Robert Kirsch,** *Los Angeles Times*

* * *

"Ross Macdonald gives to the detective story that accent of class that the late Raymond Chandler did."

—**Seymour Korman,** *Chicago Tribune*

* * *

"Ross Macdonald's work has consistently nourished me. . . . I have turned to it often to hear what I should like to call the justice of its voice and to be enlightened by its wisdom, delighted by its imagination, and, not incidentally, superbly entertained."

—**Thomas Berger**

* * *

Also by Ross Macdonald

The Moving Target
The Chill
The Galton Case
The Blue Hammer
The Way Some People Die

Published by
WARNER BOOKS

ROSS MACDONALD

◆

THE FAR SIDE OF THE DOLLAR

A LEW ARCHER NOVEL

WARNER BOOKS

A Time Warner Company

The people and events in this novel are all imaginary, and do not refer to any actual people or events.

R.M.

WARNER BOOKS EDITION

Copyright © 1964 by Ross Macdonald
All rights reserved. This book may not be reproduced in whole or in part, by mimeograph or any other means, without permission.

This Warner Books Edition is published by arrangement with
Alfred A. Knopf, Inc., 201 East 50th Street, New York, New York 10022

Cover design by Jackie Merri Meyer
Cover illustration by Gary Kelley

Warner Books, Inc.
666 Fifth Avenue
New York, N.Y. 10103

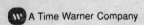 A Time Warner Company

Printed in the United States of America

First Warner Books Printing: July, 1990
10 9 8 7 6 5 4 3 2

To Alfred

1

_____

It was August, and it shouldn't have been raining. Perhaps rain was too strong a word for the drizzle that blurred the landscape and kept my windshield wipers going. I was driving south, about halfway between Los Angeles and San Diego.

The school lay off the highway to my right, in large grounds of its own which stretched along the seashore. Toward the sea I caught the dull sheen of the slough that gave the place its name, Laguna Perdida. A blue heron, tiny in the distance, stood like a figurine at the edge of the ruffled water.

I entered the grounds through automatic gates which lifted when my car passed over a treadle. A gray-headed man in a blue serge uniform came out of a kiosk and limped in my direction.

"You got a pass?"

"Dr. Sponti wants to see me. My name is Archer."

"That's right, I got your name here." He took a typewritten list out of the inside breast pocket of his jacket and brandished it as if he was proud of his literacy. "You can park in the lot in front of the administration building. Sponti's office is right inside." He gestured toward a stucco building a hundred yards down the road.

I thanked him. He started to limp back to his kiosk, then paused and turned and struck himself on the leg. "Bad knee. World War I."

"You don't look that old."

"I'm not. I was fifteen when I enlisted, told them I was eighteen. Some of the boys in here," he said with a sudden flashing look around him, "could do with a taste of fire."

There were no boys anywhere in sight. The buildings of the school, widely distributed among bare fields and dripping

1

eucalyptus groves, lay under the gray sky like scattered components of an unbuilt city.

"Do you know the Hillman boy?" I said to the guard.

"I heard about him. He's a troublemaker. He had East Hall all stirred up before he took off. Patch was fit to be tied."

"Who's Patch?"

"Mr. Patch," he said without affection, "is the supervisor for East Hall. He lives in with the boys, and it plays hell with his nerves."

"What did the Hillman boy do?"

"Tried to start a rebellion, according to Patch. Said the boys in the school had civil rights like anybody else. Which ain't so. They're all minors, and most of them are crazy in the head, besides. You wouldn't believe some of the things I've seen in my fourteen years on this gate."

"Did Tommy Hillman go out through the gate?"

"Naw. He went over the fence. Cut a screen in the boys' dorm and sneaked out in the middle of the night."

"Night before last?"

"That's right. He's probably home by now."

He wasn't or I wouldn't have been there.

Dr. Sponti must have seen me parking my car. He was waiting for me in the secretary's enclosure outside the door of his office. He had a glass of buttermilk in his left hand and a dietetic wafer in his right. He popped the wafer into his mouth and shook my hand, munching, "I'm glad to see you."

He was dark and florid and stout, with the slightly desperate look of a man who had to lose weight. I guessed that he was an emotional man—he had that liquid tremor of the eye—but one who had learned to keep his feelings under control. He was expensively and conservatively dressed in a dark pinstripe suit which hung on him a little loosely. His hand was soft and chilly.

Dr. Sponti reminded me of undertakers I had known. Even his office, with its dark mahogany furniture and the gray light at the window, had a funereal look, as if the school and its director were in continuous mourning for its students.

"Sit down," he said with a melancholy flourish. "We have a little problem, as I told you on the long-distance telephone. Ordinarily we don't employ private detectives to—ah—persuade our lost boys to come home. But this is a rather special case, I'm afraid."

"What makes it special?"

Sponti sipped his buttermilk, and licked his upper lip with the tip of his tongue. "Forgive me. Can I offer you some lunch?"

"No thanks."

"I don't mean this." Irritably, he jiggled the sluggish liquid in his glass. "I can have something hot sent over from dining commons. Veal scallopini is on the menu today."

"No thanks. I'd rather you gave me the information I need and let me get to work. Why did you call me in to pick up a runaway? You must have a lot of runaways."

"Not as many as you might think. Most of our boys become quite school-centered in time. We have a rich and varied program for them. But Thomas Hillman had been here less than a week, and he showed very little promise of becoming group-oriented. He's quite a difficult young man."

"And that's what makes him special?"

"I'll be frank with you, Mr. Archer," he said, and hesitated. "This is rather a prickly situation for the school. I accepted Tom Hillman against my better judgment, actually without full knowledge of his history, simply because his father insisted upon it. And now Ralph Hillman blames us for his son's esca—that is, his surreptitious leavetaking. Hillman has threatened to sue if any harm comes to the boy. The suit wouldn't stand up in court—we've had such lawsuits before—but it could do us a great deal of public harm." He added, almost to himself: "Patch really was at fault."

"What did Patch do?"

"I'm afraid he was unnecessarily violent. Not that I blame him as man to man. But you'd better talk to Mr. Patch yourself. He can give you all the details of Tom's—ah—departure."

"Later, I'd like to talk to him. But you can tell me more about the boy's background."

"Not as much as I'd like. We ask the families, or their doctors, to give us a detailed history of our entering students. Mr. Hillman promised to write one, but he hasn't as yet. And I've had great difficulty in getting any facts out of him. He's a very proud and very angry man."

"And a wealthy one?"

'I don't know his Dun and Bradstreet rating. Most of our parents are comfortably fixed," he added with a quick little smug smile.

"I'd like to see Hillman. Does he live in town?"

"Yes, but please don't try to see him, at least not today. He's just been on the phone to me again, and it would only stir him up further."

Sponti rose from his desk and moved to the window that overlooked the parking lot. I followed him. The fine rain outside hung like a visible depression in the air.

"I still need a detailed description of the boy, and everything I can find out about his habits."

"Patch can give you that, better than I. He's been in daily contact with him. And you can talk to his housemother, Mrs. Mallow. She's a trained observer."

"Let's hope somebody is." I was getting impatient with Sponti. He seemed to feel that the less he told me about the missing boy, the less real his disappearance was. "How old is he, or is that classified material?"

Sponti's eyes crossed slightly, and his rather pendulous cheeks became faintly mottled. "I object to your tone."

"That's your privilege. How old is Tom Hillman?"

"Seventeen."

"Do you have a picture of him?"

"None was provided by the family, though we ask for one as a matter of routine. I can tell you briefly what he looks like. He's quite a decent-looking young chap, if you overlook the sullen expression he wears habitually. He's quite big, around six feet, he looks older than his age."

"Eyes?"

"Dark blue, I think. His hair is dark blond. He has what might be called aquiline features, like his father."

"Identifying marks?"

He shrugged his shoulders. "I know of none."

"Why was he brought here?"

"For treatment, of course. But he didn't stay long enough to benefit."

"Exactly what's the matter with him? You said he was difficult, but that's a pretty general description."

"It was meant to be. It's hard to tell what ails these boys in adolescent storm. Often we help them without knowing how or why. I'm not a medical doctor, in any case."

"I thought you were."

"No. We have medical doctors associated with our staff, of course, both physicians and psychiatrists. There wouldn't be much point in talking to them. I doubt if Tom was here long enough even to meet his therapist. But there's no doubt he was high."

"High?"

"Emotionally high, running out of control. He was in a bad way when his father brought him here. We gave him tranquillizers, but they don't always work in the same way on different subjects."

"Did he cause you a lot of trouble?"

"He did indeed. Frankly, I doubt if we'll readmit him even if he does come back."

"But you're hiring me to find him."

"I have no choice."

We discussed money matters, and he gave me a check. Then I walked down the road to East Hall. Before I went in to see Mr. Patch, I turned and looked at the mountains on the far side of the valley. They loomed like half-forgotten faces through the overcast. The lonely blue heron rose from the edge of the slough and sailed toward them.

2

East Hall was a sprawling one-story stucco building which somehow didn't belong on that expansive landscape. Its mean and unprepossessing air had something to do with the high little windows, all of them heavily screened. Or with the related fact that it was a kind of prison which pretended not to be. The spiky pyracantha shrubs bordering the lawn in front of the building were more like barriers than ornaments. The grass looked dispirited even in the rain.

So did the line of boys who were marching in the front door as I came up. Boys of all ages from twelve to twenty, boys of all shapes and sizes, with only one thing in common: they marched like members of a defeated army. They reminded me of the very young soldiers we captured on the Rhine in the last stages of the last war.

Two student leaders kept them in some sort of line. I followed them, into a big lounge furnished with rather dilapidated furniture. The two leaders went straight to a ping-pong table that stood in one corner, picked up paddles, and began to play a rapid intense game with a ball that one of them produced from his windbreaker pocket. Six or seven boys began to watch them. Four or five settled down with comic books. Most of the rest of them stood around and watched me.

A hairy-faced young fellow who ought to have started to shave came up to me smiling. His smile was brilliant, but it faded like an optical illusion. He came so close that his shoulder nudged my arm. Some dogs will nudge you like that, to test your friendliness.

"Are you the new supervisor?"

"No. I thought Mr. Patch was the supervisor."

"He won't last." A few of the younger boys giggled. The hairy one responded like a successful comedian. "This is the violent ward. They never last."

"It doesn't look so violent to me. Where is Mr. Patch?"

"Over at dining commons. He'll be here in a minute. Then we have organized fun."

"You sound pretty cynical for your age. How old are you?"

"Ninety-nine." His audience murmured encouragingly. "Mr. Patch is only forty-nine. It makes it hard for him to be my father-image."

"Maybe I could talk to Mrs. Mallow."

"She's in her room drinking her lunch. Mrs. Mallow always drinks her lunch." The bright malice in his eyes alternated with a darker feeling. "Are you a father?"

"No."

In the background the ping-pong ball was clicking back and forth like mindless conversation.

A member of the audience spoke up. "He's not a father."

"Maybe he's a mother," said the hairy boy. "Are you a mother?"

"He doesn't look like a mother. He has no bosoms."

"My mother has no bosoms," said a third one. "That's why I feel rejected."

"Come off it, boys." The hell of it was, they wished I was a father, or even a mother, one of theirs, and the wish stood in their eyes. "You don't want me to feel rejected, do you?"

Nobody answered. The hairy boy smiled up at me. It lasted a little longer than his first smile. "What's your name? I'm Frederick Tyndal the Third."

"I'm Lew Archer the First."

I drew the boy away from his audience. He pulled back from my touch, but he came along and sat down with me on a cracked leather couch. Some of the younger boys had put an overplayed record on a player. Two of them began to dance together to the raucous self-parodying song. "Surfin' ain't no sin," was the refrain.

"Did you know Tom Hillman, Fred?"

"A little. Are you his father?"

"No. I said I wasn't a father."

"Adults don't necessarily tell you the truth." He plucked at the hairs on his chin as if he hated the signs of growing up. "My father said he was sending me away to military school. He's a big shot in the government," he added flatly, without pride, and then, in a different tone: "Tom Hillman didn't get along with his father, either. So he got railroaded here. The Monorail to the Magic Kingdom." He produced a fierce ecstatic hopeless grin.

"Did Tom talk to you about it?"

"A little. He wasn't here long. Five days. Six. He came in Sunday night and took off Saturday night." He squirmed uneasily on the creaking leather. "Are you a cop?"

"No."

"I just wondered. You ask questions like a cop."

"Did Tom do something that would interest the cops?"

"We all do, don't we?" His hot and cold running glance went around the room, pausing on the forlorn antics of the dancing boys. "You don't qualify for East Hall unless you're a juvie. I was a criminal mastermind myself. I forged the big shot's name on a fifty-dollar check and went to San Francisco for the weekend."

"What did Tom do?"

"Stole a car, I guess. It was a first offense, he said, and he would of got probation easy. But his father didn't want the publicity, so he put him in here. Also, I guess Tom had a fight with his father."

"I see."

"Why are you so fascinated in Tom?"

"I'm supposed to find him, Fred."

"And bring him back here?"

"I doubt that they'll readmit him."

"He's lucky." More or less unconsciously, he moved against me again. I could smell the untended odor of his hair and body, and sense his desolation. "I'd break out of here myself if I had a place to go. But the big shot would turn me over to the Youth Authority. It would save him money, besides."

"Did Tom have a place to go?"

He jerked upright and looked at my eyes from the corners of his. "I didn't say that."

"I'm asking you."

"He wouldn't tell me if he had."

"Who was closest to him in the school?"

"He wasn't close to anybody. He was so upset when he came in, they put him in a room by himself. I went in and talked to him one night, but he didn't say much to me."

"Nothing about where he planned to go?"

"He didn't *plan* anything. He tried to start a riot Saturday night but the rest of us were chicken. So he took off. He seemed to be very excited."

"Was he emotionally disturbed?"

"Aren't we all?" He tapped his own temple and made an insane face. "You ought to see my Rorschach."

"Some other time."

"Be my guest."

"This is important, Fred. Tom is very young, and excited, as you said. He's been missing for two nights now, and he could get into very serious trouble."

"Worse than this?"

"You know it, or you'd be over the fence yourself. Did Tom say anything about where he was going?"

The boy didn't answer.

"Then I assume he did tell you something?"

"No." But he wouldn't meet my eyes.

Mr. Patch came into the room and changed its carefree atmosphere. The dancing boys pretended to be wrestling. Comic books disappeared like bundles of hot money. The ping-pong players put away their ball.

Patch was a middle-aged man with thinning hair and thickening jowls. His double-breasted tan gabardine suit was creased across his rather corpulent front. His face was creased, too, into a sneer of power which didn't go with his sensitive small mouth. As he looked around the room, I could see that the whites of his eyes were tinted with red.

He strode to the record player and turned it off, insinuating his voice into the silence:

"Lunch time isn't music time, boys. Music time is after dinner, from seven to seven-thirty." He addressed one of the ping-pong players: "Bear that in mind, Deering. No music in the daytime. I'll hold you responsible."

"Yessir."

"And weren't you playing ping-pong?"

"We were just rallying, sir."

"Where did you get the ball? I understood the balls were locked up in my desk."

"They are, sir."

"Where did you get the one you were playing with?"

"I don't know, sir." Deering fumbled at his windbreaker. He was a gawky youth with an Adam's apple that looked like a hidden ping-pong ball. "I think I must of found it."

"Where did you find it? In my desk?"

"No sir. On the grounds, I think it was."

Mr. Patch walked toward him with a kind of melodramatic stealth. As he moved across the room, the boys behind him made faces, waved their arms, did bumps and grinds. One boy, one of the dancers, fell silently to the floor with a throat-slitting gesture, held the pose of a dying gladiator for a single frozen second, then got back onto his feet.

Patch was saying in a long-suffering tone: "You bought it, didn't you, Deering? You know that regulations forbid you fellows to bring in private ping-pong balls of your own. You know that, don't you? You're president of the East Hall Legislative Assembly, you helped to frame those regulations yourself. Didn't you?"

"Yessir."

"Then give it to me, Deering."

The boy handed Patch the ball. Patch stooped to place it on the floor—while a boy behind him pretended to kick him—and squashed it under his heel. He gave Deering the misshapen ball.

"I'm sorry, Deering. I have to obey the regulations just as you do." He turned to the roomful of boys, who snapped into conformity under his eyes, and said mildly: "Well, fellows, what's on the agenda—?"

"I think I am," I said, getting up from the couch. I gave him my name and asked if I could talk to him in private.

"I suppose so," he said with a worried smile, as if I might in fact be his successor. "Come into my office, such as it is. Deering and Bronson, I'm leaving you in charge."

His office was a windowless cubicle containing a cluttered desk and two straight chairs. He closed the door on the noise that drifted down the corridor from the lounge, turned on a desk lamp, and sat down sighing.

"You've got to stay on top of them." He sounded like a man saying his prayers. "You wanted to discuss one of my boys?"

"Tom Hillman."

The name depressed him. "You represent his father?"

"No. Dr. Sponti sent me to talk to you. I'm a private detective."

"I see." He pushed out his lips in a kind of a pout. "I suppose Sponti's been blaming me, as usual."

"He did say something about unnecessary violence."

"That's nonsense!" He pounded the desk between us with his clenched fist. His face became congested with blood. Then it went starkly pale, like a raw photograph. Only the reddish whites of his eyes held their color. "Sponti doesn't work down here with the animals. I ought to know when physical discipline is necessary. I've been in juvenile work for twenty-five years."

"It seems to be getting you down."

With an effort that crumpled up his face, he brought himself under control. "Oh no, I love the work, I really do. Anyway, it's the only thing I'm trained for. I love the boys. And they love me."

"I could see that."

He wasn't listening for my irony. "I'd have been pals with Tom Hillman if he'd lasted."

"Why didn't he?"

"He ran away. You know that. He stole a pair of shears from the gardener and used it to cut the screen on his bedroom window."

"Exactly when was this?"

"Sometime Saturday night, between my eleven-o'clock bed-check and my early-morning one."

"And what happened before that?"

"Saturday night, you mean? He was stirring up the other boys, inciting them to attack the resident staff. I'd left the common room after dinner, and I heard him from in here, making a speech. He was trying to convince the boys that they had been deprived of their rights and should fight for them. Some of the more excitable ones were affected. But when I ordered Hillman to shut up, he was the only one who rushed me."

"Did he hit you?"

"I hit him first," Patch said. "I'm not ashamed of it. I had to preserve my authority with the others." He rubbed his fist. "I knocked him cold. You have to make a show of manliness. When I hit them, they go down for the count. You have to give them an image to respect."

I said to stop him: "What happened after that?"

"I helped him to his room, and then I reported the incident to Sponti. I thought the boy should be put in the padded room. But Sponti countermanded my advice. Hillman would never have broken out if Sponti had let me put him in the padded room. Just between you and me, it's Sponti's fault." He brought himself up short and said in a smaller voice: "Don't quote me to him."

"All right."

I was beginning to despair of getting anything useful out of Patch. He was a little dilapidated, like the furniture in the common room. The noise coming from that direction was becoming louder. Patch rose wearily to his feet.

"I'd better get back there before they tear the place down."

"I just wanted to ask you, do you have any thoughts on where Tom Hillman went after he left here?"

Patch considered my question. He seemed to be having difficulty in imagining the outside world into which the boy had vanished. "L.A.," he said finally. "They usually head for L.A. Or else they head south for San Diego and the border."

"Or east?"

"If their parents live east, they sometimes go that way."

"Or west across the ocean?" I was baiting him.

"That's true. One boy stole a thirty-foot launch and headed for the islands."

"You seem to have a lot of runaways."

"Over the years, we have quite a turnover. Sponti's opposed to strict security measures, like we used to have at Juvenile Hall. With all the breakouts we've had, I'm surprised he wants to make such a production out of this one. The boy'll turn up, they nearly always do.''

Patch sounded as if he wasn't looking forward to the prospect.

Somebody tapped at the door behind me. "Mr. Patch?" a woman said through the panels.

"Yes, Mrs. Mallow."

"The boys are getting out of hand. They won't listen to me. What are you doing in there?"

"Conferring. Dr. Sponti sent a man."

"Good. We need a man."

"Is that so?" He brushed past me and opened the door. "Keep your cracks to yourself, please, Mrs. Mallow. I know one or two things that Dr. Sponti would dearly love to know."

"So do I," the woman said.

She was heavily rouged, with dyed red hair arranged in bangs on her forehead. She had on a dark formal dress, about ten years out of fashion, and several loops of imitation pearls. Her face was pleasant enough, in spite of eyes that had been bleared by horrors inner and outer.

She brightened up when she saw me. "Hello."

"My name is Archer," I said. "Dr. Sponti brought me in to look into Tom Hillman's disappearance."

"He's a nice-looking boy." she said. "At least he was until our local Marquis de Sade gave him a working-over."

"I acted in self-defense," Patch cried. "I don't enjoy hurting people. I'm the authority figure in East Hall, and when I'm attacked it's just like killing their father."

"You better go and make with the authority, Father. But if you hurt anybody this week I'll carve the living heart out of your body."

Patch looked at her as if he believed she might do it. Then he turned on his heel and strode away toward the roaring room. The roaring subsided abruptly, as if he had closed a soundproof door behind him.

"Poor old Patch," said Mrs. Mallow. "He's been around too long. Poor old all of us. Too many years of contact with the adolescent mind, if mind is the word, and eventually we all go blah."

"Why stay?"

"We get so we can't live in the outside world. Like old convicts. That's the real hell of it."

"People around here are extraordinarily ready to spill their problems—"

"It's the psychiatric atmosphere."

"But," I went on, "they don't tell me much I want to know. Can *you* give me clear impression of Tom Hillman?"

"I can give you my own impression."

She had a little difficulty with the word, and it seemed to affect her balance. She walked into Patch's office and leaned on his desk facing me. Her face, half-shadowed in the upward light from the lamp, reminded me of a sibyl's.

"Tom Hillman is a pretty nice boy. He didn't belong here. He found that out in a hurry. And so he left."

"Why didn't he belong here?"

"You want me to go into detail? East Hall is essentially a place for boys with personality and character problems, or with a sociopathic tendency. We keep the more disturbed youngsters, boys and girls, in West Hall."

"And Tom belonged there?"

"Hardly. He shouldn't have been sent to Laguna Perdida at all. This is just my opinion, but it ought to be worth something. I used to be a pretty good clinical psychologist." She looked down into the light.

'Dr. Sponti seems to think Tom was disturbed."

"Dr. Sponti never thinks otherwise, about any prospect. Do you know what these kids' parents pay? A thousand dollars a month, plus extras. Music lessons. Group therapy." She laughed harshly. "When half the time it's the parents who should be here. Or in some worse place."

'A thousand dollars a month," she repeated. "So Dr. Sponti so-called can draw his twenty-five thousand a year. Which is more than six times what he pays me for holding the kids' hands."

She was a woman with a grievance. Sometimes grievances made for truth-telling, but not always. "What do you mean, Dr. Sponti so-called?"

"He's not a medical doctor, or any other kind of real doctor. He took his degree in educational administration, at one of the diploma mills down south. Do you know what he wrote his dissertation on? The kitchen logistics of the medium-sized boarding school."

"Getting back to Tom," I said, "why would his father bring him here if he didn't need psychiatric treatment?"

"I don't know. I don't know his father. Probably because he wanted him out of his sight."

"Why?" I insisted.

"The boy was in some kind of trouble."

"Did Tom tell you that?"

"He wouldn't talk about it. But I can read the signs."

"Have you heard the story that he stole a car?"

'No, but it would help to explain him. He's a very unhappy young man, and a guilty one. He isn't one of your hardened j.d.'s. Not that any of them *really* are."

"You seem to have liked Tom Hillman."

"What little I saw of him. He didn't want to talk last week, and I try never to force myself on the boys. Except for class hours, he spent most of the time in his room. I think he was trying to work something out."

"Like a plan for revolution?"

Her eyes glinted with amusement. "You heard about that, did you? The boy had more gumption than I gave him credit for. Don't look so surprised. I'm on the boys' side. Why else would I be here?"

I was beginning to like Mrs. Mallow. Sensing this, she moved toward me and touched my arm. "I hope that you are, too. On Tom's side, I mean."

"I'll wait until I know him. It isn't important, anyway."

"Yes it is. It's always important."

"Just what happened between Tom and Mr. Patch Saturday night?"

"I wouldn't know, really. Saturday night is my night off. You can make a note of that if you like, Mr. Archer."

She smiled, and I caught a glimpse of her life's meaning. She cared for other people. Nobody cared for her.

3

She let me out through a side door which had to be unlocked. The rain was just heavy enough to wet my face. Dense-looking clouds were gathering over the mountains, which probably meant that the rain was going to persist.

I started back toward the administration building. Sponti was going to have to be told that I must see Tom Hillman's parents, whether he approved or not. The varying accounts of Tom I'd had, from people who liked or disliked him, gave me no distinct impression of his habits or personality. He could be a persecuted teen-ager, or a psychopath who knew how to appeal to older women, or something in between, like Fred the Third.

I wasn't looking where I was going, and a yellow cab almost ran me down in the parking lot. A man in tweeds got out of the back seat. I thought he was going to apologize to me, but he didn't appear to see me.

He was a tall, silver-haired man, well fed, well cared for, probably good-looking under normal conditions. At the moment he looked haggard. He ran into the administration building. I walked in after him, and found him arguing with Sponti's secretary.

"I'm very sorry, Mr. Hillman," she intoned. "Dr. Sponti is in conference. I can't possibly interrupt him."

"I think you'd better," Hillman said in a rough voice.

"I'm sorry. You'll have to wait."

"But I can't wait. My son is in the hands of criminals. They're trying to extort money from me."

"Is that true?" Her voice was unprofessional and sharp.

"I'm not in the habit of lying."

The girl excused herself and went into Sponti's office, closing the door carefully behind her. I spoke to Hillman, telling him my name and occupation:

"Dr. Sponti called me in to look for your son. I've been wanting to talk to you. It seems to be time I did."

"Yes. By all means."

He took my hand. He was a large, impressive-looking man. His face had the kind of patrician bony structure that doesn't necessarily imply brains or ability, or even decency, but that generally goes with money. He was deep in the chest and heavy in the shoulders. But there was no force in his grasp. He was trembling all over, like a frightened dog.

"You said something about criminals and extortion."

"Yes." But his steel-gray eyes kept shifting away to the door of Sponti's office. He wanted to talk to somebody he could blame. "What are they doing in there?" he said a little wildly.

"It hardly matters. If your son's been kidnapped, Sponti can't help you much. It's a matter for the police."

"No! The police stay out. I've been instructed to keep them out." His eyes focused on me for the first time, hard with suspicion. "You're not a policeman, are you?"

"I told you I was a private detective. I just came down from Los Angeles an hour ago. How did you find out about Tom, and who gave you your instructions?"

"One of the gang. He telephoned my house when we were just sitting down to lunch. He warned me to keep the matter quiet. Otherwise Tom will never come back."

"Did he say that?"

"Yes."

"What else did he say?"

"They want to sell me information about Tom's whereabouts. It was just a euphemism for ransom money."

"How much?"

"Twenty-five thousand dollars."

"Do you have it?"

"I'll have it by the middle of the afternoon. I'm selling some stock. I went into town to my broker's before I came here."

"You move fast, Mr. Hillman." He needed some mark of respect. "But I don't quite understand why you came out here."

"I don't trust these people," he said in a lowered voice. Apparently he had forgotten, or hadn't heard, that I was working for Sponti. "I believe that Tom was lured away from here, perhaps with inside help, and they're covering up."

"I doubt that very much. I've talked to the staff member involved. He and Tom had a fight Saturday night, and later Tom cut a screen and went over the fence. One of the students confirmed this, more or less."

"A student would be afraid to deny the official story."

"Not this student, Mr. Hillman. If your son's been kidnapped, it happened after he left here. Tell me this, did he have any criminal connections?"

"Tom? You must be out of your mind."

"I heard he stole a car."

"Did Sponti tell you that? He had no right to."

"I got it from other sources. Boys don't usually steal cars

unless they've had some experience outside the law, perhaps with a juvenile gang—"

"He didn't steal it." Hillman's eyes were evasive. "He borrowed it from a neighbor. The fact the he wrecked it was pure accident. He was emotionally upset—"

Hillman was, too. He ran out of breath and words. He opened and closed his mouth like a big handsome fish hooked by circumstance and yanked into alien air. I said:

"What are you supposed to do with the twenty-five thousand? Hold it for further instructions?"

Hillman nodded, and sat down despondently in a chair. Dr. Sponti's door had opened, and he had been listening, I didn't know for how long. He came out into the anteroom now, flanked by his secretary and followed by a man with a long cadaverous face.

"What's this about kidnapping?" Sponti said in a high voice. He forced his voice down into a more soothing register: "I'm sorry, Mr. Hillman."

Hillman's sitting position changed to a kind of crouch. "You're going to be sorrier. I want to know who took my son out of here, and under what circumstances, and with whose connivance."

"Your son left here of his own free will, Mr. Hillman."

"And you wash your hands of him, do you?"

"We never do that with any of our charges, however short their stay. I've hired Mr. Archer here to help you out. And I've just been talking to Mr. Squerry here, our comptroller."

The cadaverous man bowed solemnly. Black stripes of hair were pasted flat across the crown of his almost naked head. He said in a precise voice:

"Dr. Sponti and I have decided to refund in full the money you paid us last week. We've just written out a check, and here it is."

He handed over a slip of yellow paper. Hillman crumpled it into a ball and threw it back at Mr. Squerry. It bounced off his thin chest and fell to the floor. I picked it up. It was for two thousand dollars.

Hillman ran out of the room. I walked out after him, before Sponti could terminate my services, and caught Hillman as he was getting into the cab.

"Where are you going?"

"Home. My wife's in poor shape."

"Let me drive you."

"Not if you're Sponti's man."

"I'm nobody's man but my own. Sponti hired me to find your son. I'm going to do that if it's humanly possible. But I'll need some cooperation from you and Mrs. Hillman."

"What can we do?" He spread his large helpless hands.

"Tell me what kind of a boy he is, who his friends are, where he hangs out—"

"What's the point of all that? He's in the hands of gangsters. They want money. I'm willing to pay them."

The cab driver, who had got out of his seat to open the door for Hillman, stood listening with widening mouth and eyes.

"It may not be as simple as that," I said. "But we won't talk about it here."

"You can trust me," the driver said huskily. "I got a brother-in-law on the Highway Patrol. Besides, I never blab about my fares."

"You better not," Hillman said.

He paid the man, and came along with me to my car.

"Speaking of money," I said when we were together in the front seat, "you didn't really want to throw away two thousand dollars, did you?" I smoothed out the yellow check and handed it to him.

There's no way to tell what will make a man break down. A long silence, or a telephone ringing, or the wrong note in a woman's voice. In Hillman's case, it was a check for two thousand dollars. He put it away in his alligator wallet, and then he groaned loudly. He covered his eyes with his hands and leaned his forehead on the dash. Cawing sounds came out of his mouth as if an angry crow was tearing at his vitals.

After a while he said: "I should never have put him in this place." His voice was more human than it had been, as if he had broken through into a deeper level of self-knowledge.

"Don't cry over spilt milk."

He straightened up. "I wasn't crying." It was true his eyes were dry.

"We won't argue, Mr. Hillman. Where do you live?"

"In El Rancho. It's between here and the city. I'll tell you how to get there by the shortest route."

The guard limped out of his kiosk, and we exchanged half-salutes. He activated the gates. Following Hillman's instructions, I drove out along a road which passed through a reedy wasteland where blackbirds were chittering, then through a suburban wasteland jammed with new apartments, and around the perimeter of a college campus. We passed an airport, where a plane was taking off. Hillman looked as if he wished he were on it.

"Why did you put your son in Laguna Perdida School?"

His answer came slowly, in bits and snatches. "I was afraid. He seemed to be headed for trouble. I felt I had to prevent it somehow. I was hoping they could straighten him out so that he could go back to regular school next month. He's supposed to be starting his senior year in high school."

"Would you mind being specific about the trouble he was in? Do you mean car theft?"

"That was one of the things. But it wasn't a true case of theft, as I explained."

"You didn't explain, though."

"It was Rhea Carlson's automobile he took. Rhea and Jay Carlson are our next-door neighbors. When you leave a new Dart in an open carport all night with the key in the ignition, it's practically an invitation to a joyride. I told them that. Jay would've admitted it, too, if he hadn't had a bit of a down on Tom. Or if Tom hadn't wrecked the car. It was fully covered, by my insurance as well as theirs, but they had to take the emotional approach."

"The car was wrecked?"

"It's a total loss. I don't know how he managed to turn it over, but he did. Fortunately he came out of it without a scratch."

"Where was he going?"

"He was on his way home. The accident happened practically at our door. I'll show you the place."

"Then where had he been?"

"He wouldn't say. He'd been gone all night, but he wouldn't tell me anything about it."

"What night was that?"

"Saturday night. A week ago Saturday night. The police brought him home about six o'clock in the morning, and told me I better have our doctor go over him, which I did. He wasn't hurt physically, but his mind seemed to be affected. He went into a rage when I tried to ask him where he had spent the night. I'd never seen him like that before. He'd always been a quiet-spoken boy. He said I had no right to know about him, that I wasn't really his father, and so on and so forth. I'm afraid I lost my temper and slapped him when he said that. Then he turned his back on me and wouldn't talk at all, about anything.''

''Had he been drinking?''

''I don't think so. No. I would have smelled it on him.''

''What about drugs?''

I could see his face turn toward me, large and vague in my side vision. ''That's out of the question.''

''I hope so. Dr. Sponti told me your son had a peculiar reaction to tranquillizers. That sometimes happens with habitual users.''

''My son was not a drug user.''

''A lot of young people are, nowadays, and their parents are the last to know about it.''

''No. It wasn't anything like that,'' he said urgently. ''The shock of the accident affected his mind.''

''Did the doctor think so?''

''Dr. Shanley is an orthopedic surgeon. He wouldn't know about psychiatric disturbance. Anyway, he didn't know what happened that morning, when I went to the judge's house to arrange for bail. I haven't told anyone about it.''

I waited, and listened to the windshield wipers. A green and white sign on the shoulder of the road announced: ''El Rancho.'' Hillman said, as if he was glad to have something neutral to say:

''You turn off in another quarter mile.''

I slowed down. ''You were going to tell me what happened that Sunday morning.''

''No. I don't believe I will. It has no bearing on the present situation.''

''How do we know that?''

He didn't answer me. Perhaps the thought of home and neighbors had silenced him.

''Did you say the Carlsons had a down on Tom?''

''I said that, and it's true.''

''Do you know the reason for it?''

''They have a daughter, Stella. Tom and Stella Carlson were very close. Jay and Rhea disapproved, at least Rhea did. So did Elaine, my wife, for that matter.''

I turned off the main road. The access road passed between tall stone gateposts and became the palm-lined central road bisecting El Rancho. It was one of those rich developments whose inhabitants couldn't possibly have troubles. Their big houses sat far back behind enormous lawns. Their private golf course lay across the road we were traveling on. The diving tower of their beach club gleamed with fresh aluminum paint in the wet distance.

But like the drizzle, troubles fall in or out of season on everybody.

The road bent around one corner of the golf course. Hillman pointed ahead to a deep gouge in the bank, where the earth was still raw. Above it a pine tree with a damaged trunk was turning brown in places.

"This is where he turned the car over."

I stopped the car. "Did he explain how the accident happened?"

Hillman pretended not to hear me. We got out of the car. There was no traffic in sight, except for a foursome of diehard golfers approaching in two carts along the fairway.

"I don't see any brake- or skid-marks," I said. "Was your son an experienced driver?"

"Yes. I taught him to drive myself. I spent a great deal of time with him. In fact, I deliberately reduced my work load at the firm several years ago, partly so that I could enjoy Tom's growing up."

His phrasing was a little strange, as if growing up was something a boy did for his parents' entertainment. It made me wonder. If Hillman had been really close to Tom, why had he clapped him into Laguna Perdida School at the first sign of delinquency? Or had there been earlier signs which he was suppressing?

One of the golfers waved from his cart as he went by. Hillman gave him a cold flick of the hand and got into my car. He seemed embarrassed to be found at the scene of the accident.

"I'll be frank with you," I said as we drove away. "I wish you'd be frank with me. Laguna Perdida is a school for disturbed and delinquent minors. I can't get it clear why Tom deserved, or needed, to be put there."

"I did it for his own protection. Good-neighbor Carlson was threatening to prosecute him for car theft."

"That's nothing so terrible. He'd have rated probation, if this was a first offense. Was it?"

"Of course it was."

"Then what were you afraid of?"

"I wasn't—" he started to say. But he was too honest, or too completely conscious of his fear, to finish the sentence.

"What did he do Sunday morning, when you went to see the judge?"

"He didn't do anything, really. Nothing happened."

"But that nothing hit you so hard you won't discuss it."

"That's correct. I won't discuss it, with you or anyone. Whatever happened last Sunday, or might have happened, has been completely outdated by recent events. My son has been kidnapped. He's a passive victim, don't you understand?"

I wondered about that, too. Twenty-five thousand dollars was a lot of money in my book, but it didn't seem to be in Hillman's. If Tom was really in the hands of professional criminals, they would be asking for all that the traffic would bear.

"How much money could you raise if you had to, Mr. Hillman?"

He gave me a swift look. "I don't see the point."

"Kidnappers usually go the limit in their demands. I'm trying to find our if they have in this case. I gather you could raise a good deal more than twenty-five thousand."

"I could, with my wife's help."

"Let's hope it won't be necessary."

4

The Hillmans' private drive meandered up an oak-covered rise and circled around a lawn in front of their house. It was a big old Spanish mansion, with white stucco walls, wrought-iron ornamentation at the windows, red tile roof gleaming dully in the wet. A bright black Cadillac was parked in the circle ahead of us.

"I meant to drive myself this morning," Hillman said. "But then I didn't trust myself to drive. Thanks for the lift."

It sounded like a dismissal. He started up the front steps, and I felt a keen disappointment. I swallowed it and went after him, slipping inside the front door before he closed it.

It was his wife he was preoccupied with. She was waiting for him in the reception hall, bowed forward in a high-backed Spanish chair which made her look tinier than she was. Her snakeskin shoes hung clear of the polished tile floor. She was a beautifully made thin blonde woman in her forties. An aura of desolation hung about her, a sense of uselessness, as if she was in fact the faded doll she resembled. Her green dress went poorly with her almost greenish pallor.

"Elaine?"

She had been sitting perfectly still, with her knees and fists together. She looked up at her husband, and then over his head at the huge Spanish chandelier suspended on a chain from the beamed ceiling two stories up. Its bulbs protruded like dubious fruit from clusters of wrought-iron leaves.

"Don't stand under it," she said. "I'm always afraid it's going to fall. I wish you'd have it taken down, Ralph."

"It was your idea to bring it back and put it there."

"That was a long time ago," she said. "I thought the space needed filling."

"It still does, and it's still perfectly safe." He moved toward her and touched her head. "You're wet. You shouldn't have gone out in your condition."

"I just walked down the drive to see if you were coming. You were gone a long time."

"I couldn't help it."

She took his hand as it slid away from her head and held it against her breast. "Did you hear anything?"

"We can't expect to hear anything yet for a while. I made arrangements for the money. Dick Leandro will bring it out later this afternoon. In the meantime we wait for a phone call."

"It's hideous, waiting."

"I know. You should try to think about something else."

"What else is there?"

"Lots of things." I think he tried to name one, and gave up. "Anyway, it isn't good for you to be sitting out here in the cold hall. You'll give yourself pneumonia again."

"People don't give it to *themselves*, Ralph."

"We won't argue. Come into the sitting room and I'll make you a drink."

He remembered me and included me in the invitation, but he didn't introduce me to his wife. Perhaps he considered me unworthy, or perhaps he wanted to discourage communication between us. Feeling rather left out, I followed them up three tile steps into a smaller room where a fire was burning. Elaine Hillman stood with her back to it. Her husband went to the bar, which was in an alcove decorated with Spanish bullfight posters.

She held out her hand to me. It was ice cold. "I don't mean to monopolize the heat. Are you a policeman? I thought we weren't using them."

"I'm a private detective. Lew Archer is my name."

Her husband called from the alcove: "What will you drink, darling?"

"Absinthe."

"Is that such a good idea?"

"It has wormwood in it, which suits my mood. But I'll settle for a short Scotch."

"What about you, Mr. Archer?"

I asked for the same. I needed it. While I rather liked both of the Hillmans, they were getting on my nerves. Their joint handling of their anxiety was almost professional, as if they were actors improvising a tragedy before an audience of one. I don't mean the anxiety wasn't sincere. They were close to dying of it.

Hillman came back across the room with three lowball glasses on a tray. He set it down on a long table in front of the fireplace and handed each of us a glass. Then he shook up the wood fire with a poker. Flames hissed up the chimney. Their reflection changed his face for a moment to a red savage mask.

His wife's face hung like a dead moon over her drink. "Our son is very dear to us, Mr. Archer. Can you help us get him back?"

"I can try. I'm not sure it's wise to keep the police out of this. I'm only one man, and this isn't my normal stomping ground."

"Does that make a difference?"

"I have no informers here."

"Do you hear him, Ralph?" she said to her crouching husband. "Mr. Archer thinks we should have the police in."

"I hear him. But it isn't possible." He straightened up with a sigh, as if the whole weight of the house was on his shoulders. "I'm not going to endanger Tom's life by anything I do."

"I feel the same way," she said. "I'm willing to pay through the nose to get him back. What use is money without a son to spend it on?"

That was another phrase that was faintly strange. I was getting the impression that Tom was the center of the household, but a fairly unknown center, like a god they made sacrifices to and expected benefits from, and maybe punishments, too. I was beginning to sympathize with Tom.

"Tell me about him, Mrs. Hillman."

Some life came up into her dead face. But before she could open her mouth Hillman said: "No. You're not going to put Elaine through that now."

"But Tom's a pretty shadowy figure to me. I'm trying to get some idea of where he might have gone yesterday, how he got tangled up with extortionists."

"*I* don't know where he went," the woman said.

"Neither do I. If I had," Hillman said, "I'd have gone to him yesterday."

"Then I'm going to have to go out and do some legwork. You can let me have a picture, I suppose."

Hillman went into an adjoining room, twilit behind pulled drapes, where the open top of a grand piano leaned up out of the shadows. He came back with a silver-framed studio photograph of a boy whose features resembled his own. The boy's dark eyes were rebellious, unless I was projecting my own sense of the household into them. They were also intelligent and imaginative. His mouth was spoiled.

"Can I take this out of the frame? Or if you have a smaller one, it would be better to show around."

"To show around?"

"That's what I said, Mr. Hillman. It's not for my memory book."

Elaine Hillman said: "I have a smaller one upstairs on my dressing table. I'll get it."

"Why don't I go up with you? It might help if I went through his room."

"You can look at his room," Hillman said, "but I don't want you searching it."

"Why?"

"I just don't like the idea. Tom has the right to some privacy, even now."

The three of us went upstairs, keeping an eye on each other. I wondered what Hillman was afraid I might find, but I hesitated to ask him. While everything seemed to be under control, Hillman could flare up at any moment and order me out of his house.

He stood at the door while I gave the room a quick once-over. It was a front bedroom, very large, furnished with plain chests of drawers and chairs and a table and a bed which all looked hand-finished and expensive. A bright red telephone sat on the bedside table. There were engravings of sailing ships and Audubon prints hung with geometric precision around the walls, Navajo rugs on the floor, and a wool bedspread matching one of them.

I turned to Hillman. "Was he interested in boats and sailing?"

"Not particularly. He used to come out and crew for me occasionally, on the sloop, when I couldn't get anyone else. Does it matter?"

"I was just wondering if he hung around the harbor much."

"No. He didn't."

"Was he interested in birds?"

"I don't think so."

"Who chose the pictures?"

"I did," Elaine Hillman said from the hallway. "I decorated the room for Tom. He liked it, didn't he, Ralph?"

Hillman mumbled something. I crossed the room to the deeply set front windows, which overlooked the semicircular driveway. I could see down the wooded slope, across the golf course, all the way to the highway, where cars rolled back and forth like children's toys out of reach. I could imagine Tom sitting here in the alcove and watching the highway lights at night.

A thick volume of music lay open on the leather seat. I looked at the cover. It was a well-used copy of *The Well-Tempered Clavier*.

"Did Tom play the piano, Mr. Hillman?"

"Very well. He had ten years of lessons. But then he wanted—"

His wife made a small dismayed sound at his shoulder. "Why go into all that?"

"All what?" I said. "Trying to get information out of you people is like getting blood out of a stone."

"I *feel* like a bloodless stone," she said with a little grimace. "This hardly seems the time to rake up old family quarrels."

"We didn't quarrel," her husband said. "It was the one thing Tom and I ever disagreed on. And he went along with me on it. End of subject."

"All right. Where did he spend his time away from home?"

The Hillmans looked at each other, as if the secret of Tom's whereabouts was somehow hidden in each other's faces. The red telephone interrupted their dumb communion, like a loud thought. Elaine Hillman gasped. The photograph in her hand fell to the floor. She wilted against her husband.

He held her up. "It wouldn't be for us. That's Tom's private telephone."

"You want me to take it?" I said through the second ring.

"Please do."

I sat on the bed and picked up the receiver. "Hello."

"Tom?" said a high, girlish voice. "Is that you, Tommy?"

"Who is this calling?" I tried to sound like a boy.

The girl said something like "Augh" and hung up on me.

I set down the receiver: "It was a girl or a young woman. She wanted Tom."

The woman spoke with a touch of malice that seemed to renew her strength: That's nothing unusual. I'm sure it was Stella Carlson. She's been calling all week."

"Does she always hang up like that?"

"No. I talked to her yesterday. She was full of questions, which of course I refused to answer. But I wanted to make sure that she hadn't seen Tom. She hadn't."

"Does she know anything about what's happened?"

"I hope not," Hillman said. 'We've got to keep it in the family. The more people know, the worse—" He left another sentence dangling in the air.

I moved away from the telephone and picked up the fallen photograph. In a kind of staggering march step, Elaine Hillman went to the bed and straightened out the bedspread where I had been sitting. Everything had to be perfect in the room, I thought, or the god would not be appeased and would never return to them. When she had finished smoothing the bed, she flung herself face down on it and lay still.

Hillman and I withdrew quietly and went downstairs to wait

for the call that mattered. There was a phone in the bar alcove off the sitting room, and another in the butler's pantry, which I could use to listen in. To get to the butler's pantry we had to go through the music room, where the grand piano loomed, and across a formal dining room which had a dismal air, like a reconstructed room in a museum.

The past was very strong here, like an odor you couldn't quite place. It seemed to be built into the very shape of the house, with its heavy dark beams and thick walls and deep windows; it would almost force the owner of the house to feel like a feudal lord. But the role of hidalgo hung loosely on Hillman, like something borrowed for a costume party. He and his wife must have rattled around in the great house, even when the boy was there.

Back in the sitting room, in front of the uncertain fire, I had a chance to ask Hillman some more questions. The Hillmans had two servants, a Spanish couple named Perez who had looked after Tom from infancy. Mrs. Perez was probably out in the kitchen. Her husband was in Mexico, visiting his family.

"You *know* he's in Mexico?"

"Well," Hillman said, "his wife has had a card from Sinaloa. Anyway, the Perezes are devoted to us, and to Tom. We've had them with us ever since we moved here and bought this house."

"How long ago was that?"

"Over sixteen years. We moved here, the three of us, after I was separated from the Navy. Another engineer and I founded our own firm here, Technological Enterprises. We've had very gratifying success, supplying components to the military and then NASA. I was able to go into semiretirement not long ago."

"You're young to retire, Mr. Hillman."

"Perhaps." He looked around a little restlessly, as if he disliked talking about himself. "I'm still the chairman of the board, of course. I go down to the office several mornings a week. I play a lot of golf, do a lot of hunting and sailing." He sounded weary of his life. "This summer I've been teaching Tom calculus. It isn't available in his high school. I thought it would come in handy if he made it to Cal Tech or M.I.T. I went to M.I.T. myself. Elaine was a student at Radcliffe. She was born on Beacon Street, you know."

We're prosperous and educated people, he seemed to be

saying, first-class citizens: how can the world have aimed such a dirty blow at us? He leaned his large face forward until his hands supported it again.

The telephone rang in the alcove. I heard it ring a second time as I skidded around the end of the dining-room table. At the door of the butler's pantry I almost knocked down a small round woman who was wiping her hands on her apron. Her emotional dark eyes recoiled from my face.

"I was going to answer it," she said.

"I will, Mrs. Perez."

She retreated into the kitchen and I closed the door after her. The only light in the pantry came through the semicircular hatch to the dining room. The telephone was on the counter inside it, no longer ringing. Gently I raised the receiver.

"What was that?" a man's voice said. "You got the FBI on the line or something?" The voice was a western drawl with a faint whine in it.

"Certainly not. I've followed your instructions to the letter."

"I hope I can believe you, Mr. Hillman. If I thought you were having this call traced I'd hang up and goodbye Tom." The threat came easily, with a kind of flourish, as if the man enjoyed this kind of work.

"Don't hang up." Hillman's voice was both pleading and loathing. "I have the money for you, at least I'll have it here in a very short while. I'll be ready to deliver it whenever you say."

"Twenty-five thousand in small bills?"

"There will be nothing larger than a twenty."

"All unmarked?"

"I told you I've obeyed you to the letter. My son's safety is all I care about."

"I'm glad you get the picture, Mr. Hillman. You pick up fast, and I like that. Matter of fact, I hate to do this to you. And I'd certainly hate to do anything to this fine boy of yours."

"Is Tom with you now?" Hillman said.

"More or less. He's nearby."

"Could I possibly talk to him?"

"No."

"How do I know he's alive?"

The man was silent for a long moment. "You don't trust me, Mr. Hillman. I don't like that."

"How can I trust—?" Hillman bit the sentence in half.

"I know what you were going to say. How can you trust a lousy creep like me? That isn't our problem, Hillman. Our problem is can I trust a creep like you. I know more about you than you think I do, Hillman."

Silence, in which breath wheezed.

"Well, can I?"

"Can you what?" Hillman said in near-despair.

"Can I trust you, Hillman?"

"You can trust me."

Wheezing silence. The wheeze was in the man's voice when he spoke again: "I guess I'll have to take your word for it, Hillman. Okay. You'd probably like to talk all day about what a creep I am, but it's time to get down to brass tacks. I want my money, and this isn't ransom money, get that straight. Your son wasn't kidnapped, he came to us of his own free will—"

"I don't—" Hillman strangled the words in his throat.

"You don't believe me? Ask him, if you ever have a chance. You're throwing away your chances, you realize that? I'm trying to help you pay me the money—the information money, that's all it is—but you keep calling me names, liar and creep and God knows what else."

"No. There's nothing personal."

"That's what you think."

"Look here," Hillman said. "You said it's time to get down to brass tacks. Simply tell me where and when you want the money delivered. It will be delivered. I guarantee it."

Hillman's voice was sharp. The man at the other end of the line reacted to the sharpness perversely:

"Don't be in such a hurry. I'm calling the shots, you better not forget it."

"Then call them," Hillman said.

"In my own good time. I think I better give you a chance to think this over, Hillman. Get down off your high horse and down on your knees. That's where you belong." He hung up.

Hillman was standing in the alcove with the receiver still in his hand when I got back to the sitting room. Absently he replaced it on its brackets and came toward me, shaking his silver head.

"He wouldn't give me any guarantees about Tom."

"I heard him. They never do. You have to depend on his mercy."

"His *mercy!* He was talking like a maniac. He seemed to revel in the—in the pain."

"I agree, he was getting his kicks. Let's hope he's satisfied with the kicks he's already got, and the money."

HIllman's head went down. "You think Tom is in danger, don't you?"

"Yes. I don't think you're dealing with an outright maniac, but the man didn't sound too well-balanced. I think he's an amateur, or possibly a petty thief who saw his chance to move in on the heavy stuff. More likely a gifted amateur. Is he the same man who called this morning?"

"Yes."

"He may be working alone. Is there any chance that you could recognize his voice? There was some hint of a personal connection, maybe a grievance. Could he be a former employee of yours, for example?"

"I very much doubt it. We only employ skilled workers. This fellow sounded practically subhuman." His face became gaunter. "And you tell me I'm at his mercy."

"Your son is. Could there be any truth in what he said about Tom going to him voluntarily?"

"Of course not. Tom is a good boy."

"How is his judgment?"

HIllman didn't answer me, except by implication. He went to the bar, poured himself a stiff drink out of a bourbon bottle, and knocked it back. I followed him to the bar.

"Is there any possible chance that Tom cooked up this extortion deal himself, with the help of one of his buddies, or maybe with hired help?"

He hefted the glass in his hand, as if he was thinking of throwing it at my head. I caught a glimpse of his red angry mask before he turned away. "It's quite impossible. Why do you have to torment me with these ideas?"

"I don't know your son. You ought to."

"He'd never do a thing like that to me."

"You put him in Laguna Perdida School."

"I had to."

"Why?"

He turned on me furiously. "You keep hammering away at the same stupid question. What has it got to do with anything?"

"I'm trying to find out just how far gone Tom is. If there

was reason to think that he kidnapped himself, to punish you or raise money, we'd want to turn the police loose—''

"You're crazy!''

"Is Tom?''

"Of course not. Frankly, Mr. Archer, I'm getting sick of you and your questions. If you want to stay in my house, it's got to be on my terms.''

I was tempted to walk out, but something held me. The case was getting its hooks into my mind.

HIllman filled his glass with whisky and drank half of it down.

"If I were you, I'd lay off the sauce," I said. "You have decisions to make. This could be the most important day of your life.''

He nodded slowly. "You're right." He reached across the bar and poured the rest of his whisky into the metal sink. Then he excused himself, and went upstairs to see to his wife.

5

I let myself out the front door, quietly, got a hat and raincoat out of the trunk of my car, and walked down the winding driveway. In the dead leaves under the oak trees the drip made rustling noises, releasing smells and memories. When I was seventeen I spent a summer working on a dude ranch in the foothills of the Sierra. Toward the end of August, when the air was beginning to sharpen, I found a girl, and before the summer was over we met in the woods. Everything since had been slightly anticlimactic.

Growing up seemed to be getting harder. The young people were certainly getting harder to figure out. Maybe Stella Carlson, if I could get to her, could help me understand Tom.

The Carlsons' mailbox was a couple of hundred yards down the road. It was a miniature replica, complete with shutters, of their green-shuttered white colonial house, and it rubbed me the wrong way, like a tasteless advertisement. I went up the drive to the brick stoop and knocked on the door.

A handsome redheaded woman in a linen dress opened the door and gave me a cool green look. "Yes?"

I didn't think I could get past her without lying. "I'm in the insurance—"

"Soliciting is not allowed in El Rancho."

"I'm not selling, Mrs. Carlson, I'm a claims adjuster." I got an old card out of my wallet which supported the statement. I had worked for insurance companies in my time.

"If it's about my wrecked car," she said, "I thought that was all settled last week."

"We're interested in the cause of the accident. We keep statistics, you know."

"I'm not particularly interested in becoming a statistic."

"Your car already is. I understand it was stolen."

She hesitated, and glanced behind her, as if there was a witness in the hallway. "Yes," she said finally. "It was stolen."

"By some young punk in the neighborhood, is that right?"

She flushed in response to my incitement. "Yes, and I doubt very much that it was an accident. He took my car and wrecked it out of sheer spite." The words boiled out as if they had been simmering in her mind for days.

"That's an interesting hypothesis, Mrs. Carlson. May I come in and talk it over with you?"

"I suppose so."

She let me into the hallway. I sat at a telephone table and took out my black notebook. She stood over me with one hand on the newel post at the foot of the stairs.

"Do you have anything to support that hypothesis?" I said with my pencil poised.

"You mean that he wrecked the car deliberately?"

"Yes."

Her white teeth closed on her full red lower lip, and left a brief dent in it. "It's something you couldn't make a statistic out of. The boy—his name is Tom Hillman—was interested in our daughter. He used to be a much nicer boy than he is now. As a matter of fact, he used to spend most of his free time over here. We treated him as if he were our own son. But the relationship went sour. Very sour." She sounded both angry and regretful.

"What soured it?"

She made a violent sideways gesture. "I prefer not to discuss it. It's something an insurance company doesn't have to know. Or anybody else."

"Perhaps I could talk to the boy. He lives next door, doesn't he?"

"His parents do, the Hillmans. I believe they've sent him away somewhere. We no longer speak to the Hillmans," she said stiffly. "They're decent enough people, I suppose, but they've made awful fools of themselves over that boy."

"Where did they send him?"

"To some kind of reform school, probably. He needed it. He was running out of control."

"In what way?"

"Every way. He smashed up my car, which probably means he was drinking. I know he was spending time in the bars on lower Main Street."

"The night before he wrecked your car?"

"All summer. He even tried to teach his bad habits to Stella. That's what soured the relationship, if you want to know."

I made a note. "Could you be a little more specific, Mrs. Carlson? We're interested in the whole social background of these accidents."

"Well, he actually dragged Stella with him to one of those awful dives. Can you imagine, taking an innocent sixteen-year-old girl to a wino joint on lower Main? That was the end of Tom Hillman, as far as we were concerned."

"What about Stella?"

"She's a sensible girl." She glanced up toward the head of the stairs. "Her father and I made her see that it wasn't a profitable relationship."

"So she wasn't involved in the borrowing of your car?"

"Certainly not."

A small clear voice said from the head of the stairs: "That isn't true, Mother and you know it. I told you—"

"Be quiet, Stella. Go back to bed. If you're ill enough to stay home from camp, you're ill enough to stay in bed."

As she was talking, Mrs. Carlson surged halfway up the stairs. She had very good calves, a trifle muscular. Her daughter came down toward her, a slender girl with lovely eyes that seemed to take up most of her face below the forehead. Her brown hair was pulled back tight. She had on slacks and a high-necked blue sweater which revealed the bud-sharp outlines of her breasts.

"I'm feeling better, thank you," she said with adolescent iciness. "At least I was, until I heard you lying about Tommy."

"How dare you? Go to your room."

"I will if you'll stop telling lies about Tommy."

"You shut up."

Mrs. Carlson ran up the three or four steps that separated them, grabbed Stella by the shoulders, turned her forcibly, and marched her up out of sight. Stella kept repeating the word "Liar," until a door slammed on her thin clear voice.

Five minutes later Mrs. Carlson came down wearing fresh makeup, a green hat with a feather in it, a plaid coat, and gloves. She walked straight to the door and opened it wide.

"I'm afraid I have to rush now. My hairdresser gets very angry with me when I'm late. We were getting pretty far afield from what you wanted, anyway."

"On the contrary. I was very interested in your daughter's remarks."

She smiled with fierce politeness. "Pay no attention to Stella. She's feverish and hysterical. The poor child's been upset ever since the accident."

"Because she was involved in it?"

"Don't be silly." She rattled the door knob. "I really have to go now."

I stepped outside. She followed, and slammed the door hard behind me. She'd probably had a lot of practice slamming doors.

"Where's your car?" she called after me.

"I parachuted in."

She stood and watched me until I reached the foot of the driveway. Then she went back into her house. I plodded back to the Hillmans' mailbox and turned up their private lane. The rustling in the woods were getting louder. I thought it was a towhee scratching in the undergrowth. But it was Stella.

She appeared suddenly beside the trunk of a tree, wearing a blue ski jacket with the hood pulled up over her head and tied under her chin. She looked about twelve. She beckoned me with the dignity of a full-grown woman, ending the motion with her finger at her lips.

"I better stay out of sight. Mother will be looking for me."

"I thought she had an appointment with the hairdresser."

"That was just another lie," she said crisply. "She's always lying these days."

"Why?"

"I guess people get in the habit of it or something. Mother always used to be a very straight talker. So did Dad. But this business about Tommy has sort of thrown them. It's thrown me, too," she added, and coughed into her hand.

"You shouldn't be out in the wet," I said. "You're sick."

"No, really, I mean not physically. I just don't feel like facing the kids at camp and having to answer their questions."

"About Tommy?"

She nodded. "I don't even know where he is. Do you?"

"No, I don't."

"Are you a policeman, or what?"

"I used to be a policeman. Now I'm a what."

She wrinkled her nose and let out a little giggle. Then she tensed in listening attitude, like a yearling fawn. She threw off her hood.

"Do you hear her? That's Mother calling me."

Far off through the trees I heard a voice calling: "Stella."

"She'll kill me," the girl said. "But somebody has to tell the truth some time. *I know.* Tommy has a tree house up the slope, I mean he used to have when he was younger. We can talk there."

I followed her up a half-overgrown foot trail. A little redwood shack with a tar-paper roof sat on a low platform among the spreading branches of an oak. A homemade ladder, weathered gray like the tree house, slanted up to the platform. Stella climbed up first and went inside. A red-capped woodpecker flew out of an unglazed window into the next tree, where he sat and harangued us. Mrs. Carlson's voice floated up from the foot of the slope. She had a powerful voice, but it was getting hoarse.

"Swiss Family Robinson," Stella said when I went in. She was sitting on the edge of a built-in cot which had a mattress but no blankets. "Tommy and I used to spend whole days up here, when we were children." At sixteen, there was nostalgia in her voice. "Of course when we reached puberty it had to stop. It wouldn't have been proper."

"You're fond of Tommy."

"Yes. I love him. We're going to be married. But don't get the wrong idea about us. We're not even *going* steady. We're not making out and we're not soldered." She wrinkled her nose, as if she didn't like the smell of the words. 'We'll be married when the time is right, when Tommy's through college or at least has a good start. We won't have any money problems, you see."

I thought she was using me to comfort herself a little with a story, a simple story with a happy ending. "How is that?"

"Tommy's parents have lots of money."

"What about your parents? Will they let you marry him?"

"They won't be able to stop me."

I believed her, if Tommy survived. She must have seen the "if" cross my eyes like a shadow. She was a perceptive girl.

"Is Tommy all right?" she said in a different tone.

"I hope so."

She reached up and plucked at my sleeve. "Where is he, Mister—?"

"I don't know, Stella. My name is Lew Archer. I'm a private detective working on Tommy's side. And you were going to tell me truth about the accident."

"Yes. It was my fault. Mother and Dad seem to think they have to cover up for me, but it only makes things worse for Tommy. I was the one responsible, really." Her direct upward look, her earnest candor, reminded me of a child saying her prayers.

"Were you driving the car?"

"No. I don't mean I was with him. But I told him he could take it and I got the key for him out of Mother's room. It's really my car, too—I mean, to use."

"She knows this?"

"Yes. I told her and Dad on Sunday. But they had already talked to the police, and after that they wouldn't change their story, or let me. They said it didn't alter the fact that he took it."

"Why did you let him take it?"

"I admit it wasn't such a good idea. But he had to go someplace to see somebody and his father wouldn't let him use one of their cars. He was grounded. Mother and Dad were gone for the evening, and Tommy said he'd be back in a couple of hours. It was only about eight o'clock, and I thought it would be okay. I didn't know he was going to be out all night." She closed her eyes and hugged herself. "I was awake all night, listening for him."

"Where did he go?"

"I don't know."

"What was he after?"

"I don't know that, either. He said it was the most important thing in his life."

"Could he have been talking about alcohol?"

"Tommy doesn't drink. It was somebody he had to see, somebody very important."

"Like a drug pusher?"

She opened her wonderful eyes. "You're twisting meanings, the way Dad does when he's mad at me. Are you mad at me, Mr. Archer?"

"No. I'm grateful to you for being honest."

"Then why do you keep dragging in crummy meanings?"

"I'm used to questioning crummy people, I guess. And sometimes an addict's own mother, or own girl, doesn't know he's using drugs."

"I'm sure Tommy wasn't. He was dead against it. He knew what it had done to some—" She covered her mouth with her hand. Her nails were bitten.

"You were going to say?"

"Nothing."

Our rapport was breaking down. I did my best to save it. "Listen to me, Stella, I'm not digging dirt for the fun of it. Tommy's in real danger. If he had contacts with drug users, you should tell me."

"They were just some of his musician friends," she mumbled. "They wouldn't do anything to hurt him."

"They may have friends who would. Who are these people?"

"Just some people he played the piano with this summer, till his father made him quit. Tommy used to sit in on their jam sessions on Sunday afternoon at The Barroom Floor."

"Is that one of the dives your mother mentioned?"

"It isn't a dive. He didn't take me to dives. It was merely a place where they could get together and play their instruments. He wanted me to hear them play."

"And Tommy played with them?"

She nodded brightly. "He's a very good pianist, good enough to make his living at it. They even offered him a weekend job."

"Who did?"

"The combo at The Barroom Floor. His father wouldn't let him take it, naturally."

"Tell me about the people in the combo."

"Sam Jackman is the only one I know. He used to be a locker boy at the beach club. He plays the trombone. The there was a saxophonist and a trumpeter and a drummer. I don't remember their names."

"What did you think of them?"

"I didn't think they were very good. But Tommy said they were planning to make an album."

"Every combo is. I mean, what kind of people were they?"

"They were just musicians. Tommy seemed to like them."

"How much time had he been spending with them?"

"Just Sunday afternoons. And I guess he used to drop in to hear them some nights. He called it his other life."

"His other life?"

"Uh-huh. *You* know, at home he had to hit the books and make his parents feel good and all that stuff. The same way I have to do when I'm at home. But it hasn't been working too well since the accident. Nobody feels good."

She shivered. A cold wet wind was blowing through the windows of the tree house. Mrs. Carlson's voice could no longer be heard. I felt uneasy about keeping the girl away from her mother. But I didn't want to let her go until she had told me everything she could.

I squatted on my heels in front of her. "Stella, do you think Tommy's appointment that Saturday night had to do with his musician friends?

"No. He would have told me if it had. It was more of a secret than that."

"Did he say so?"

"He didn't have to. It was something secret and terribly important. He was terribly excited."

"In a good way or a bad way?"

"I don't know how you tell the difference. He wasn't afraid, it that's what you mean."

"I'm trying to ask you if he was sick."

"Sick?"

"Emotionally sick."

"No. I—That's foolish."

"Then why did his father have him put away?"

"You mean, put away in a mental hospital?" She leaned toward me, so close I could feel her breath on my face.

"Something like that—Laguna Perdida School. I didn't mean to tell you, and I'm going to ask you not to tell your parents."

"Don't worry, I'll never tell them anything. So that's where he is! Those hypocrites!" Her eyes were fixed and wet. "You said he was in danger. Are they trying to cut out his frontal lobe like in Tennessee Williams?"

"No. He was in no danger where he was. But he escaped from the place, the night before last, and fell into the hands of thieves. Now, I'm not going to load your mind with any more of this. I'm sorry it came out."

"Don't be." She gave me a second glimpse of the woman she was on her way to becoming. "If it's happening to Tommy, it's just like it was happening to me." Her forefinger tapped through nylon at the bone between her little breasts. "You said he fell into the hands of thieves. Who are they?"

"I'm trying to answer that question, in a hurry. Could they be his friends from The Barroom Floor?"

She shook her head. "Are they holding him prisoner or something?"

"Yes. I'm trying to get to them before they do something worse. If you know of any other contacts he had in his other life, particularly underworld contacts—"

"No. He didn't have any. He didn't have another life, really. It was just talk, talk and music."

Her lips were turning blue. I had a sudden evil image of myself: a heavy hunched figure seen from above in the act of tormenting a child who was already tormented. A sense went through me of the appalling ease with which the things you do in a good cause can slip over into bad.

"You'd better go home, Stella."

She folded her arms. "Not until you tell me everything. I'm not a child."

"But this is confidential information. I didn't intend to let any of it out. If it got to the wrong people, it would only make things worse."

She said with some scorn: "You keep beating around the bush, like Dad. Is Tommy being held for ransom?"

"Yes, but I'm pretty sure it's no ordinary kidnapping. He's supposed to have gone to these people of his own free will."

"Who said so?"

"One of them."

Her clear brow puckered. "Then why would Tommy be in any danger from them?"

"If he knows them," I said, "they're not likely to let him come home. He could identify them."

"I see." Her eyes were enormous, taking in all at once the horror of the world and growing dark with it. "I was *afraid* he was in some awful jam. His mother wouldn't tell me anything. I thought maybe he'd killed himself and they were keeping it quiet."

"What made you think that?"

"Tommy did. He called me up and I met him here in the tree house the morning after the accident. I wasn't supposed to tell anyone. But you've been honest with me. He wanted to see me one more time—just as friends, you know—and say goodbye forever. I asked him if he was going away, or what he planned to do. He wouldn't tell me."

"Was he suicidal?"

"I don't know. I was afraid that that was what it all meant. Not hearing from him since, I got more and more worried. I'm not as worried now as I was before you told me all those things." She did a mental double take on one of them. "But why would he deliberately go and stay with criminals?"

"It isn't clear. He may not have known they were criminals. If you can think of anyone—"

"I'm trying." She screwed up her face, and finally shook her head again. "I can't, unless they were the same people he had to see that other Saturday night. When he borrowed our car."

"Did he tell you anything at all about those people?"

"Just that he was terribly keen about seeing them."

"Were they men or women?"

"I don't even know that."

"What about the Sunday morning, when you met him here? Did he tell you anything at all about the night before?"

"No. He was feeling really low, after the accident and all, and the terrible row with his parents. I didn't ask him any questions. I guess I should have, shouldn't I? I always do the wrong thing, either by commission or omission."

"I think you do the right thing more often than most."

"Mother doesn't think so. Neither does Dad."

"Parents can be mistaken."

"Are you a parent?" The question reminded me of the sad boys in Laguna Perdida School.

"No, I never have been. My hands are clean."

"You're making fun of me," she said with a glum face.

"Never. Hardly ever."

She gave me a quick smile. "Gilbert and Sullivan. I didn't know detectives were like you."

"Neither do most of the other detectives." Our rapport, which came and went, was flourishing again. "There's one other thing I've been meaning to ask you, Stella. Your mother seems to believe that Tommy wrecked her car on purpose."

"I know she does."

"Could there be any truth in it?"

She considered the question. "I don't see how. He wouldn't do it to me, *or* her, unless—" She looked up in dark surmise.

"Go on."

"Unless he was trying to kill himself, and didn't care about anything any more."

"Was he?"

"He may have been. He didn't want to come home, he told me that much. But he didn't tell me why."

"I might learn something from examining the car. Do you know where it is?"

"It's down in Ringo's wrecking yard. Mother went to see it the other day."

"Why?"

"It helps her to stay mad, I guess. Mother's really crazy about Tommy, at least she used to be, and so was Dad. This business has been terribly hard on them. And I'm not making it any easier staying away from home now." She got to her feel, stamping them rapidly. "Mother will be calling out the gendarmes. Also she'll kill me."

"No she won't."

"Yes she will." But she wasn't basically afraid for herself. "If you find out anything about Tommy, will you let me know?"

"That might be a little tough to do, in view of your mother's attitude. Why don't you get in touch with me when you can? This number will always get me, through my answering service." I gave her a card.

She climbed down the ladder and flitted away through the

trees, one of those youngsters who make you feel like apologizing for the world.

6

I made my way back to the Hillmans' house. It resembled a grim white fortress under the lowering sky. I didn't feel like going in just now and grappling with the heavy, smothering fear that hung in the rooms. Anyway, I finally had a lead. Which Hillman could have given me if he'd wanted to.

Before I got into my car I looked up at the front window of Tom's room. The Hillmans were sitting close together in the niche of the window, looking out. Hillman shook his head curtly: no phone call.

I drove into town and turned right off the highway onto the main street. The stucco and frame buildings in this segment of town, between the highway and the railroad tracks, had been here a long time and been allowed to deteriorate. There were tamale parlors and pool halls and rummage stores and bars. The wet pavements were almost empty of people, as they always were when it rained in California.

I parked and locked my car in front of a surplus and sporting goods store and asked the proprietor where The Barroom Floor was. He pointed west, toward the ocean:

"I don't think they're open, in the daytime. There's lots of other places open."

"What about Ringo's auto yard?"

"Three blocks south on Sanger Street, that's the first stoplight below the railroad tracks."

I thanked him.

"You're welcome, I'm sure." He was a middle-aged man with a sandy moustache, cheerfully carrying a burden of unsuccess. "I can sell you a rainproof cover for your hat."

"How much?"

"Ninety-eight cents. A dollar-two with tax."

I bought one. He put it on my hat. "It doesn't do much for the appearance, but—"

"Beauty is functional."

He smiled and nodded. "You took the words out of my mouth. I figured you were a smart man. My name's Botkin, by the way, Joseph Botkin."

"Lew Archer." We shook hands.

"My pleasure, Mr. Archer. If I'm not getting too personal, why would a man like you want to do your drinking at The Barroom Floor?"

"What's the matter with The Barroom Floor?"

"I don't like the way they handle their business, that's all. It lowers the whole neighborhood. Which is low enough already, God knows."

"How do they handle their business?"

"They let young kids hang out there, for one thing—I'm not saying they serve them liquor. But they shouldn't let them in at all."

"What do they do for another thing?"

"I'm talking too much." He squinted at me shrewdly. "And you ask a lot of questions. You wouldn't be from the Board of Equalization by any chance?"

"No, but I probably wouldn't tell you if I was. Is The Barroom Floor under investigation?"

"I wouldn't be surprised. I heard there was a complaint put in on them."

"From a man named Hillman?"

"Yeah. You are from the Board of Equalization, eh? If you want to look the place over for yourself, it opens at five."

It was twenty past four. I wandered along the street, looking through the windows of pawnshops at the loot of wrecked lives. The Barroom Floor was closed all right. It looked as if it was never going to reopen. Over the red-checked half-curtains at the windows, I peered into the dim interior. Red-checked tables and chairs were grouped around a dime-size dance floor; and farther back in the shadows was a bandstand decorated with gaudy paper. It looked so deserted you'd have thought all the members of the band had hocked their instruments and left town years ago.

I went back to my car and drove down Sanger Street to Ringo's yard. It was surrounded by a high board fence on which his name was painted in six-foot white letters. I pushed in through the gate. A black German shepherd glided out of the open door of a shack and delicately grasped my right wrist between his large yellow teeth. He didn't growl or anything. He merely held me, looking up brightly at my face.

A wide fat man, with a medicine ball of stomach badly concealed under his plaid shirt, came to the door of the shack.

"That's all right, Lion."

The dog let go of me and went to the fat man.

"His teeth are dirty," I said. "You should give him bones to chew. I don't mean wristbones."

"Sorry. We weren't expecting any customers. But he won't hurt you, will you, Lion?"

Lion rolled his eyes and let his tongue hang out about a foot.

"Go ahead, pet him."

"I'm a dog lover," I said, "but is he a man lover?"

"Sure. Go ahead and pet him."

I went ahead and petted him. Lion lay down on his back with his feet in the air, grinning up at me with his fangs.

"What can I do you for, mister?" Ringo said.

"I want to look at a car."

He waved his hand toward the yard. "I got hundreds of them. But there isn't a one of them you could drive away. You want one to cannibalize?"

"This is a particular car I want to examine." I produced my adjuster's card. "It's a fairly new Dodge, I think, belonged to a Mrs. Carlson, wrecked a week or so ago."

"Yeah. I'll show it to you."

He put on a black rubber raincoat. Lion and I followed him down a narrow aisle between two lines of wrecked cars. With their crumpled grilles and hoods, shattered windshields, torn fenders, collapsed roofs, disemboweled seats, and blown-out tires, they made me think of some ultimate freeway disaster. Somebody with an eye for detail should make a study of automobile graveyards, I thought, the way they study the ruins and potsherds of vanished civilizations. It could provide a clue as to why our civilization is vanishing.

"All the ones in this line are totaled out," Ringo said. "This is the Carlson job, second from the end. That Pontiac came in since. Head-on collision, two dead." He shuddered. "I never go on the highway when I can help it."

"What caused the accident to the Carlson car?"

"It was taken for a joy ride by one of the neighbors' kids, a boy name of Hillman. You know how these young squirts are—if it isn't theirs, they don't care what happens to it. According to the traffic detail, he missed a curve and went off the road and probably turned it over trying to get back on. He must of rolled over several times and ended up against a tree."

I walked around the end of the line and looked over the Dart from all sides. There were deep dents in the roof and hood and all four fenders, as if it had been hit with random sledgehammers. The windshield was gone. The doors were sprung.

Leaning in through the left-hand door, I noticed an oval piece of white plastic, stamped with printing, protruding from the space between the driver's seat and the back. I reached in and pulled it out. It was a brass door key. The printing on the plastic tab said: DACK'S AUTO COURT 7.

"Watch the glass in there," Ringo said behind me. "What are you looking for?"

I put the key in my pocket before I turned around. "I can't figure out why the boy didn't get hurt."

"He had the wheel to hang on to, remember. Lucky for him it didn't break."

"Is there any chance he wrecked the car on purpose?"

"Naw. He'd have to be off his rocker to do that. Course you can't put anything past these kids nowadays. Can you, Lion?" He stooped to touch the dog's head and went on talking, either to it or to me. "My own son that I brought up in the business went off to college and now he don't even come home for Christmas some years. I got nobody to take over the business." He straightened up and looked around at his wrecks with stern affection, like the emperor of a wasteland.

"Could there have been anybody with him in the car?"

"Naw. They would of been really banged up, with no seat belts and nothing to hang on to." He looked at the sky, and added impatiently: "I don't mind standing around answering your questions, mister. But if you really want the dope on the accident, talk to the traffic detail. I'm closing up."

It was ten minutes to five. I made my way back to The Barroom Floor. Somebody had turned on a few lights inside. The front door was still locked. I went back to my car and waited. I took out the Dack's Auto Court key and looked at it, wondering if it meant anything. It could have meant, among other farfetched possibilities, that the handsome Mrs. Carlson was unfaithful to her husband.

Shortly after five a short dark man in a red jacket unlocked the front door of The Barroom Floor and took up his position behind the bar. I went in and sat down on a stool opposite him. He seemed much taller behind the bar. I looked over it and saw that he was standing on a wooden platform about a foot off the floor.

"Yeah," he said, "it keeps me on the level. Without it I can barely see over the bar." He grinned. "My wife, now, is five foot six and built in proportion. She ought to be here now," he added in a disciplinary tone, and looked at the wristwatch on his miniature wrist. "What will you have?

"Whisky sour. You own this place?"

"Me and the wife, we have an interest in it."

"Nice place," I said, though it wasn't particularly nice. It was no cleaner and no more cheerful than the average bar and grill with cabaret pretensions. The old waiter leaning against the wall beside the kitchen door seemed to be sleeping on his feet.

"Thank you. We have plans for it." As he talked, he made my drink with expert fingers. "You haven't been in before. I don't remember your face."

"I'm from Hollywood. I hear you have a pretty fair jazz combo."

"Yeah."

"Will they be playing tonight?"

"They only play Friday and Saturday nights. We don't get the weekday trade to justify 'em."

"What about the Sunday jam sessions? Are they still on?"

"Yeah. We had one yesterday. The boys were in great form. Too bad you missed them." He slid my drink across the bar. "You in the music business?"

"I represent musicians from time to time. I have an office on the Strip."

"Sam would want to talk to you. He's the leader."

"Where can I get in touch with him?"

"I have his address somewhere. Just a minute, please."

A couple of young men in business suits with rain-sprinkled shoulders had taken seats at the far end of the bar. They were talking in carrying voices about a million-dollar real estate deal. Apparently it was somebody else's deal, not theirs, but they seemed to enjoy talking about it.

The small man served them short whiskeys without being asked. A lavishly built young woman came in and struggled out of a transparent raincoat which she rolled up and tossed under the bar. She had a Sicilian nose. Her neck was hung with jewelry like a bandit princess's.

The small man looked at her sternly. "You're late. I can't operate without a hostess."

"I'm sorry, Tony. Rachel was late again."

"Hire another baby sitter."

"But she's so good with the baby. You wouldn't want just anybody feeding him.

"We won't talk about it now. You know where you're supposed to be."

"Yes, Mr. Napoleon."

With a rebellious swing of the hip, she took up her post by the door. Customers were beginning to drift in by twos and fours. Most of them were young or young middle-aged. They looked respectable enough. Talking and laughing vivaciously, clinking her jewelry, the hostess guided them to the red-checked tables.

Her husband remembered me after a while. "Here's Sam Jackman's address. He has no phone, but it isn't far from here."

He handed me a sheet from a memo pad on which he had written in pencil: "169 Mimosa, apt. 2."

It was near the railroad tracks, an old frame house with Victorian gingerbread on the facade half chewed away by time. The heavy carved front door was standing open, and I went into the hallway, feeling warped parquetry under my feet. On a closed door to my right, a number 2 stamped from metal hung upside down by a single nail. It rattled when I knocked.

A yellow-faced man in shirt sleeves looked out. "Who is it you want?"

"Sam Jackman."

"That's me." He seemed surprised that anybody should want him. "Is it about a job?" He asked the question with a kind of hollow hopefulness that answered itself in the negative.

"No, but I want to talk to you about something important, Mr. Jackman."

He caught the "mister" and inclined his head in acknowledgement. "All right."

"May I come in? My name is Lew Archer. I'm a private detective."

"I dunno, the place is a mess. With the wife working all day—but come on in."

He backed into his apartment, as if he was afraid to expose his flank. It consisted of one large room which might once have been the drawing room of the house. It still had its fine proportions, but the lofty ceiling was scabbed and watermarked, the windows hung with torn curtains. A cardboard wardrobe, a gas plate behind a screen, stood against the inner wall. Run-down furniture, including an unmade double bed in one corner, cluttered the bare wooden floor. On a table beside the bed, a small television set was reeling of the disasters of the day in crisp elocutionary sentences.

Jackman switched it off, picked up a smoking cigarette from the lid of a coffee can on the table, and sat on the edge of the bed. It wasn't a marihuana cigarette. He was completely still and silent, waiting for me to explain myself. I sat down facing him.

"I'm looking for Tom Hillman."

He gave me a swift glance that had fear in it, then busied himself putting out his cigarette. He dropped the butt into the pocket of his shirt.

"I didn't know he was missing."

"He is."

"That's too bad. What would make you think that he was here?" He looked around the room with wide unblinking eyes. "Did Mr. Hillman send you?"

"No."

He didn't believe me. "I just wondered. Mr. Hillman has been on my back."

"Why?"

"I interested myself in his boy," he said carefully.

"In what way?"

"Personally." He turned his hands palms upward on his knees. "I heard him doodling on the piano at the beach club. That was one day last spring. I did a little doodling of my own. Piano isn't my instrument, but he got interested in some chords I showed him. That made me a bad influence."

"Were you?"

"Mr. Hillman thought so. He got me fired from the beach club. He didn't want his precious boy messing with the likes of me." His upturned hands lay like helpless pink-bellied animals on their backs. "If Mr. Hillman didn't send you, who did?"

"A man named Dr. Sponti."

I thought the name would mean nothing to him, but he gave me another of his quick fearful looks. "Sponti? You mean—?" He fell silent.

"Go on, Mr. Jackman. Tell me what I mean."

He huddled down into himself, like a man slumping into sudden old age. He let his speech deteriorate: "I wouldn't know nothin' about nothin', mister." He opened his mouth in an idiotic smile that showed no teeth.

"I think you know a good deal. I think I'll sit here until you tell me some of it."

"That's your privilege," he said, although it wasn't.

He took the butt out of his shirt pocket and lit it with a kitchen match. He dropped the distorted black match-end into the coffee lid. We looked at each other through smoke that drifted like ectoplasm from his mouth.

"You know Dr. Sponti, do you?"

"I've heard the name," Jackman said.

"Have you seen Tom Hillman in the last two days?"

He shook his head, but his eyes stayed on my face in a certain way, as if he was expecting to be challenged.

"Where have you heard Sponti's name?"

"A relative of mine. She used to work in the kitchen at L.P.S." He said with irony: "That makes me an accessory, I guess."

"Accessory to what?"

"Any crime in the book. I wouldn't even have to know what happened, would I?" He doused his butt in a carefully restricted show of anger.

"That sort of talk gets us nowhere."

"Where does your sort of talk get us? Anything I tell you is evidence against me, isn't it?"

"You talk like a man with a record."

"I've had my troubles." He added after a long silence: "I'm sorry Tommy Hillman is having his."

"You seem to be fond of him."

"We took to each other." He threw the line away.

"I wish you'd tell me more about him. That's really what I came here for."

My words sounded slightly false. I was suspicious of Jackman, and he knew it. He was a watcher and a subtle listener.

"Now I got a different idea," he said. "I got the idea you're after Tommy to put him back in the L.P. School. Correct me if I'm wrong."

"You're wrong."

"I don't believe you." He was watching my hands to see if I might hit him. There were marks on his face where he had been hit before. "No offense, but I don't believe you, mister—"

I repeated my name. "Do you know where Tommy is?"

"No. I do know this. If Mr. Hillman put him in the L.P. School, he's better off on the loose than going home. His father had no right to do it to him."

"So I've been told."

"Who told you?"

"One of the women on the staff there. She said Tom wasn't disturbed in her opinion, and didn't belong in the school. Tom seemed to agree with her. He broke out Saturday night."

"Good."

"Not so good. At least he was safe there."

"He's safe," Jackman said, and quickly regretted saying it. He opened his mouth in its senseless toothless smile, a tragic mask pretending to be comic.

"Where is he then?"

Jackman shrugged his thin shoulders. "I told you before and I'll tell you again, I don't know."

"How did you know that he was on the loose?"

"Sponti wouldn't send you to me otherwise."

"You're quick on the uptake."

"I have to pick up what I can," he said. "You talk a lot without saying much."

"You say even less. But you'll talk, Sam."

He rose in a quick jerky movement and went to the door. I thought he was going to tell me to leave, but he didn't. He stood against the closed door in the attitude of a man facing a rifle squad.

"What do you expect me to do?" he cried. "Put my neck in the noose so Hillman can hang me?"

I walked toward him.

"Stay away from me!" The fear in his eyes was burning brightly, feeding on a long fuse of experience. He lifted one crooked arm to shield his head. "Don't touch me!"

"Calm down. That's hysterical talk, about a noose."

"It's a hysterical world. I lost my job for teaching his kid some music. Now Hillman is raising the ante. What's the rap this time?"

"There is no rap if the boy is safe. You said he was. Didn't you?"

No answer, but he looked at me under his arm. He had tears in his eyes.

"For God's sake, Sam, we ought to be able to get together on this. You like the boy, you don't want anything bad to happen to him. That's all I have in mind."

"There's bad and bad." But he lowered his defensive arm and kept on studying my face.

"I know there's bad and bad," I said. "The line between them isn't straight and narrow. The difference between them isn't black and white. I know you favor Tom against his father. You don't want him to cut off from you or your kind of music. And you think I want to drag him back to a school where he doesn't belong."

"Aren't you?"

"I'm trying to save his life. I think you can help me."

"How?"

"Let's sit down again and talk quietly the way we were. Come on. And stop seeing Hillman when you look at me."

Jackman returned to the bed and I sat near him.

"Well, Sam, have you seen him in the last two days?"

"See who? Mr. Hillman?"

"Don't go into the idiot act again. You're an intelligent man. Just answer my question."

"Before I do, will you answer one of mine?"

"If I possibly can."

"When you say you're trying to save his life, you mean save him from bad influences, don't you, put him back in Squaresville with all the other squares?"

"Worse things can happen to a boy."

"You didn't answer my question."

"You could have asked a better one. I mean save him from death. He's in the hands of people who may or may not decide to kill him, depending on how the impulse takes them. Am I telling you anything you don't know?"

"You sure are, man." His voice was sincere, and his eyes filled up with compunction. But he and I could talk for a year, and he would still be holding something back. Among the things he was holding back was the fact that he didn't believe me.

"Why don't you believe me, Sam?"

"I didn't say that."

"You don't have to. You're acting it out, by sitting on the information you have."

"I ain't sittin' on nothin', 'ceptin' this here old raunchy bed," he said in broad angry parody.

"Now I know you are. I've got an ear for certain things, the way you've got an ear for music. You play the trombone, don't you?"

"Yeah." He looked surprised.

"I hear you blow well."

"Don't flatter me. I ain't no J. C. Higginbotham."

"And I ain't no Sherlock Holmes. But sooner or later you're going to tell me when you saw Tommy Hillman last. You're not going to sit on your raunchy ole bed and wait for the television to inform you that they found Tommy's body in a ditch."

"Did they?"

"Not yet. It could happen tonight. When did you see him?" He drew a deep breath. "Yesterday. He was okay."

"Did he come here?"

"No sir. He never has. He stopped in at The Barroom Floor yesterday afternoon. He came in the back way and only stayed five minutes."

"What was he wearing?"

"Slacks and a black sweater. He told me once his mother knitted that sweater for him."

"Did you talk to him yesterday afternoon?"

"I played him a special riff and he came up and thanked me. That was all. I didn't know he was on the run. Shucks, he even had his girl friend with him."

"Stella?"

"The other one. The older one."

"What's her name?"

"He never told me. I only seen her once or twice before that. Tommy knew I wouldn't approve of him squiring her around. She's practically old enough to be his mother."

"Can you describe her?"

"She's a bottle blonde, with a lot of hair, you know how they're wearing it now." He swept his hand up from his wrinkled forehead. "Blue eyes, with a lot of eye shadow. It's hard to tell what she looks like under that makeup."

I got out my notebook and made some notes. "What's her background?"

"Show business, maybe. Like I say, I never talked to her. But she has the looks."

"I gather she's attractive."

"She appears to be to Tom. I guess she's his first. A lot of young boys start out with an older woman. But," he added under his breath, "he could do better than that."

"How old is she?"

"Thirty, anyway. She didn't show me her birth certificate. She dresses younger—skirts up over the knees. She isn't a big girl, and maybe in some lights she can get away with the youth act."

"What was she wearing yesterday?"

"A dark dress, blue satin or something like that, with sequins on it, a neckline down to here." He touched his solar plexus. "It grieved me to see Tom with his arm around her."

"How did she seem to feel about him?"

"You're asking me more than I can answer. He's a good-looking boy, and she makes a show of affection. But I don't need X-ray eyes to know what is in her mind."

"Would she be a hustler?"

"Could be."

"Did you ever see her with any other man?"

"I never did. I only saw her once or twice with Tom."

"Once, or twice?"

He ruminated. "Twice before yesterday. The first time was two weeks ago yesterday. That was a Sunday, he brought her to our jam session that afternoon. The woman had been drinking and first she wanted to sing and then she wanted to dance. We don't allow dancing at these sessions, you have to pay cabaret tax. Somebody told her that and she got mad and towed the boy away."

"Who told her not to dance?"

"I disremember. One of the cats sitting around, I guess, they object to dancing. The music we play Sundays isn't to dance to, anyway. It's more to the glory of God," he said surprisingly.

"What about the second time you saw her?"

He hesitated, thinking. "That was ten nights ago, on a Friday. They came in around midnight and had a sandwich. I drifted by their table, at the break, but Tom didn't introduce me or ask me to sit down. Which was all right with me. They seemed to have things to talk about."

"Did you overhear any part of their conversation?"

"I did." His face hardened. "She needed money, she was telling him, money to get away from her husband."

"You're sure you heard that?"

"Sure as I'm sitting here."

"What was Tom's attitude?"

"Looked to me like he was fascinated."

"Had he been drinking?"

"*She* was. He didn't drink. They don't serve drinks to minors at the Floor. No sir. She had him hyped on something worse than drink."

"Drugs?"

"You know what I mean." His hands molded a woman's figure in the air.

"You used the word 'hyped.' "

"It was just a manner of speaking," he said nervously, rubbing his upper arm through the shirt sleeve.

"Are you on the needle?"

"No sir. I'm on the TV," he said with a sudden downward smile.

"Show me your arms."

"I don't have to. You got no right."

"I want to test your veracity. Okay?"

He unbuttoned his cuffs and pushed his sleeves up his thin yellow arms. The pitted scars in them were old and dry.

"I got out of Lexington seven years ago," he said, "and I haven't fallen since, I thank the good Lord."

He touched his scars with a kind of reverence. They were like tiny extinct volcanoes in his flesh. He covered them up.

"You're doing all right, Mr. Jackman. With your background, you'd probably know if Tom was on drugs."

"I probably would. He wasn't. More than once I lectured him on the subject. Musicians have their temptations. But he took my lectures to heart." He shifted his hand to the region of his heart. "I ought to of lectured him on the subject of women."

"I never heard that it did much good. Did you ever see Tom and the blonde with anyone else?"

"No."

"Did he introduce her to anyone?"

"I doubt it. He was keeping her to himself. Showing her off, but keeping her to himself."

"You don't have any idea what her name is?"

"No. I don't."

I got up and thanked him. "I'm sorry if I gave you a rough time."

"I've had rougher."

7

Dack's Auto Court was on the edge of the city, in a rather rundown suburb named Ocean View. The twelve or fifteen cottages of the court lay on the flat top of a bluff, below the highway and above the sea. They were made of concrete block and painted an unnatural green. Three or four cars, none of them recent models, were parked on the muddy gravel.

The rain had let up and fresh yellow light slanted in from a hole in the west, as if to provide a special revelation of the ugliness of Dack's Auto Court. Above the hutch marked "Office," a single ragged palm tree leaned against the light. I parked beside it and went in.

A hand-painted card taped to the counter instructed me to "Ring for Proprietor." I punched the handbell beside it. It didn't work.

Leaning across the counter, I noticed on the shelf below it a telephone and a metal filing box divided into fifteen numbered sections. The registration card for number seven was dated three weeks before, and indicated that "Mr. and Mrs. Robt. Brown" were paying sixteen dollars a week for that cottage. The spaces provided on the card for home address and license number were empty.

The screen door creaked behind me. A big old man with a naked condor head came flapping into the office. He snatched the card from my fingers and looked at me with hot eyes. "What do you think you're doing?"

"I was only checking."

"Checking what?"

"To see if some people I know are here. Bob Brown and his wife."

He held the card up to the light and read it, moving his lips laboriously around the easy words. "They're here," he said without joy. "Leastways, they were this morning."

He gave me a doubtful look. My claim of acquaintanceship with the Browns had done nothing for my status. I tried to improve it. "Do you have a cottage vacant?"

"Ten of them. Take your pick."

"How much?"

"Depends on if you rent by the day or the week. They're three-fifty a day, sixteen a week."

"I'd better check with the Browns first, see if they're planning to stay."

"I wouldn't know about that. They been here three weeks." He had a flexible worried mouth in conflict with a stupid stubborn chin. He stroked his chin as if to educate it. "I can let you have number eight for twelve a week single. That's right next door to the Browns' place."

"I'll check with them."

"I don't believe they're there. You can always try."

I went outside and down the dreary line of cottages. The door of number seven was locked. Nobody answered my repeated rapping.

When I turned away, the old man was standing in front of number eight. He beckoned to me and opened the door with a flourish:

"Take a look. I can let you have it for ten if you really like it."

I stepped inside. The room was cold and cheerless. The inside walls were concrete block, and the same unnatural green as the outside. Through a crack in the drawn blind, yellow light slashed at the hollow bed, the threadbare carpet. I'd spent too many nights in places like it to want to spend another.

"It's clean," the old man said.

"I'm sure it is, Mr. Dack."

"I cleaned it myself. But I'm not Dack. I'm Stanislaus. Dack sold out to me years ago. I just never got around to having the signs changed. What's the use? They'll be tearing everything down and putting up high-rise apartments pretty soon." He smiled and stroked his bald skull as if it was a kind of golden egg. "Well, you want the cottage?"

"It really depends on Brown's plans."

"If I was you," he said, "I wouldn't let too much depend on him."

"How is that, Mr. Stanislaus?"

"He's kind of a blowtop, ain't he? I mean, the way he treats that little blonde wife. I always say these things are between a man *and* his wife. But it rankles me," he said. "I got a deep respect for women."

"So have I. I've never liked the way he treated women."

"I'm glad to hear that. A man should treat his wife with love and friendship. I lost my own wife several years ago, and I know what I'm talking about. I tried to tell him that, he told me to mind my own business. I know he's a friend of yours—"

"He's not exactly a friend. Is he getting worse?"

"Depends on what you mean, *worse*. This very day he was slapping her around. I felt like kicking him out of my place. Only, how would that help *her*? And all she did was make a little phone call. He tries to keep her cooped up like she was in jail." He paused, listening, as if the word *jail* had associations for him. "How long have you known this Brown?"

"Not so long," I said vaguely. "I ran into him in Los Angeles."

"In Hollywood?"

"Yeah. In Hollywood."

"Is it true she was in the movies? She mentioned one day she used to be in the movies. He told her to shut up."

"Their marriage seems to be deteriorating."

"You can say that again." He leaned toward me in the doorway. "I bet you she's the one you're interested in. I see a lot of couples, one way and another, and I'm willing to bet you she's just about had her fill of him. If I was a young fellow like you, I'd be tempted to make her an offer." He nudged me; the friction seemed to warm him. "She's a red-hot little bundle."

"I'm not young enough."

"Sure you are." He handled my arm, and chuckled. "It's true she likes 'em young. I been seeing her off and on with a teen-ager, even."

I produced the photograph of Tom that Elaine Hillman had given me. "This one?"

The old man lifted it to the daylight, at arm's length. "Yeah. That's a might good picture of him. He's a good-looking boy." He handed the photograph back to me, and fondled his chin. "How do you come to have a picture of him?"

I told him the truth, or part of it: "He's a runaway from a boarding school. I'm a private detective representing the school."

The moist gleam of lechery faded out of Stanislaus's eyes. Something bleaker took its place, a fantasy of punishment perhaps. His whole face underwent a transformation, like quick-setting concrete.

"You can't make me responsible for what the renters do."

"Nobody said I could."

He didn't seem to hear me. "Let's see that picture again." I showed it to him. He shook his head over it. "I made a mistake. My eyes ain't what they used to be. I never seen him before."

'You made a positive identification."

"I take it back. You were talking to me under false pretenses, trying to suck me in and get something on me. Well, you got nothing on me. It's been tried before," he said darkly. "And you can march yourself off my property."

"Aren't you going to rent me the cottage?"

He hesitated a moment, saying a silent goodbye to the ten dollars. "No sir, I want no spies and peepers in my place."

"You may be harboring something worse."

I think he suspected it, and the suspicion was the source of his anger.

"I'll take my chances. Now you git. If you're not off my property in one minute, I'm going to call the sheriff."

That was the last thing I wanted. I'd already done enough to endanger the ransom payment and Tom's return. I got.

8

A blue sports car stood in the drive behind the Hillman Cadillac. An athletic-looking young man who looked as if he belonged in the sports car came out of the house and confronted me on the front steps. He wore an Ivy League suit and had an alligator coat slung over his arm and hand, with something bulky and gun-shaped under it.

"Point that thing away from me. I'm not armed."

"I w-want to know who you are." He had a faint stammer.

"Lew Archer. Who are you?"

"I'm Dick Leandro." He spoke the words almost questioningly, as if he didn't quite know what it meant to be Dick Leandro.

"Lower that gun," I reminded him. "Try pointing it at your leg."

He dropped his arm. The alligator coat slid off it, onto the flagstone steps, and I saw that he was holding a heavy old revolver. He picked up the coat and looked at me in a rather confused way. He was a handsome boy in his early twenties, with brown eyes and dark curly hair. A certain little dancing light in his eyes told me that he was aware of being handsome.

"Since you're here," I said, "I take it the money's here, too."

"Yes. I brought it out from the office several hours ago."

"Has Hillman been given instructions for delivering it?"

He shook his head. "We're still waiting."

I found Ralph and Elaine Hillman in the downstairs room where the telephone was. They were sitting close together as if for warmth, on a chesterfield near the front window. The waiting had aged them both.

The evening light fell like gray paint across their faces. She was knitting something out of red wool. Her hands moved rapidly and precisely as if they had independent life.

Hillman got to his feet. He had been holding a newspaper-wrapped parcel in his lap, and he laid it down on the chesterfield, gently, like a father handling an infant.

"Hello, Archer," he said in a monotone.

I moved toward him with some idea of comforting him. But the expression in his eyes, hurt and proud and lonely, discouraged me from touching him or saying anything very personal.

60

"You've had a long hard day."

He nodded slowly, once. His wife let out a sound like a dry sob. "Why haven't we heard anything from that man?"

"It's hard to say. He seems to be putting on the screws deliberately."

She pushed her knitting to one side, and it fell on the floor unnoticed. Her faded pretty face wrinkled up as if she could feel the physical pressure of torture instruments. "He's keeping us in hell, in absolute hell. But why?"

"He's probably waiting for dark," I said. "I'm sure you'll be hearing from him soon. Twenty-five thousand dollars is a powerful attraction."

"He's welcome to the money, five times over. Why doesn't he simply take it and give us back our boy?" Her hand flung itself out, rattling the newspaper parcel beside her.

"Don't fret yourself, Ellie." Hillman leaned over her and touched her pale gold hair. "There's no use asking questions that can't be answered. Remember, this will pass." His words of comfort sounded hollow and forced.

"So will I," she said wryly and bitterly, "if this keeps up much longer."

She smoothed her face with both hands and stayed with her hands in a prayerful position at her chin. She was trembling. I was afraid she might snap like a violin string. I said to Hillman:

"May I speak to you in private? I've uncovered some facts you should know."

"You can tell me in front of Elaine, and Dick for that matter."

I noticed that Leandro was standing just inside the door.

"I prefer not to."

"You're not calling the shots, however." It was a curious echo of the man on the telephone. "Let's have your facts."

I let him have them: "Your son has been seen consorting with a married woman named Brown. She's a blonde, show-business type, a good deal older than he is, and she seems to have been after him for money. The chances are better than even that Mrs. Brown and her husband are involved in this extortion bid. They seem to be on the uppers—"

Elaine raised her open hands in front of her face, as if too many words were confusing her. "What do you mean, consorting?"

"He's been hanging around with the woman, publicly and privately. They were seen together yesterday afternoon."

"Where?" Hillman said.

"At The Barroom Floor."

"Who says so?"

"One of their employees. He's seen them before, and he referred to Mrs. Brown as 'Tom's girl friend, the older one.' I've had corroborating evidence from the man who owns the court where the Browns are living. Tom has been hanging around there, too."

"How old is this woman?"

"Thirty or more. She's quite an attractive dish, apparently."

Elaine Hillman lifted her eyes. There seemed to be real horror in them. "Are you implying that Tom has been having an affair with her?"

"I'm simply reporting facts."

"I don't believe your facts, not any of them."

"Do you think I'm lying to you?"

"Maybe not deliberately. But there must be some ghastly mistake."

"I agree," Dick Leandro said from the doorway. "Tom has always been a very clean-living boy."

Hillman was silent. Perhaps he knew something about his son that the others didn't. He sat down beside his wife and hugged the paper parcel defensively.

"His virtue isn't the main thing right now," I said. "The question is what kind of people he's mixed up with and what they're doing to him. Or possibly what they're doing to you with his cooperation."

"What is that supposed to mean?" Hillman said.

"We have to reconsider the possibility that Tom is in on the extortion deal. He was with Mrs. Brown yesterday. The man on the telephone, who may be Brown, said Tom came to them voluntarily."

Elaine Hillman peered up into my face as if she was trying to grasp such a possibility. It seemed to be too much for her to accept. She closed her eyes and shook her head so hard that her hair fell untidily over her forehead. Pushing it back with spread fingers, she said in a small voice that sent chills through me:

"You're lying, I know my son, he's an innocent victim. You're trying to do something terrible, coming to us in our affliction with such a filthy rotten smear."

Her husband tried to quiet her against his shoulder. "Hush now, Elaine. Mr. Archer is only trying to help."

She pushed him away from her. "We don't want that kind of help. He has no right. Tom is an innocent victim, and God knows what is happening to him." Her hand was still at her head, with her pale hair sprouting up between her fingers. "I can't take any more of this, Ralph—this dreadful man with his dreadful stories."

"I'm sorry, Mrs. Hillman. I didn't want you to hear them."

"I know. You wanted to malign my son without anyone to defend him."

"That's nonsense, Ellie," Hillman said. "I think you better come upstairs and let me give you a sedative."

He helped her to her feet and walked her out past me, looking at me sorrowfully across her rumpled head. She moved like an invalid leaning on his strength.

Dick Leandro drifted into the room after they had left it, and sat on the chesterfield to keep the money company. He said in a slightly nagging way:

"You hit Elaine pretty hard with all that stuff. She's a sensitive woman, very puritanical about sex and such. And incidentally she's crazy about Tommy. She won't listen to a word against him."

"*Are* there words against him?"

"Not that I know about. But he has been getting into trouble lately. *You* know, with the car wreck and all. And now you t-tell me he's dipping into the fleshpots."

"I didn't say that."

"Yeah, but I got the message. Where does the g-girl live, anyway? Somebody ought to go and question her."

"You're full of ideas."

He had a tin ear for tone. "Well, how about it? I'm game."

"You're doing more good here, guarding the money. How did Hillman happen to pick you to bring the money, by the way? Are you an old family friend?"

"I guess you could say that. I've been crewing for Mr. Hillman since I was yay-high." He held out his hand at knee level. "Mr. Hillman is a terrific guy. Did you know he made Captain in the Navy? But he won't let anybody call him Captain except when we're at sea.

"And generous," the young man said. "As a matter of fact, he helped me through college and got me a job at his broker's. I owe him a lot. He's treated me like a father." He spoke with some emotion, real but intended, like an actor's. "I'm an orphan, you might say. My family broke up when I was yay-high, and my father left town. He used to work for Mr. Hillman at the plant.''

"Do you know Tom Hillman well?"

"Sure. He's a pretty good kid. But a little too much of an egghead in my book. Which keeps him from being popular. No wonder he has his troubles." Leandro tapped his temple with his knuckles. "Is it true that Mr. Hillman put him in the booby—I mean, in a sanatorium?"

"Ask him yourself."

The young man bored me. I went into the alcove and made myself a drink. Night was closing in. The garish bullfight posters on the walls had faded into darkness like long-forgotten *corridas*. There were shadows huddling with shadows behind the bar. I raised my glass to them in a gesture I didn't quite understand, except that there was relief in darkness and silence and whisky.

I could hear Hillman's footsteps dragging down the stairs. The telephone on the bar went off like an alarm. Hillman's descending footsteps became louder. He came trotting into the room as the telephone rang a second time. He elbowed me out of his way.

I started for the extension phone in the pantry. He called after me:

"No! I'll handle this myself."

There was command in his voice. I stood and watched him pick up the receiver, hold it to his head like a black scorpion, and listen to what it said.

"Yes, this is Mr. Hillman. Just a minute." He brought a business envelope and a ballpoint pen out of his inside pocket, turned on an overhead light, and got ready to write on the bar. "Go ahead."

For about half a minute he listened and wrote. Then he said: "I think so. Aren't there steps going down to the beach?"

He listened and wrote. "Where shall I walk to?" He turned the envelope over and wrote some more. "Yes," he said. "I park two blocks away, at Seneca, and approach the steps on foot. I put the money under the right side of the top step. Then I go down to the beach for half an hour. Is that all?"

There was a little more. He listened to it. Finally he said: "Yes. But the deal is very much one as far as I'm concerned. I'll be there at nine sharp."

There was a pathetic note in his voice, the note of a salesman trying to nail down an appointment with a refractory client.

"Wait," he said, and groaned into the dead receiver.

Dick Leandro, moving like a cat, was in the alcove ahead of me. "What is it, Mr. Hillman? What's the trouble?"

"I wanted to ask about Tom. He didn't give me a chance." He lifted his face to the plaster ceiling. "I don't know if he's alive or dead."

"They wouldn't *kill* him, would they?" the young man said. He sounded as though he'd had a first frightening hint of his own mortality.

"I don't know, Dick. I don't know." Hillman's head rolled from one side to the other.

The young man put his arm around his shoulder. "Take it easy now, Skipper. We'll get him back."

Hillman poured himself a heavy slug of bourbon and tossed it down. It brought a little color into his face. I said:

"Same man?"

"Yes."

"And he told you where to make the money-drop."

"Yes."

"Do you want company?"

"I have to go there alone. He said he'd be watching."

"Where are you to go?"

Hillman looked at each of our faces in turn, lingeringly, as if he was saying goodbye. "I'll keep that to myself. I don't want anything to wreck the arrangements."

"Somebody should know about them, though, in case anything does go wrong. You're taking a chance."

"I'd rather take a chance with my own life than my son's." He said it as if he meant it, and the words seemed to renew his courage. He glanced at his wristwatch. "It's twenty-five to nine. It will take me up to twenty minutes to get there. He didn't give me much leeway."

"Can you drive okay?" Leandro said.

"Yes. I'm all right. I'll just go up and tell Ellie that I'm leaving. You stay in the house with her, won't you, Dick?"

"I'll be glad to."

Hillman went upstairs, still clutching his scribbled-over envelope. I said to Leandro: "Where is Seneca Street?"

"Seneca Road. In Ocean View."

"'Are there steps going down to the beach anywhere near there?''

"Yeah, but you're not supposed to go there. You heard Mr. Hillman.''

"I heard him.''

Hillman came down and took the parcel of money out of Leandro's hands. He thanked the young man, and his voice was deep and gentle as well as melancholy.

We stood on the flagstone steps and watched him drive away into the darkness under the trees. In the hole in the dark west a little light still persisted, like the last light there was ever going to be.

I went through the house to the kitchen and asked Mrs. Perez to make me a plain cheese sandwich. She grumbled, but she made it. I ate it leaning against the refrigerator. Mrs. Perez wouldn't talk about the trouble in the family. She seemed to have a superstitious feeling that trouble was only amplified by words. When I tried to question her about Tom's habits, she gradually lost her ability to understand my English.

Dick Leandro had gone upstairs to sit with Elaine. He seemed more at home than Tom appeared to have been with his own family. I went out through the reception hall. It was nine o'clock, and I couldn't wait any longer.

Driving along the highway to Ocean View, I argued jesuitically with myself that I had stayed clear of the money-drop, I wasn't double-dealing with Hillman, who wasn't my client in any case, and besides I had no proof that Mrs. Brown and her husband were connected with the extortion attempt.

It was deep night over the sea, moonless and starless. I left my car at a view-point near Dack's Auto Court. The sea was a hollow presence with a voice. I hiked down the access road to the court, not using the flashlight that I carried with me.

The office was lighted and had a neon "Vacancy" sign above the door. Avoiding the spill of light from it, I went straight to cottage number seven. It was dark. I knocked, and got no answer. I let myself in with the key I had and closed the self-locking door behind me.

Mrs. Brown was waiting. I stumbled over her foot and almost fell on top of her before I switched on my flashlight. She lay in her winking sequined gown under the jittery beam. Blood was tangled like tar in her bright hair. Her face was mottled with bruises, and misshapen. She looked as thought she had been beaten to death.

I touched her hand. She was cold. I turned the light away from her lopsided grin.

The beam jumped around the green walls, the newspaper-littered floor. It found a large strapped canvas suitcase standing at the foot of the bed with two paper bags beside it. One of the bags contained a bottle of cheap wine, the other sandwiches that were drying out.

I unstrapped the suitcase and opened it. An odor rose from its contents like sour regret. Men's and women's things were bundled indiscriminately together, dirty shirts and soiled slips, a rusting safety razor and a dabbled jar of cold cream and a bottle of mascara, a couple of dresses and some lingerie, a man's worn blue suit with a chain-store label and nothing in the pockets but tobacco powder and, tucked far down in the outer breast pocket, a creased yellow business card poorly printed on cheap paper:

> Harold "Har" Harley
>
> *Application Photos Our Specialty*

I found the woman's imitation snakeskin purse on a chair by the side window. It contained a jumble of cosmetics and some frayed blue chip stamps. No wallet, no identification, no money except for a single silver dollar in the bottom of the bag.

There were also a pack of cards, slick with the oil of human hands, and a dice which came up six all three times I rolled it.

I heard a car approaching, and headlights swept the window on the far side. I switched off my flashlight. The wheels of the car crunched in the gravel and came to a halt directly in front of the cottage. Someone got out of the car and turned the cottage doorknob. When the door refused to open, a man's voice said:

"Let me in."

It was the slightly wheezing, whining voice I'd heard that afternoon on Hillman's phone. I moved toward the door with the dark flashlight raised in my hand. The man outside rattled the knob.

"I know you're in there, I saw the light. This is no time to carry a grudge, hon."

The woman lay in her deep waiting silence. I stepped around her and stood against the wall beside the door. I shifted the flash to my left hand and fumbled for the spring lock with my right.

"I hear you, damn you. You want another taste of what you had today?" He waited, and then said: "If you won't open the door, I'll shoot the lock out."

I heard the click of a hammer. I stayed where I was beside the door, holding the flashlight like a club. But he didn't fire.

"On the other hand," he said, "there's nothing in there I need, including you. You can stay here on your can if you want to. Make up your mind right now."

He waited. He couldn't outwait her.

"This is your last chance. I'll count to three. If you don't open up, I'm traveling alone." He counted, one, two, three, but it would take bigger magic to reach her. "Good riddance to bad rubbish," he said.

His footsteps moved away on the stones. The car door creaked. I couldn't let him go.

I snapped back the lock and opened the door and rushed him. His shadowy hatted figure was halfway into his car, with one foot on the ground. He whirled. The gun was still in his hand. It gave out a hot little flame. I could feel it sear me.

I staggered across the gravel and got hold of his twisting body. He hammered my hands loose with the butt of his gun. I had blood in my eyes, and I couldn't avoid the gun butt when it smashed into my skull. A kind of chandelier lit up in my head and then crashed down into darkness.

Next thing I was a V.I.P. traveling with a police guard in the back of a chauffeured car. The turban I could feel on my head suggested to the joggled brain under it that I was a rajah or a maharajah. We turned into a driveway under a red light, which excited me. Perhaps I was being taken to see one of my various concubines.

I raised the question with the uniformed men sitting on either side of me. Gently but firmly, they helped me out of the patrol car and walked me through swinging doors, which a man in white held open, into a glaring place that smelled of disinfectants.

They persuaded me to sit down on a padded table and then to lie down. My head hurt. I felt it with my hands. It had a towel around it, sticky with blood.

A large young face with a moustache leaned over me upside down. Large hairy hands removed the towel and did some probing and scouring in my scalp. It stung.

"You're a lucky man. It parted your hair for you, kind of permanently."

"How bad is it, Doctor?"

"The bullet wound isn't serious, just a crease. As I said, you're lucky. This other lesion is going to take longer to heal. What did you get hit with?"

"Gun butt. I think."

"More fun and games," he said.

"Did they catch him?"

"You'll have to ask them. They haven't told me a thing."

He clipped parts of my head and put some clamps in it and gave me a drink of water and an aspirin. Then he left me lying alone in the white-partitioned cubicle. My two guards moved rapidly into the vacuum.

They were sheriff's men, wearing peaked hats and tan uniforms. They were young and hearty, with fine animal bodies and rather animal, not so fine, faces. Good earnest boys, but a little dull. They said they wanted to help me.

"Why did you kill her?" the dark one said.

"I didn't. She'd been dead for some time when I found her."

"That doesn't let you out. Mr. Stanislaus said you were there earlier in the day."

"He was with me all the time."

"That's what you say," the fair one said.

This repartee went on for some time, like a recording of an old vaudeville act which some collector had unwisely preserved. I tried to question them. They wouldn't tell me anything. My head was feeling worse, but oddly enough I began to think better with it. I even managed to get up on my elbows and look at them on the level.

"I'm a licensed private detective from Los Angeles."

"We know that," the dark one said.

I felt for my wallet. It was missing. "Give me my wallet."

"You'll get it back all in good time. Nobody's going to steal it."

"I want to talk to the sheriff."

"He's in bed asleep."

"Is there a captain or lieutenant on duty?"

"The lieutenant is busy at the scene of the crime. You can talk to him in the morning. The doctor says you stay here overnight. Concussion. What did the woman hit you with, anyway?"

"Her husband hit me, with a gun butt."

"I hardly blame him," the fair one said emotionally, "after what you did to his wife."

"Were you shacked up with her?" the dark one said.

I looked from one healthy smooth face to the other. They didn't look sadistic, or sound corrupt, and I wasn't afraid for myself. Sooner or later the mess would be straightened out. But I was afraid.

"Listen," I said, "you're wasting time on me. I had legitimate business at the court. I was investigating—" The fear came up in my throat and choked off the rest of the sentence. It was fear for the boy.

"Investigating what?" the dark one said.

"Law enforcement in this county. It stinks." I wasn't feeling too articulate.

"We'll law-enforcement you," the dark one said. He was broad, with muscular shoulders. He moved them around in the air a little bit and pretended to catch a fly just in front of my face.

"Lay off, muscle," I said.

The large, moustached face of the doctor appeared in the entrance to the cubicle. "Everything okay in here?"

I said above the deputies' smiling assurances: "I want to make a phone call."

The doctor looked doubtfully from me to the officers. "I don't know about that."

"I'm a private detective investigating a crime. I'm not free to talk about it without the permission of my principal. I want to call him."

"There's no facilities for that," the dark deputy said.

"How about it, Doctor? You're in charge here, and I have a legal right to make a phone call."

He was a very young man behind his moustache. "I don't know. There's a telephone booth down the hall. Do you think you can make it?"

"I never felt better in my life."

But when I swung my legs down, the floor seemed distant and undulant. The deputies had to help me to the booth and prop me up on the stool inside of it. I pulled the folding door shut. Their faces floated outside the wired glass like bulbous fishes, a dark one and a fair one, nosing around a bathyscaphe on the deep ocean floor.

Technically Dr. Sponti was my principal, but it was Ralph Hillman's number I asked Information for. I had a dime in my pocket, fortunately, and Hillman was there. He answered the phone himself on the first ring:

"Yes?"

"This is Archer."

He groaned.

"Have you heard anything from Tom?" I said.

"No. I followed instructions to the letter, and when I came up from the beach the money was gone. He's double-crossed me," he said bitterly.

"Did you see him?"

"No. I made no attempt to."

"I did." I told Hillman what had happened, to me and to Mrs. Brown.

His voice came thin and bleak over the wire. "And you think these are the same people?"

"I think Brown's your man. Brown is probably an alias. Does the name Harold Harley mean anything to you?"

"What was that again?"

"Harold or 'Har' Harley. He's a photographer."

"I never heard of him."

I wasn't surprised. Harley's yellow card was the kind that businessmen distributed by the hundred, and had no necessary connection with Brown.

"Is that all you wanted?" Hillman said. "I'm trying to keep this line open."

"I haven't got to the main thing. The police are on my back. I can't explain what I was doing at the auto court without dragging in the extortion bit, and your son."

"Can't you give them a story?"

"It wouldn't be wise. This is a capital case, a double one."

"Are you trying to tell me that Tom is dead?"

"I meant that kidnapping is a capital crime. But you are dealing with a killer. I think at this point you should level with the police, and get their help. Sooner or later I'm going to have to level with them."

"I forbid—" He changed his tone, and started the sentence over: "I beg of you, please hold off. Give him until morning to come home. He's my only son."

"All right. Till morning. We can't bottle it up any longer than that, and we shouldn't."

I hung up and stepped out into the corridor. Instead of taking me back to the emergency ward, my escort took me up in an elevator to a special room with heavy screens on the windows. They let me lie down on the bed, and took turns questioning me. It would be tedious to recount the dialogue. It was tedious at the time, and I didn't listen to all of it.

Some time around midnight a sheriff's lieutenant named Bastian came into the room and ordered the deputies out into the hall. He was a tall man, with iron-gray hair clipped short. The vertical grooves in his cheeks looked like the scars inflicted by a personal discipline harsher than saber cuts.

He stood over me frowning. "Dr. Murphy says you're feeling critical of law enforcement in this county."

"I've had reason."

"It isn't easy recruiting men at the salaries the supervisors are willing to pay. We can hardly compete with the wages for unskilled labor. And this is a *tough* job."

"It has its little extra compensations."

"What does that mean?"

"I seem to be missing my wallet."

Bastian's face went grim. He marched out into the hall, made some remarks in a voice that buzzed like a hornet, and came back carrying my wallet. I counted the money in it, rather obtrusively.

"It was used to check you out," Bastian said. "L.A. County

gives you a good rating, and I'm sorry if you weren't treated right."

"Think nothing of it. I'm used to being pushed around by unskilled labor."

"You heard me apologize," he said, in a tone that closed the subject.

Bastian asked me a number of questions about Mrs. Brown and the reason for my interest in her. I told him I'd have to check with my client in the morning, before I could open up. Then he wanted everything I could give him about Brown's appearance and car.

The moments before and after the shot were vague in my memory. I dredged up what I could. Brown was a man of better than medium size, physically powerful, not young, not old. He was wearing a dark gray or blue jacket and a wide-brimmed grayish hat which shadowed his eyes. The lower part of his face was heavy-jawed. His voice was rough, with a slight wheeze in it. The car was a dirty white or tan two-door sedan, probably a Ford, about eight years old.

I learned two facts from Lieutenant Bastian: the car had an Idaho license, according to other tenants of the court, and Stanislaus was in trouble for keeping no record of the license number. I think Bastian gave me these facts in the hope of loosening my tongue. But he finally agreed to wait till morning.

They shifted me to another room on the same floor, unguarded. I spent a good part of the night, waking and sleeping, watching a turning wheel of faces. The faces were interspersed from time to time with brilliant visions of Dack's Auto Court. It's green ugliness was held in the selective sunset glare, as if it was under a judgment, and so was I.

10

Morning was welcome, in spite of the pain in my head. I couldn't remember eating anything but Mrs. Perez's cheese sandwich since the previous morning. The tepid coffee and overscrambled eggs tasted like nectar and ambrosia.

I was finishing breakfast when Dr. Sponti arrived, breathing rapidly and audibly. His plump face bore the marks of a bad night. He had sleepless bruises around the eyes, and a gash in his upper lip where his razor had slipped. The chilly hand he offered me reminded me of the dead woman's, and I dropped it.

"I'm surprised you knew I was here."

"I found out in a rather circuitous way. A Lieutenant Bastian phoned me in the middle of the night. Evidently he saw the check I gave you yesterday morning. He asked me a great many questions."

"About me?"

"About the whole situation involving you and Tom Hillman."

"You told him about Tom Hillman?"

"I had no choice, really." He picked at the fresh scab on his lip. "A woman has been murdered in Ocean View. I was honor bound to provide the authorities with all the information I could. After all—"

"Does this include the business of the ransom money?"

"Naturally it does. Lieutenant Bastian considered it highly important. He thanked me effusively, and promised that the name of the school would be kept out of the papers."

"Which is the main thing."

"It is to me," Sponti said. "I'm in the school business."

It was frustrating to have held out for nothing, and to have no secrets to trade with Bastian. But it was relieving, too, that the thing was out in the open. Hillman's imposition of silence had made it hard for me to do my job. I said:

"Have you had any repercussions from Ralph Hillman?"

"He phoned early this morning. The boy is still on the missing list." Sponti's voice was lugubrious, and his eyes rolled heavily toward me. "The parents are naturally quite frantic by this time. Mr. Hillman said things I'm sure he'll regret later."

"Is he still blaming you for the kidnapping?"

"Yes, and he blames me for bringing you into the case. He seems to feel you broke faith with him, shall we say."

"By going to the auto court and getting myself shot?"

"You frightened off the kidnappers, in his opinion, and

prevented them from returning his son to him. I'm very much afraid he wants nothing more to do with you, Mr. Archer.''

"And neither do you?"

Dr. Sponti pursed his lips and brought his ten fingers together in the air. They made a Norman arch and then a Gothic one. "I'm sure you understand the pressures I'm under. I'm virtually obliged to do as Mr. Hillman wishes in his extremity."

"Sure."

"And I'm not going to ask you to refund any part of your check. The entire two hundred and fifty dollars is yours, even though you've been in my employ"—he looked at his watch—"considerably less than twenty-four hours. The unearned surplus will take care of your medical expenses, I'm sure." He was backing toward the door. "Well, I have to run."

"Go to hell," I said as he went out.

He poked his head in again: "You may regret saying that. I'm tempted to stop payment on that check after all."

I made an obscene suggestion as to the disposition of the check. Dr. Sponti turned as blue as a Santa Clara plum and went away. I lay and enjoyed my anger for a while. It went so nicely with the reciprocating ache in my head. And it helped to cover over the fact that I had let myself in for this. I shouldn't have gone the second time to Dack's Auto Court, at least not when I did.

A nurse's aide came in and took away my tray. Later a doctor palpated my skull, looked into my eyes with a tiny light, and told me I probably had a slight concussion but so had a lot of other people walking around. I borrowed a safety razor from an orderly, shaved and dressed, and went down to the cashier's window and paid my bill with Sponti's check.

I got over two hundred dollars change. Riding downtown in a taxi, I decided I could afford to spend another day on the case, whether Dr. Sponti liked it or not. I told the driver to let me off at the telephone company.

"You said the courthouse."

"The telephone company. We've had a change of plan."

"You should have said so in the first place."

"Forgive my failure of leadership."

I was feeling bitter and bright. It had to do with the weather, which had turned sunny, but more to do with my decision to spend my own time on a boy I'd never seen. I didn't tip the driver.

One end of the main public room in the telephone building was lined with long-distance booths and shelves of out-of-town directories. Only the main cities in Idaho, like Boise and Pocatello and Idaho Falls, were represented. I looked through their directories for a photographer named Harold Harley. He wasn't listed. Robert Brown was, by the legion, but the name was almost certainly an alias.

I installed myself in one of the booths and placed a long-distance call to Arnie Walters, a Reno detective who often worked with me. I had no Idaho contact, and Reno was on the fastest route to Idaho. Reno itself had a powerful attraction for thieves with sudden money.

"Walters Agency," Arnie said.

"This is Lew." I told him where I was calling from, and why.

"You come up with some dillies. Murder and kidnapping, eh?"

"The kidnapping may be a phony. Tom Hillman, the supposed victim, has been palling around with the murdered woman for a couple of weeks."

"How old did you say he was?"

"Seventeen. He's big for his age." I described Tom Hillman in detail. "He may be traveling with Brown either voluntarily or involuntarily."

"Or not traveling at all?" Arnie said.

"Or not traveling at all."

"You know this boy?"

"No."

"I thought maybe you knew him. Okay. Where does this photographer Harold Harley come in?"

"Harley may be Brown himself, or he may know Brown. His card is the only real lead I have so far. That and the Idaho license. I want you to do two things. Check Idaho and adjoining states for Harley. You have the business directories, don't you?"

"Yeah, I'll get Phyllis on them." She was his wife and partner.

"The other thing, I want you to look out for Brown and the boy, you and your informers in Tahoe and Vegas."

"What makes you think they're headed in this direction?"

"It's a hunch. The woman had a silver dollar and a loaded dice in her purse."

"And no identification?"

"Whoever did her in got rid of everything she had in that line. But we'll identify her. We have *her*."

"Let me know when you do."

I walked across town to the courthouse, under a sky that yesterday's rain had washed clean. I asked the deputy on duty in the sheriff's department where to find Lieutenant Bastian. He directed me to the identification laboratory on the second floor.

It was more office than laboratory, a spacious room with pigeons murmuring on the window ledges. The walls were crowded with filing cabinets and hung with maps of the city and county and state. A large adjacent closet was fitted out as a darkroom, with drying racks and a long metal sink.

Bastian got up smiling. His smile wasn't greatly different from last night's frown. He laid down a rectangular magnifying glass on top of the photograph he had been studying. Leaning across the desk to take his outstretched hand, I could see that it was a picture of Mrs. Brown in death.

"What killed her, Lieutenant?" I said when we were seated.

"This." He held up his right hand and clenched it. His face clenched with it. "The human hand."

"Robert Brown's?"

"It looks like it. He gave her a beating early yesterday afternoon, according to Stanislaus. The deputy coroner says she's been dead that long."

"Stanislaus told me they quarreled over a telephone call she made."

"That's right. We haven't been able to trace the call, which means it was probably local. She used the phone in Stanislaus's office, but he claims to know nothing more about it."

"How does he know Brown gave her a beating?" I said.

"He says a neighbor woman told him. That checks out." Bastian wiped his left hand across his tense angry face, without really changing his expression. "It's terrible the way some people live, that a woman could be killed within a neighbor's hearing and nobody knows or cares."

"Not even Brown," I said. "He thought she was alive at nine-thirty last night. He talked to her through the door, trying to get her to open up. Or he may have been trying to con himself into thinking he hadn't killed her after all. I don't think he's too stable."

Bastian looked up sharply. "Were you in the cottage when Brown was talking through the door?"

"I was. Incidentally, I recognized his voice. He's the same man who extorted twenty-five thousand dollars from Ralph Hillman last night. I listened in on a phone call he made to Hillman yesterday."

Bastian's right fist was still clenched. He used it to strike the desk top, savagely. The pigeons on the window ledge flew away.

"It's too damn bad," he said, "you didn't bring us in on this yesterday. You might have saved a life, not to mention twenty-five thousand dollars."

"Tell that to Hillman."

"I intend to. This morning. Right now I'm telling you."

"The decision wasn't mine. I tried to change it. Anyway, I entered the case after the woman was killed."

"That's a good place to begin," Bastian said after a pause. "Go on from there. I want the full record."

He reached down beside his desk and turned on a recorder. For an hour or more the tape slithered quietly from wheel to wheel as I talked into it. I was clientless and free and I didn't suppress anything. Not even the possibility that Tom Hillman had cooperated with Brown in extorting money from his father.

"I'd almost like to think that that was true," Bastian said. "It would mean that the kid is still alive, anyway. But it isn't likely."

"Which isn't likely?"

"Both things. I doubt that he hoaxed his old man, and I doubt that he's still alive. It looks as if the woman was used as a decoy to get him in position for the kill. We'll probably find his body in the ocean week after next."

His words had the weight of experience behind them. Kidnap victims were poor actuarial risks. But I said:

"I'm working on the assumption that he's alive."

Bastian raised his eyebrows. "I thought Dr. Sponti took you off the case."

"I still have some of his money."

Bastian gave me a long cool appraising look. "L. A. was right. You're not the usual peeper."

"I hope not."

"If you're staying with it, you can do something for me, as well as for yourself. Help me to get this woman identified." He slid the picture of Mrs. Brown out from under the magnifying glass. "This postmortem photo is too rough to circularize. But you could show it around in the right circles. I'm having a police artist make a composite portrait, but that takes time."

"What about fingerprints?"

"We're trying that, too, but a lot of women have never been fingerprinted. Meantime, will you try and get an identification? You're a Hollywood man, and the woman claimed that she was in pictures at one time."

"That doesn't mean a thing."

"It might."

"But I was planning to try and pick up Brown's trail in Nevada. If the boy's alive, Brown knows where to find him."

"The Nevada police already have our APB on Brown. And you have a private operative on the spot. Frankly, I'd appreciate it if you'll take this picture to Hollywood with you. I don't have a man I can spare. By the way, I had your car brought into the county garage."

Cooperation breeds cooperation. Besides, the woman's identity was important, if only because the killer had tried to hide it. I accepted the picture, along with several others taken from various angles, and put them in the same pocket as my picture of Tom.

"You can reverse any telephone charges," Bastian said in farewell.

Halfway down the stairs I ran into Ralph Hillman. At first glance he looked fresher than he had the previous evening. But it was an illusory freshness. The color in his cheeks was hectic, and the sparkle in his eyes was the glint of desperation. He sort of reared back when he saw me, like a spooked horse.

"Can you give me a minute, Mr. Hillman?"

"Sorry. I have an appointment."

"The lieutenant can wait. I want to say this. I admit I made a mistake last night. But you made a mistake in getting Sponti to drop me."

He looked at me down his patrician nose. "*You'd* naturally think so. It's costing you money."

"Look, I'm sorry about last night. I was overeager. That's the defect of a virtue. I want to carry on with the search for your son."

"What's the use? He's probably dead. Thanks to you."

"That's a fairly massive accusation, Mr. Hillman."

"Take it. It's yours. And please get out of my way." He looked compulsively at his wristwatch. "I'm already late."

He brushed past me and ran upstairs as if I might pursue him. It wasn't a pleasant interview. The unpleasantness stuck in my crop all the way to Los Angeles.

11

I bought a hat a size too large, to accommodate my bandages, and paid a brief visit to the Hollywood division of the L. A. P. D. None of the detective-sergeants in the upstairs offices recognized Mrs. Brown in her deathly disguise. I went from the station to the news room of the Hollywood *Reporter*. Most of the people at work there resented being shown such pictures. The ones who gave them an honest examination failed to identify Mrs. Brown.

I tried a number of flesh peddlers along the Strip, with the same lack of success and the same effect. The photographs made me unpopular. These guys and dolls pursuing the rapid buck hated to be reminded of what was waiting on the far side of the last dollar. The violence of the woman's death only made it worse. It could happen to anybody, any time.

I started back to my office. I intended to call Bastian and ask him to rush me a Xerox copy of the composite sketch as soon as the artist had completed it. Then I thought of Joey Sylvester.

Joey was an old agent who maintained an office of sorts two blocks off Sunset and two flights up. He hadn't been able to adapt to the shift of economic power from the major studios to the independent producers. He lived mainly on his share of residuals from old television movies, and on his memories.

I knocked on the door of his cubbyhole and heard him hiding his bottle, as if I might be the ghost of Louis B. Mayer or an emissary from J. Arthur Rank. Joey looked a little disappointed when he opened the door and it was only me. But he resurrected the bottle and offered me a drink in a paper cup. He had a glass tumbler for his own use, and I happened to know that nearly every day he sat at his desk and absorbed a quart of bourbon and sometimes a quart and a half.

He was a baby-faced old man with innocent white hair and crafty eyes. His mind was like an old-fashioned lamp with its wick in alcohol, focused so as to light up the past and its chauffeur-driven Packard, and cast the third-floor-walkup present into cool shadow.

It wasn't long past noon, and Joey was still in fair shape. "It's good to see you, Lew boy. I drink to your health." He did so, with one fatherly hand on my shoulder.

"I drink to yours."

The hand on my shoulder reached up and took my hat off. "What did you do to your head?"

"I was slightly shot last night."

"You mean you got drunk and fell down?"

"Shot with a gun," I said.

He clucked. "You shouldn't expose yourself the way you do. Know what you ought to do, Lew boy? Retire and write your memoirs. The unvarnished sensational truth about Hollywood."

"It's been done a thousand times, Joey. Now they're even doing it in the fan mags."

"Not the way you could do it. Give 'em the worm's-eye view. There's a title!" He snapped his fingers. "I bet I could sell your story for twenty-five G's, make it part of a package with Steve McQueen. Give some thought to it, Lew boy. I could open up a lovely jar of olives for you."

"I just opened a can of peas, Joey, and I wonder if you can help me with it. How is your tolerance for pictures of dead people?"

"I've seen a lot of them die." His free hand fluttered toward the wall above his desk. It was papered with inscribed photographs of vanished players. His other hand raised his tumbler. "I drink to them."

I cluttered his desk top with the angry pictures. He looked them over mournfully. "Ach!" he said. "What the human animal does to itself! Am I supposed to know her?"

"She's supposed to have worked in pictures. You know more actors than anybody."

"I did at one time. No more."

"I doubt that she's done any acting recently. She was on the skids."

"It can happen overnight." In a sense, it had happened to him. He put on his glasses, turned on a desk lamp, and studied the pictures intensively. After a while he said: "Carol?"

"You know her."

He looked at me over his glasses. "I couldn't swear to it in court. I once knew a little blonde girl, natural blonde, with ears like that. Notice that they're small and close to the head and rather pointed. Unusual ears for a girl."

"Carol who?"

"I can't remember. It was a long time ago, back in the forties. I don't think she was using her own name, anyway."

"Why not?"

"She had a very stuffy family back in Podunk. They disapproved of the acting bit. I seem to remember she told me she ran away from home."

"In Podunk?"

"I didn't mean that literally. Matter of fact, I think she came from some place in Idaho."

"Say that again."

"Idaho. Is your dead lady from Idaho?"

"Her husband drives a car with an Idaho license. Tell me more about Carol. When and where did you know her?"

"Right here in Hollywood. A friend of mine took an interest in the girl and brought her to me. She was a lovely child. Untouched." His hands flew apart in the air, untouching her. "All she had was high-school acting experience, but I got her a little work. It wasn't hard in those days, with the war still going on. And I had a personal in with all the casting directors on all the lots."

"What year was it, Joey?"

He took off his glasses and squinted into the past. "She came to me in the spring of '45, the last year of the war."

Mrs. Brown, if she was Carol, had been around longer than I'd thought. "How old was she then?"

"Very young. Just a child, like I said. Maybe sixteen."

"And who was the friend who took an interest in her?"

"It isn't like you think. It was a woman, one of the girls in the story department at Warner's. She's producing a series now at Television City. But she was just a script girl back in the days I'm talking about."

"You wouldn't be talking about Susanna Drew?"

"Yeah. Do you know Susanna?"

"Thanks to you. I met her at a party at your house, when you were living in Beverly Hills."

Joey looked startled, as though the shift from one level of the past to another had caught him unawares. "I remember. That must have been ten years ago."

He sat and thought about ten years ago, and so did I. I had taken Susanna home from Joey's party, and we met at other parties, by agreement. We had things to talk about. She picked my brains for what I knew about people, and I picked hers for what she knew about books. I was crazy about her insane sense of humor.

The physical thing came more slowly, as it often does when it promises to be real. I think we tried to force it. We'd both been drinking, and a lot of stuff boiled up from Susanna's childhood. Her father had been a professor at UCLA, who lost his wife young, and he had supervised Susanna's studies. Her father was dead, but she could still feel his breath on the back of her neck.

We had a bad passage, and Susanna stopped going to parties, at least the ones I went to. I heard she had a marriage which didn't take. Then she had a career, which took.

"How did she happen to know Carol?" I said to Joey.

"You'll have to ask her yourself. She told me at the time, but I don't remember. My memory isn't what it was." The present was depressing him. He poured himself a drink.

I refused the offer of one. "What happened to Carol?"

"She dropped out of sight. I think she ran off with a sailor, or something like that. She didn't have what it takes, anyway, after the first bloom." Joey sighed deeply. "If you see Susanna, mention my name, will you, Lew? I mean, if you can do it gracefully." He moved one hand in an undulating horizontal curve. "She acts like she thought I was dead."

I used Joey's phone to make a call to Susanna Drew's office. Her secretary let me talk to her:

"This is Lew Archer, Susanna."

"How nice to hear from you."

'The occasion isn't so nice," I said bluntly. "I'm investigating a murder. The victim may or may not be a girl you knew back in the forties, named Carol."

"Not Carol Harley?"

"I'm afraid she's the one."

Her voice roughened. "And you say she's dead?"

"Yes. She was murdered yesterday in a place called Ocean View."

She was silent for a moment. When she spoke again, her voice was softer and younger. "What can I do?"

"Tell me about your friend Carol."

"Not on the telephone, *please*. The telephone dehumanizes everything."

"A personal meeting would suit me much better," I said rather formally. "I have some pictures to show you, to make the identification positive. It should be soon. We're twenty-four hours behind—"

"Come over now. I'll send your name out front."

I thanked Joey and drove to Television City. A guard from the front office escorted me through the building to Susanna Drew's office. It was large and bright, with flowers on the desk and explosive-looking abstract expressionist paintings on the walls. Susanna was standing at the window, crying. She was a slim woman with short straight hair so black the eye stayed on it. She kept her back to me for some time after her secretary went out and closed the door. Finally she turned to face me, still dabbing at her wet cheeks with a piece of yellow Kleenex.

She was fortyish now, and not exactly pretty, but neither did she look like anybody else. Her black eyes, even in sorrow, were furiously alive. She had style, and intelligence in the lines and contours of her face. Legs still good. Mouth still good. It said:

"I don't know why I'm carrying on like this. I haven't seen or heard from Carol in seventeen or eighteen years." She paused. "I really do know, though. 'It is Margaret I mourn for.' Do you know Hopkins's poem?"

"You know I don't. Who's Margaret?"

"The girl in the poem," she said. "She's grieving over the fallen autumn leaves. And Hopkins tells her she's grieving for herself. Which is what I'm doing." She breathed deeply. "I used to be so *young*."

"You're not exactly over the hill now."

"Don't flatter me. I'm old old old. I was twenty in 1945

when I knew Carol. Back in the pre-atomic era." On the way to her desk she paused in front of one of the abstract paintings, as if it represented what had happened to the world since. She sat down with an air of great efficiency. "Well, let me look at your pictures."

"You won't like them. She was beaten to death."

"God. Who would do that?"

"Her husband is the prime suspect."

"Harley? Is she—was she still with that *schmo?*"

"Evidently she still was."

"I knew he'd do her in sooner or later."

I leaned on the end of her desk. "How did you know that?"

"It was one of those fated things. Elective affinities with a reverse twist. She was a really nice child, as tender as a soft-boiled egg, and he was a psychopathic personality. He just couldn't leave her alone."

"How do you know he was a psychopathic personality?"

"I know a psychopathic personality when I see one," she said, lifting her chin. "I was married to one, briefly, back in the fabulous fifties. Which constitutes me an authority. If you want a definition, a psychopathic personality is a man you can't depend on for anything except trouble."

"And that's the way Harley was?"

"Oh yes."

"What was his first name?"

"Mike. He was a sailor, a sailor in the Navy."

"And what was the name of his ship?"

She opened her mouth to tell me, I believe. But something shifted rapidly and heavily in her mind, and closed off communication. "I'm afraid I don't remember." She looked up at me with black opaque eyes.

"What did he do before he went into the Navy? Was he a photographer?"

She looked back over the years. "I think he had been a boxer, a professional boxer, not a very successful one. He may have been a photographer, too. He was the sort of person who had been a number of things, none of them successfully."

"Are you sure his name wasn't Harold?"

"Everybody *called* him Mike. It may have been a *nom de guerre.*"

"A what?"

"A fighting name. You know." She breathed deeply. "You were going to show me some pictures, Lew."

"They can wait. You could help me most right now by telling me what you can remember about Carol and Harley and how you got to know them."

Tensely, she looked at her watch. "I'm due in a story conference in one minute."

"This is a more important story conference."

She breathed in and out. "I suppose it is. Well, I'll make it short and simple. It's a simple story, anyway, so simple I couldn't use it in my series. Carol was a country girl from Idaho. She ran away from home with an awol sailor. Mike Harley came from the same hick town, I think, but he'd already been in the Navy for a couple of years and seen the world. He promised to take her out to the coast and get her into the movies. She was about sixteen and so naive it made you want to weep or burst out laughing."

"I can hear you laughing. When and where did you happen to meet her?"

"In the early spring of 1945. I was working at Warner's in Burbank and spending weekends in various places. You know the old Barcelona Hotel near Santa Monica? Carol and Harley were staying there, and it's where I—well, I got interested in her."

"Were they married?"

"Carol and Harley? I think they'd gone through some sort of ceremony in Tia Juana. At least Carol thought they were married. She also thought Harley was on extended leave, until the Shore Patrol picked him up. They whisked him back to his ship and Carol was left with nothing to live on, literally nothing. Harley hadn't bothered to make an allotment or anything. So I took her under my wing."

"And brought her to see Joe Sylvester."

"Why not? She was pretty enough, and she wasn't a stupid girl. Joey got her a couple of jobs, and I spent a lot of time with her on grooming and diction and posture. I'd just been through an unhappy love affair, in my blue period, and I was glad to have somebody to occupy my mind with. I let Carol share my apartment, and I actually think I could have made something out of her. A really wholesome Marilyn, perhaps." She caught herself going into Hollywood patter, and stopped abruptly. "But it all went blah."

"What happened?"

"Harley had left her pregnant, and it began to show. Instead of grooming a starlet, I found myself nursing a pregnant teen-ager with a bad case of homesickness. But she refused to go home. She said her father would kill her."

"Do you remember her father's name?"

"I'm afraid not. She was using the name Carol Cooper for professional purposes, but that wasn't her true surname. I *think* her father lived in Pocatello, if that's any help."

"It may be. You say she was pregnant. What happened to the baby?"

"I don't know. Harley turned up before the baby was born—the Navy had finally kicked him out, I believe—and she went back to him. This was in spite of everything I could say or do. They were elective affinities, as I said. The Patient Griselda and the nothing man. So seventeen years later he had to kill her."

"Was he violent when you knew him?"

"Was he not." She crossed her arms over her breast. "He knocked me down when I tried to prevent her from going back to him. I went out to find help. When I got back to my apartment with a policeman they were both gone, with all the money in my purse. I didn't press charges, and that was the last I saw of them."

"But you still care about Carol."

"She was nice to have around. I never had a sister, or a daughter. In fact, when I think back, *feel* back, I never had a happier time than that spring and summer in Burbank when Carol was pregnant. We didn't know how lucky we were."

"How so?"

"Well, it was a terribly hot summer and the refrigerator kept breaking down and we only had the one bedroom and Carol got bigger and bigger and we had no men in our lives. We thought we were suffering many deprivations. Actually all the deprivations came later." She looked around her fairly lavish office as if it was a jail cell, then at her watch. "I really have to go now. My writers and directors will be committing mayhem on each other."

"Speaking of mayhem," I said, "I'll ask you to look at these pictures if you can stand it. The identification should be nailed down."

"Yes."

I spread the photographs out for her. She looked them over carefully.

"Yes. It's Carol. The poor child."

She had become very pale. Her black eyes stood out like the coal eyes of a snowgirl. She got to her feet and walked rather blindly into an adjoining room, shutting the door behind her.

I sat at her desk, pinched by her contour chair, and used the phone to ask her secretary to get me Lieutenant Bastian. He was on the line in less than a minute. I told him everything Susanna Drew had told me.

She came out of the next room and listened to the end of the conversation. "You don't waste any time," she said when I hung up.

"Your evidence is important."

"That's good. I'm afraid it's taken all I've got." She was still very pale. She moved toward me as if the floor under her feet was teetering. "Will you drive me home?"

Home was an apartment on Beverly Glen Boulevard. It had a mezzanine and a patio and African masks on the walls. She invited me to make us both a drink, and we sat and talked about Carol and then about Tom Hillman. She seemed to be very interested in Tom Hillman.

I was becoming interested in Susanna. Something about her dark intensity bit into me as deep as memory. Sitting close beside her, looking into her face, I began to ask myself whether, in my present physical and financial and moral condition, I could take on a woman with all those African masks.

The damn telephone rang in the next room. She got up, using my knee as a place to rest her hand. I heard her say:

"So it's you. What do you want from me now?"

That was all I heard. She closed the door. Five minutes later, when she came out, her face had changed again. A kind of angry fear had taken the place of sorrow in her eyes, as if they had learned of something worse than death.

"Who was that, Susanna?"

"You'll never know."

I drove downtown in a bitter mood and bullyragged my friend Colton, the D. A.'s investigator, into asking Sacramento for Harold or Mike Harley's record, if any. While I was waiting for an answer I went downstairs to the newsstand and bought an early evening paper.

The murder and kidnapping were front-page news, but there

was nothing in the newspaper story I didn't already know, except that Ralph Hillman had had a distinguished combat record as a naval aviator and later (after Newport Line School) as a line officer. He was also described as a millionaire.

I sat in Colton's outer office trying to argue away my feeling that Bastian had shoved me onto the fringes of the case. The feeling deepened when the word came back from Sacramento that neither a Harold nor a Mike Harley had a California record, not even for a traffic violation. I began to wonder if I was on the track of the right man.

I drove back to the Strip through late afternoon traffic. It was nearly dusk when I reached my office. I didn't bother turning on the light for a while, but sat and watched the green sky at the window lose its color. Stars and neons came out. A plane like a moving group of stars circled far out beyond Santa Monica.

I closed the venetian blind, to foil snipers, and turned on the desk lamp and went through the day's mail. It consisted of three bills, and a proposition from the Motel Institute of St. Louis. The Institute offered me, in effect, a job at twenty thousand a year managing a million-dollar convention motel. All I had to do was fill out a registration form for the Institute's mail-order course in motel management and send it to the Institute's registrar. If I had a wife, we could register as a couple.

I sat toying with the idea of filling out the form, but decided to go out for dinner first. I was making very incisive decisions. I decided to call Susanna Drew and ask her to have dinner with me, telling myself that it was in line of business. I could even deduct the tab from my income tax.

She wasn't in the telephone book. I tried Information. Unlisted number. I couldn't afford her anyway.

Before I went out for dinner by myself, I checked my answering service. Susanna Drew had left her number for me.

"I've been trying to get you," I said to her.

"I've been right here in my apartment."

"I mean before I knew you left your number."

"Oh? What did you have in mind?"

"The Motel Institute of St. Louis is making a very nice offer to couples who want to register for their course in motel management."

"It sounds inviting. I've always wanted to go out to sunny California and manage a motel."

"Good. We'll have dinner and talk strategy. Television won't last, you know that in your heart. None of these avant-garde movements last."

"Sorry, Lew. I'd love dinner, another night. Tonight I'm not up to it. But I did want to thank you for looking after me this afternoon. I was in a bad way for a while."

"I'm afraid I did it to you."

"No. My whole lousy life reared up and did it to me. You and your pictures were just the catalytic agent."

"Could you stand a visit from a slightly catalytic agent? I'll bring dinner from the delicatessen. I'll buy you a gardenia."

"No. I don't want to see you tonight."

"And you haven't changed your mind about that telephone call you wouldn't tell me about?"

"No. There are things about me you needn't know."

"I suppose that's encouraging in a way. Why did you leave your number for me, then?"

"I found something that might help you—a picture of Carol taken in 1945."

"I'll come and get it. You haven't really told me how you met her, you know."

"Please don't come. I'll send a messenger with it."

"If you insist. I'll wait in my office." I gave her the address.

"Lew?" Her voice was lighter and sweeter, almost poignant. "You're not just putting on an act, are you? To try and pry out my personal secrets, I mean?"

"It's no act," I said.

"Likewise," she said. "Thank you."

I sat in the echoing silence thinking that she had been badly treated by a man or men. It made me angry to think of it. I didn't go out for dinner after all. I sat and nursed my anger until Susanna's messenger arrived.

He was a young Negro in uniform who talked like a college graduate. He handed me a sealed manila envelope, which I ripped open.

It contained a single glossy print, preserved between two sheets of corrugated cardboard, of a young blond girl wearing a pageboy bob and a bathing suit. You couldn't pin down the reason for her beauty. It was partly in her clear low forehead, the high curve of her cheek, her perfect round chin; partly in the absolute femaleness that looked out of her eyes and informed her body.

Wondering idly who had taken the photograph, I turned it over. Rubber-stamped in purple ink on the back was the legend: "Photo Credit: Harold 'Har' Harley, Barcelona Hotel."

"Will that be all?" the messenger said at the door.

"No." I gave him ten dollars.

"This is too much, sir. I've already been paid."

"I know. But I want you to buy a gardenia and deliver it back to Miss Drew."

He said he would.

12

1945 was a long time ago, as time went in California. The Barcelona Hotel was still standing, but I seemed to remember hearing that it was closed. I took the long drive down Sunset to the coastal highway on the off-chance of developing my lead to Harold Harley. Also I wanted to take another look at the building where Harley and Carol had lived.

It was a huge old building, Early Hollywood Byzantine, with stucco domes and minarets, and curved verandahs where famous faces of the silent days had sipped their bootleg rum. Now it stood abandoned under the bluff. The bright lights of a service station across the highway showed that its white paint was flaking off and some of the windows were broken.

I parked on the weed-ruptured concrete of the driveway and walked up to the front door. Taped to the glass was a notice of bankruptcy, with an announcement that the building was going to be sold at public auction in September.

I flashed my light through the glass into the lobby. It was still completely furnished, but the furnishings looked as though they hadn't been replaced in a generation. The carpet was worn threadbare, the chairs were gutted. But the place still had atmosphere, enough of it to summon up a flock of ghosts.

I moved along the curving verandah, picking my way among the rain-warped wicker furniture, and shone my light through a french window into the dining room. The tables were set, complete with cocked-hat napkins, but there was dust lying thick on the napery. A good place for ghosts to feed, I thought, but not for me.

Just for the hell of it, though, and as a way of asserting myself against the numerous past, I went back to the front door and tapped loudly with my flashlight on the glass. Deep inside the building, at the far end of a corridor, a light showed itself. It was a moving light, which came toward me.

The man who was carrying it was big, and he walked as if he had sore feet or legs. I could see his face now in the upward glow of his electric lantern. A crude upturned nose, a bulging forehead, a thirsty mouth. It was a face of a horribly ravaged baby who had never been weaned from the bottle. I could also see that he had a revolver in his other hand.

He pointed it at me and flashed the light in my eyes. "This place is closed. Can't you read?" he shouted through the glass.

"I want to talk to you."

"I don't want to talk to you. Beat it. Amscray."

He waved the gun at me. I could tell from his voice and look that he had been drinking hard. A drunk with a gun and an excuse to use it can be murder, literally. I made one more attempt:

"Do you know a photographer named Harold Harley who used to be here?"

"Never heard of him. Now you get out of here before I blow a hole in you. You're trespassing."

He lifted the heavy revolver. I withdrew, as far as the service station across the street. A quick-moving man in stained white coveralls came out from under a car on a hoist and offered to sell me gas.

"It ought to take ten," I said. "Who's the character in the Barcelona Hotel? He acts like he was bitten by a bear."

The man gave a one-sided smile. "You run into Otto Sipe?"

"If that's the watchman's name."

"Yeah. He worked there so long he thinks he owns the place."

"How long?"

"Twenty years or more. I been here since the war myself, and he goes back before me. He was their dick."

"Hotel detective?"

"Yeah. He told me once he used to be an officer of the law. If he was, he didn't learn much. Check your oil?"

"Don't bother, I just had it changed. Were you here in 1945?"

"That's the year I opened. I went into the service early and got out early. Why?"

"I'm a private detective. The name is Archer." I offered him my hand.

He wiped his on his coveralls before he took it. "Daly. Ben Daly."

"A man named Harold Harley used to stay at the Barcelona in 1945. He was a photographer."

Daly's face opened. "Yeah. I remember him. He took a picture of me and the wife to pay for his gas bill once. We still have it in the house."

"You wouldn't know where he is now?"

"Sorry, I haven't seen him in ten years."

"What was the last you saw of him?"

"He had a little studio in Pacific Palisades. I dropped in once or twice to say hello. I don't think he's there any more."

"I gather you liked him."

"Sure. There's no harm in Harold."

Men could change. I showed Carol's picture to Daly. He didn't know her.

"You couldn't pin down the address in Pacific Palisades for me?"

He rubbed the side of his face. It needed retreading, but it was a good face. "I can tell you where it is."

He told me where it was, on a side street just off Sunset, next door to a short-order restaurant. I thanked him, and paid him for the gas.

The short-order restaurant was easy to find, but the building next door to it was occupied by a paperback bookstore. A young woman wearing pink stockings and a ponytail presided over the cash register. She looked at me pensively through her eye makeup when I asked her about Harold Harley.

"It seems to me I heard there was a photographer in here at one time."

"Where would he be now?"

"I haven't the slightest idea, honestly. We've only been here less than a year ourselves—a year in September."

"How are you doing?"

"We're making the rent, at least."

"Who do you pay it to?"

"The man who runs the lunch counter. Mr. Vernon. He ought to give us free meals for what he charges. Only don't quote me if you talk to him. We're a month behind now on the rent."

I bought a book and went next door for dinner. It was a place where I could eat with my hat on. While I was waiting for my steak, I asked the waitress for Mr. Vernon. She turned to the white-hatted short-order cook who had just tossed my steak onto the grill.

"Mr. Vernon, gentleman wants to speak to you."

He came over to the counter, an unsmiling thin-faced man with glints of gray beard showing on his chin. "You said you wanted it bloody. You'll get it bloody." He brandished his spatula.

"Good. I understand you own the store next door."

"That and the next one to it." The thought encouraged him a little. "You looking for a place to rent?"

"I'm looking for a man, a photographer named Harold Harley."

"He rented that store for a long time. But he couldn't quite make a go of it. There's too many photographers in this town. He held on for seven or eight years after the war and then gave up on it."

"You don't know where he is now?"

"No sir, I do not."

The sizzling of my steak reached a certain intensity, and he heard it. He went and flipped it with his spatula and came back to me. "You want french fried?"

"All right. What's the last you saw of Harley?"

"The last I heard of him he moved out to the Valley. That was a good ten years ago. He was trying to run his business out of the front room of his house in Van Nuys. He's a pretty good photographer—he took a fine picture of my boy's christening party—but he's got no head for business. I ought to know, he still owes me three months' rent."

Six young people came in and lined up along the counter. They had wind in their hair, sand in their ears, and the word

"Surfbirds" stenciled across the backs of their identical yellow sweatshirts. All of them, girls and boys, ordered two hamburgers apiece.

One of the boys put a quarter in the jukebox and played "Surfin' ain't no sin." Mr. Vernon got twelve hamburger patties out of the refrigerator and lined them up on the grill. He put my steak on a plate with a handful of fried potatoes and brought it to me personally.

"I could look up that Van Nuys address if it's important. I kept it on account of the rent he owed me."

"It's important." I showed him Carol's picture, the young one Harley had taken. "Do you recognize his wife?"

"I didn't even know he had a wife. I didn't think he'd rate with a girl like that."

"Why not?"

"He's no ladies' man. He never was. Harold's the quiet type."

Doubt was slipping in again that I was on the right track. It made my head ache. "Can you describe him to me?"

"He's just an ordinary-looking fellow, about my size, five foot ten. Kind of a long nose. Blue eyes. Sandy hair. There's nothing special about him. Of course he'd be older now."

"How old?"

"Fifty at least. I'm fifty-nine myself, due to retire next year. Excuse me, mister."

He flipped the twelve hamburger patties over, distributed twelve half-buns on top of them and went out through a swinging door at the back. I ate at my steak. Mr. Vernon returned with a slip of paper on which he had written Harley's Van Nuys address: 956 Elmhurst.

The waitress delivered the hamburgers to the surfbirds. They munched them in time to the music. The song the jukebox was playing as I went out had a refrain about "the day that I caught the big wave and made you my slave." I drove up Sunset onto the San Diego Freeway headed north.

Elmhurst was a working-class street of prewar bungalows built too close together. It was a warm night in the Valley, and some people were still on their porches and lawns. A fat man drinking beer on the porch of 956 told me that Harley had sold him the house in 1960. He had his present address because he was still paying Harley monthly installments on a second trust deed.

That didn't sound like the Harley I knew. I asked him for a description.

"He's kind of a sad character," the fat man said. "One of these guys that wouldn't say 'boo' to a goose. He's had his troubles, I guess."

"What kind of troubles?"

"Search me. I don't know him well. I only saw him the twice when I bought the house from him. He wanted out in a hurry, and he gave me a good buy. He had this chance for a job in Long Beach, developing film, and he didn't want to commute."

He gave me Harley's address in Long Beach, which is a long way from Van Nuys. It was close to midnight when I found the house, a tract house near Long Beach Boulevard. It had brown weeds in the front yard, and was lightless, like most of the houses in the street.

I drove past a street light to the end of the block and walked back. The all-night traffic on the boulevard filled the air with a kind of excitement, rough and forlorn. I was raised in Long Beach, and I used to cruise its boulevards in a model-A Ford. Their sound, whining, threatening, rising, fading, spoke to something deep in my mind which I loved and hated. I didn't want to knock on Harley's door. I was almost certain I had the wrong man.

The overhead door of the attached garage was closed but not locked. I opened it quietly. The street light down the block shone on the rear of a dirty white Ford sedan with an Idaho license plate.

I went to the lefthand door of the car and opened it. The dome light came on. The car was registered in the name of Robert Brown, with an address in Pocatello. My heart was pounding so hard I could scarcely breathe.

The door from the garage into the house was suddenly outlined by light. The door sprung open. The light slapped me across the eyes and drenched me.

"Mike?" said the voice of a man I didn't know. He looked around the corner of the door frame. "Is that you, Mike?"

"I saw Mike yesterday."

"Who are you?"

"A friend." I didn't say whose friend. "He left his car for you, I see."

"That's between him and I."

His defensive tone encouraged me. I moved across the

lighted space between us and stepped up into his kitchen, closing the door behind me. He didn't try to keep me out. He stood barefoot in his pajamas facing me, gray-haired and haggard-faced, with drooping hound eyes.

"My brother didn't tell me about a partner."

"Oh? What did he tell you?"

"Nothing. I mean—" He tried to bite his lower lip. His teeth were false, and slipped. Until he sucked them back into place he looked as if I had scared him literally to death. "He didn't tell me a thing about you or anything. I don't know why you come to me. That car is mine. I traded him my crate for it."

"Was that wise?"

"I dunno, maybe not." He glanced at the unwashed dishes piled in the sink as if they shared responsibility for his lack of wisdom. "Anyway, it's none of your business."

"It's everybody's business, Harold. You must know that by now."

His lips formed the word "Yes" without quite saying it. Tears came into his eyes. It was Harold he mourned for. He named the most terrible fear he could conjure up:

"Are you from the FBI?"

"I'm a police agent. We need to have a talk."

"Here?"

"This is as good a place as any."

He looked around the dingy little room as if he was seeing it with new eyes. We sat on opposite sides of the kitchen table. The checkered oilcloth that covered it was threadbare in places.

"I didn't want any part of this," he said.

"Who would?"

"And it isn't the first time he got me into trouble, not by a long shot. This has been going on for the last thirty-five years, ever since Mike got old enough to walk and talk. I kid you not."

"Just what do you mean when you say he's got you into trouble? This time."

He shrugged crookedly and raised his open hands as if I should plainly be able to see the stigmata in his palms. "He's mixed up in a kidnapping, isn't he?"

"Did he tell you that?"

"He never told me anything straight in his life. But I can read. Since I saw the papers today I've been scared to go out of the house. And you know what my wife did? She left me. She took a taxi to the bus station and went back to her mother in Oxnard. She didn't even wash last night's dishes.''

"When was your brother here?''

"Last night. He got here around ten-thirty. We were on our way to bed but I got up again. I talked to him right here where we're sitting. I thought there was something screwy going on—he had that wild look in his eye—but I didn't know what. He gave me one of his stories, that he won a lot of money in a poker game from some sailors in Dago, and they were after him to take the money back. That's why he wanted to change cars with me. He said.''

"Why did you agree to it?''

"I dunno. It's hard to say no when Mike wants something.''

"Did he threaten you?''

"Not in so many words. I knew he had a gun with him. I saw him take it out of his car.'' He lifted his eyes to mine. ''You always feel sort of under a threat when Mike has something going. Stand in his way and he'll clobber you soon as look at you.''

I had reason to believe him. "What was the make and model and license number of your car?''

"1958 Plymouth two-door, license IKT 449.''

"Color?''

"Two-tone blue.''

I made some notes. "I'm going to ask you a very important question. Was the boy with Mike? This boy?''

I showed him Tom's picture. He shook his head over it. "No sir.''

"Did he say where the boy was?''

"He didn't mention any boy, and I didn't know about it, then.''

"Did you know he was coming here last night?''

"In a way. He phoned me from Los Angeles yesterday afternoon. He said he might be dropping by but I wasn't to tell anybody.''

"Did he say anything about changing cars when he phoned you?''

"No *sir*.''

"Did you and your brother have any previous agreement to change cars?''

"*No* sir.''

"And you didn't know about the kidnapping until you read about it in the paper today?"

"That's correct. Or the murder either."

"Do you know who was murdered?"

His head hung forward, moving up and down slightly on the cords of his neck. He covered the back of his neck with his hand as if he feared a blow there from behind. "I guess—it sounded like Carol."

"It was Carol."

"I'm sorry to hear about that. She was a good kid, a lot better than he deserved."

"You should have come forward with information, Harold."

"I know that. Lila said so. It's why she left me. She said I was setting myself up for a patsy again."

"I gather it's happened before."

"Not this bad, though. The worst he ever did to me before was when he sold me a camera he stole from the Navy. He turned around and claimed I stole it when I visited him on his ship on visiting day."

"What was the name of the ship?"

"The *Perry Bay*. It was one of those jeep carriers. I went aboard her in Dago the last year of the war, but I wisht I never set foot on her. The way they talked to me, I thought I was gonna end up in the federal pen. But they finally took my word that I didn't know the camera was hot."

"I'm taking your word now about several things, or have you noticed?"

"I didn't know what to think."

"I believe you're an honest man in a bind, Harold."

My spoken sympathy was too much for him. It made his eyes water again. He removed his hand from the back of his neck and wiped his eyes with his fingers.

"I'm not the only one you have to convince, of course. But I think you can probably work your way out of this bind by telling the whole truth."

"You mean in court?"

"Right now."

"I want to tell the truth," he said earnestly. "I would have come forward, only I was ascared to. I was ascared they'd send me up for life."

"And Mike too?"

"It wasn't him I was worried about," he said. "I'm through

with my brother. When I found out about Carol—'' He shook his head.

"Were you fond of her?"

"Sure I was. I didn't see much of her these last years when they were in Nevada. But Carol and me, we always got along."

"They were living in Nevada?"

"Yeah. Mike had a job bartending in one of the clubs on the South Shore. Only he lost it. I had to—" His slow mind overtook his words and stopped them.

"You had to—?"

"Nothing. I mean, I had to help them out a little these last few months since he lost his job."

"How much money did you give them?"

"I dunno. What I could spare. A couple of hundred dollars." He looked up guiltily.

"Did Mike pay you back last night by any chance?"

He hung his head. The old refrigerator in the corner behind him woke up and started to throb. Above it I could still heard the sound of the boulevard rising and falling, coming and going.

"No he didn't," Harold said.

"How much did he give you?"

"He didn't *give* me anything."

"You mean he was only paying you back?"

"That's right."

"How much?"

"He gave me five hundred dollars," he said in horror.

"Where is it?"

"Under my mattress. You're welcome *to* it. I don't want any part of it."

I followed him into the bedroom. The room was in disarray, with bureau drawers pulled out, hangers scattered on the floor.

"Lila took off in a hurry," he said, "soon as she saw the paper. She probably filed suit for divorce already. It wouldn't be the first time she got a divorce."

"From you?"

"From the other ones."

Lila's picture stood on top of the bureau. Her face was dark and plump and stubborn-looking, and it supported an insubstantial dome of upswept black hair.

Harold stood disconsolately by the unmade bed. I helped him to lift up the mattress. Flattened under it was an oilskin tobacco pouch containing paper money visible through the oilskin. He handed it to me.

"Did you see where this came from, Harold?"

"He got it out of the car. I heard him unwrapping some paper."

I put the pouch in my pocket without opening it. "And you honestly didn't know it was hot?"

He sat on the bed. "I guess I knew there was something the matter with it. He couldn't win that much in a poker game, I mean and keep it. He always keeps trying for the one more pot until he loses his wad. But I didn't think about *kidnapping*, for gosh sake." He struck himself rather feebly on the knee. "Or murder."

"Do you think he murdered the boy?"

"I meant poor little Carol."

"I meant the boy."

"He wouldn't do that to a young kid," Harold said in a small hushed voice. He seemed not to want the statement to be heard, for fear it would be denied.

"Have you searched the car?"

"No sir. Why would I do that?"

"For blood or money. You haven't opened the trunk?"

"No. I never went near the lousy car." He looked sick, as if its mere presence in his garage had infected him with criminality.

"Give me the keys to it."

He picked up his limp trousers, groped in the pockets, and handed me an old leather holder containing the keys to the car. I advised him to put on his clothes while I went out to the garage.

I found the garage light and turned it on, unlocked the trunk, and with some trepidation, lifted the turtleback. The space inside was empty, except for a rusty jack and a balding spare tire. No body.

But before I closed the trunk I found something in it that I didn't like. A raveled piece of black yarn was caught in the lock. I remembered Sam Jackman telling me that Tom had been wearing a black sweater on Sunday. I jerked the yarn loose, angrily, and put it away in an envelope in my pocket. I slammed the turtleback down on the possibility which the black yarn suggested to my mind.

13

I went back into the house. The bedroom door was closed. I knocked and got no answer and flung it open. Harold was sitting on the edge of the bed in his underwear and socks. He was holding a .22 rifle upright between his knees. He didn't point it at me. I took it away from him and unloaded the single shell.

"I don't have the nerve to kill myself," he said.

"You're lucky."

"Yeah, very lucky."

"I mean it, Harold. When I was a kid I knew a man who lost his undertaking business in the depression. He decided to blow out his brains with a twenty-two. But all it did was blind him. He's been sitting around in the dark for the last thirty years. And his sons have the biggest mortuary in town."

"So I should be in the mortuary business." He sighed. "Or anything but the brother business. I know what I have to go through."

"It's like a sickness. It'll pass."

"My brother," he said, "is a sickness that never passes."

"He's going to, this time, Harold. He'll be taken care of for the rest of his life."

"If you catch him."

"We'll catch him. Where did he head from here?"

"He didn't tell me."

"Where do you think?"

"Nevada, I guess. It's always been his favorite hangout. When he has money he can't stay away from the tables."

"Where did he live when he worked on the South Shore of Tahoe?"

"They were buying a trailer but he lost that when he lost his barkeep job. His boss said he got too rough with the drunks. After that they moved from one place to another, mostly motels and lodges around the lake. I couldn't give you any definite address."

"What was the name of the club he worked at?"

"The Jet. Carol worked there, too, off and on. She was sort of a singing waitress. We went to hear her sing there once. Lila thought she was lousy, but I thought she was okay. She sang pretty sexy songs, and that's why Lila—"

102

I interrupted him. "Do you have a phone? I want to make a couple of collect calls."

"It's in the front room."

I took the rifle with me, in case he got further ideas about shooting himself, or me. The walls of the front room were as crowded as the walls of a picture gallery with Harold's photographs. Old Man, Old Woman, Young Woman, Sunset, Wildflowers, Mountain, Seascape; and Lila. Most of them had been hand-tinted, and three portraits of Lila smiled at me from various angles, so that I felt surrounded by toothy, flesh-colored face.

I went back to the bedroom. Harold was putting on his shoes. He looked up rather resentfully.

"I'm okay. You don't have to keep checking up on me."

"I was wondering if you had a picture of Mike."

"I have one. It's nearly twenty years old. After he got into trouble he never let me take him."

"Let's see it."

"I wouldn't know where to find it. Anyway, it was done when he was a kid and he doesn't look like that anymore. It's an art study, like, of his muscles, in boxing trunks."

"What does he look like now?"

"I thought you saw him."

"It was dark at the time."

"Well, he's still a fairly nice-looking man, I mean his features. He quit fighting before he got banged up too bad. He has brown hair—no gray—he parts it on the side. Mike always did have a fine head of hair." He scratched at his own thin hair. "Greenish-gray eyes, with kind of a wild look in them when he's got something going. Thin mouth. I always thought it was kind of a cruel mouth. Teeth not so good. But I dunno, he's still a nice-looking fellow, and well set-up. He keeps himself in pretty good physical shape."

"Height and weight?"

"He's an inch or so under six feet. He used to fight light-heavy, but he must be heavier now. Maybe one eighty-five."

"Any scars or distinguishing marks?"

Harold jerked his head up. "Yeah. He's got scars on his back where Dad used to beat him. I got some of my own." He pulled up his undershirt and showed me the white scars all up and down his back, like hieroglyphs recording history. Harold seemed to take his scars as a matter of course.

"Are your parents still living?"

"Sure. Dad's still running the farm. It's on the Snake River," he said without nostalgia. "Pocatello Rural Route 7. But Mike wouldn't be going there. He hates Idaho."

"You never can tell, though," I said as I made some notes.

"Take my word. He broke with Dad over twenty years ago." As an afterthought, he said: "There's a portrait I did of Dad in the front room. I call it 'Old Man.' "

Before I sat down with the telephone I looked more closely at the portrait: a grizzled farmer with flat angry eyes and a mouth like a bear trap. Then I called Arnie Walters in Reno and gave him a rundown on the old man's son, Mike Harley, ex-sailor, ex-fighter, ex-bartender, gambler, kidnapper, wife-beater, putative murderer and driver of a 1958 Plymouth, two-door, California license number IKT 449.

"You've been busy," Arnie said when he finished recording my facts. "We have, too, but we haven't come up with anything. We will now." He hesitated. "Just how much muscle do you want put into the operation?"

"You mean how much can I pay for?"

"Your client."

"I lost my client. I'm hoping this stuff I've uncovered will get me another one, but it hasn't yet."

Arnie whistled. "What you're doing isn't ethical."

"Yes it is. I'm temporarily an investigator for the local sheriff's office."

"Now I know you've flipped. I hate to bring this up, Lew, but you owe me three hundred dollars and that's a charity price for what we've done. Tomorrow at this time it'll be six hundred anyway, if we stay with it. With our overhead we just can't work for nothing."

"I know that. You'll be paid."

"When?"

"Soon. I'll talk to you in the morning."

"What do we do in the meantime?"

"Carry on."

"If you say so."

Arnie hung up on me and left me feeling a little shaky. Six hundred dollars was what I got for working a full week, and I didn't work every week. I had about three hundred dollars in the bank, about two hundred in cash. I owned an equity in the car and some clothes and furniture. My total net worth, after nearly twenty years in the detective business, was in the neighborhood of thirty-five hundred dollars. And Ralph Hillman, with his money, was letting me finance my own search for his son.

On the other hand, I answered my self-pity, I was doing what I wanted to be doing. I wanted to take the man who had taken me. I wanted to find Tom. I couldn't drop the case just as it was breaking. And I needed Arnie to backstop me in Nevada. Carry on.

I made a second collect call, to Lieutenant Bastian. It was long past midnight, but he was still on duty in his office. I told him I was bringing in a witness, and I gave him a capsule summary of what the witness was going to say. Bastian expressed a proper degree of surprise and delight.

Harold was still in the bedroom, standing pensively beside the tie rack attached to the closet door. He was fully dressed except for a tie.

"What kind of a tie do you think I ought to wear? Lila always picks out the tie I wear."

"You don't need a tie."

"They'll be taking my picture, won't they? I've got to be properly dressed." He fingered the tie rack distraughtly.

I chose one for him, a dark blue tie with a conservative pattern, the kind you wear to the funerals of friends. We closed up the house and garage and drove south out of Long Beach.

It was less than an hour's drive to Pacific Point. Harold was intermittently talkative, but his silences grew longer. I asked him about his and his brother's early life in Idaho. It had been a hard life, in an area subject to blizzards in the winter and floods in the spring and extreme heat in the summer. Their father believed that boys were a kind of domestic animal that ought to be put to work soon after weaning. They were hoeing corn and digging potatoes when they were six, and milking the cows at eight or nine.

They could have stood the work, if it hadn't been for the punishment that went with it. I'd seen Harold's scars. The old man used a piece of knotted wire on them. Mike was the first to run away. He lived in Pocatello for a couple of years with a man named Robert Brown, a high-school coach and counselor who took him in and tried to give him a chance.

Robert Brown was Carol's father. Mike paid him back for his kindness eventually by running away with his daughter.

"How old was Mike then?"

"Twenty or so. Let's see, it was about a year after they drafted him into the Navy. Yeah, he'd be about twenty. Carol was only sixteen."

"Where were you at the time?"

"Working here in Los Angeles. I was 4-F. I had a job taking pictures for a hotel."

"The Barcelona Hotel," I said.

"That's right." He sounded a little startled by my knowledge of his life. "It wasn't much of a job, but it gave me a chance to freelance on the side."

"I understand that Carol and your brother stayed there, too."

"For a little. That was when he was awol and hiding out. I let them use my room for a couple of weeks."

"You've done a lot for your brother in your time."

"Yeah. He paid me back by trying to frame me for stealing a Navy camera. There's one extra thing I could have done for him."

"What was that?"

"I could have drowned him in the river when he was a kid. That's all the use he's been to anybody. Especially Carol."

"Why did she stick to him?"

He groaned. "She wanted to, I guess."

"Were they married?"

He answered slowly. "I think so. She thought so. But I never saw any papers to prove it."

"Lately," I said, "they've been calling themselves Mr. and Mrs. Robert Brown. The car he left with you is registered to Robert Brown."

"I wondered where he got it. Now I suppose I'll have to give it back to the old guy."

"First the police will be wanting it."

"Yeah. I guess they will at that."

The thought of the police seemed to depress him profoundly. He sat without speaking for a while. I caught a glimpse of him in the headlights of a passing car. He was sitting with his chin on his chest. His body appeared to be resisting the movement which was carrying him toward his meeting with the police.

"Do you know Carol's father?" I asked him finally.

"I've met Mr. Brown. Naturally he holds Mike against me. God knows what he'll think of me now, with Carol dead and all."

"You're not your brother, Harold. You can't go on blaming yourself for what he's done."

"It's my fault, though."

"Carol's death?"

"That, too, but I meant the kidnapping. I set it up for Mike without meaning to. I gave him the idea of the whole thing."

"How did you do that?"

"I don't want to talk about it."

"You brought it up, Harold. You seem to want to get it off your chest."

"I've changed my mind."

I couldn't get him to change it back. He had a passive stubbornness which wouldn't be moved. We drove in complete silence the rest of the way.

I delivered Harold and the five hundred dollars to Lieutenant Bastian, who was waiting in his office in the courthouse, and checked in at the first hotel I came to.

14

At nine o'clock in the morning, with the taste of coffee still fresh in my mouth, I was back at the door of the lieutenant's office. He was waiting for me.

"Did you get any sleep at all?" I said.

"Not much." The loss of sleep had affected him hardly at all, except that his voice and bearing were less personal and more official. "You've had an active twenty-four hours. I have to thank you for turning up the brother. His evidence is important, especially if this case ever gets into court."

"I have some other evidence to show you."

But Bastian hadn't finished what he was saying: "I talked the sheriff into paying you twenty-five dollars per diem plus ten cents a mile, if you will submit a statement."

"Thanks, but it can wait. You could do me a bigger favor by talking Ralph Hillman into bankrolling me."

"I can't do that, Archer."

"You could tell him the facts. I've spent several hundred dollars of my own money, and I've been getting results."

"Maybe, if I have an opportunity." He changed the subject abruptly: "The pathologist who did the autopsy on Mrs. Brown has come up with something that will interest you. Actual cause of death was a stab wound in the heart. It wasn't noticed at first because it was under the breast."

"That does interest me. It could let Harley out."

"I don't see it that way. He beat her and then stabbed her."

"Do you have the weapon?"

"No. The doctor says it was a good-sized blade, thin but quite broad, and very sharp, with a sharp point. It went into her like butter, the doctor says." He took no pleasure in the image. His face was saturnine. "Now what was the evidence you referred to just now?"

I showed Bastian the piece of black yarn and told him where I had found it. He picked up the implication right away:

"The trunk, eh? I'm afraid it doesn't look too promising for the boy. He was last seen wearing a black sweater. I believe his mother knitted it for him." He studied the scrap of wool under his magnifying glass. "This looks like knitting yarn to me, too. Mrs. Hillman ought to be shown this."

He put the piece of yarn under glass on an evidence board. Then he picked up the phone and made an appointment with the Hillmans at their house in El Rancho, an appointment for both of us. We drove out through morning fog in two cars. At the foot of the Hillman's driveway a man in plain clothes came out of the fog-webbed bushes and waved us on.

Mrs. Perez, wearing black shiny Sunday clothes, admitted us to the reception hall. Hillman came out of the room where the bar was. His movements were somnambulistic and precise, as if they were controlled by some external power. His eyes were still too bright.

He shook hands with Bastian and, after some hesitation, with me. "Come into the sitting room, gentlemen. It's good of you to make the trip out here. Elaine simply wasn't up to going downtown. If I could only get her to eat," he said.

She was sitting on the chesterfield near the front window. The morning light was unkind to her parched blonde face. It was two full days and nights since the first telephone call on Monday morning. She looked as if all the minutes in those forty-eight hours had passed through her body like knots in wire. The red piece of knitting on the seat beside her hadn't grown since I'd seen it last.

She managed a rather wizened smile and extended her hand to Bastian. "Ralph says you have something to show me."

"Yes. It's a piece of yarn which may or may not have come off your boy's sweater."

"The black one I knitted for him?"

"It may be. We want to know if you recognize the yarn." Bastian handed her the evidence board. She put on reading glasses and examined it. Then she put it aside, rose abruptly, and left the room. Hillman made a move to follow her. He stopped with his hands out in a helpless pose which he was still in when she returned.

She was carrying a large, figured linen knitting bag. Crouching on the chesterfield, she rummaged among its contents and tossed out balls of wool of various colors. Her furiously active hand came to rest holding a half-used ball of black wool.

"This is what I had left over from Tom's sweater. I think it's the same. Can you tell?"

Bastian broke off a piece of yarn from the ball and compared it under a glass with my piece. He turned from the window:

"The specimens appear identical to me. If they are, we can establish it under the microscope."

"What does it mean if they are identical?" Ralph Hillman said.

"I prefer not to say until we have microscopic confirmation."

Hillman took hold of Bastian's arm and shook him. "Don't double-talk me, Lieutenant."

Bastian broke loose and stepped back. There were white frozen-looking patches around his nose and mouth. His eyes were somber.

"Very well, I'll tell you what I know. This piece of yarn was found by Mr. Archer here, caught in the lock of a car trunk. The car was one driven by the alleged kidnapper, Harley."

"You mean that Tom was riding in the trunk?"

"He may have been, yes."

"But he wouldn't do that if—" Hillman's mouth worked. "You mean Tom is dead?"

"He may be. We won't jump to any conclusions."

Elaine Hillman produced a noise, a strangled gasp, which made her the center of attention. She spoke in a thin voice, halfway between a child's and an old woman's: "I wish I had never recognized the yarn."

"It wouldn't change the facts, Mrs. Hillman."

"Well, I don't want any more of your dreadful facts. The waiting is bad enough, without these refinements of torment."

Hillman bent over and tried to quiet her. "That isn't fair, Elaine. Lieutenant Bastian is trying to help us." He had said the same thing about me. It gave me the queer feeling that time was repeating itself and would go on endlessly repeating itself, as it does in hell.

She said: "He's going about it in a strange way. Look what he's made me do. All my balls of yarn are spilled on the floor." She kicked at them with her tiny slippered feet.

Hillman got down on his knees to pick them up. She kicked at him, without quite touching him. "Get away, you're no help, either. If you'd been a decent father, this would never have happened."

Bastian picked up the evidence board and turned to me. "We'd better go."

Nobody asked us not to. But Hillman followed us out into the hall.

"Please forgive us, we're not ourselves. You haven't really *told* me anything."

Bastian answered him coolly: "We have no definite conclusions to report."

"But you think Tom's dead."

"I'm afraid he may be. We'll learn more from an analysis of the contents of that car trunk. If you'll excuse me, Mr. Hillman, I don't have time for further explanations now."

"I do," I said.

For the first time that morning Hillman looked at me as if I might be good for something more than a scapegoat. "Are you willing to tell me what's been going on?"

"So far as I understand it."

"I'll leave you men together then," Bastian said. He went out, and a minute later I heard his car go down the drive.

Hillman deputed Mrs. Perez to stay with his wife. He led me into a wing of the house I hadn't visited, down an arching corridor like a tunnel carved through chalk, to a spacious study. Two of the oak-paneled walls were lined with books, most of them in calfbound sets, as if Hillman had bought or inherited a library. A third wall was broken by a large deep window overlooking the distant sea.

The fourth wall was hung with a number of framed photographs. One was a blownup snapshot of Dick Leandro crouching in the cockpit of a racing yacht with his hand on the helm and the white wake boiling at his back. One showed a group of Navy fliers posing together on a flight deck. I recognized a younger Hillman on the far right of the group. There were other similar pictures, taken ashore and afloat; one of a torpedo-bomber squadron flying formation in old World War II Devastators; one of an escort carrier photographed from far overhead, so that it lay like a shingle on the bright, scarified water.

It seemed to me that Hillman had brought me to this specific room, this wall, for a purpose. The somnambulistic precision of his movements was probably controlled by the deep unconscious. At any rate, we were developing the same idea at the same time, and the photograph of the escort carrier was the catalyst.

"That was my last ship," Hillman said. "The fact is, for a few weeks at the end I commanded her."

"A few weeks at the end of the war?"

"A few weeks at *her* end. The war was long since over. We took her from Dago through the Canal to Boston and put her in mothballs." His voice was tender and regretful. He might have been talking about the death of a woman.

"She wasn't the *Perry Bay* by any chance?"

"Yes." He swung around to look at me. "You've heard of her?"

"Just last night. This whole thing is coming together, Mr. Hillman. Does the name Mike Harley mean anything to you?"

His eyes blurred. "I'm afraid you're confusing me. The name you mentioned earlier was Harold Harley."

"I had the wrong name. Harold is Mike's brother, and he's the one I talked to last night. He told me Mike served on the *Perry Bay*."

Hillman nodded slowly. "I remember Mike Harley. I have reason to. He caused me a lot of trouble. In the end I had to recommend an undesirable discharge."

"For stealing a Navy camera."

He gave me a swift responsive look. "You do your homework thoroughly, Mr. Archer. Actually we let him off easy, because he wasn't quite responsible. He could have been sent to Portsmouth for stealing that expensive camera." He backed up into a chair and sat down suddenly, as if he'd been struck by the full impact of the past. "So eighteen years later he has to steal my son."

I stood by the window and waited for him to master the immense coincidence. It was no coincidence in the usual sense, of course. Hillman had been in authority over Harley, and had given Harley reason to hate him. I had heard the hatred speak on the telephone Monday.

The fog over the sea was burning off. Ragged blue holes opened and closed in the grayness. Hillman came to the window and stood beside me. His face was more composed, except for the fierce glitter of his eyes.

"When I think of what that man has done to me," he said. "Tell me the rest of it, Archer. All you know."

I told him the rest of it. He listened as if I was an oracle telling him the story of his future life. He seemed particularly interested in the murdered woman, Carol, and I asked him if he had ever met her.

He shook his head. "I didn't know Harley was married."

"The marriage may not have been legal. But it lasted."

"Did Harley have children?"

"One at least."

"How could a man with a child of his own—?" He didn't finish the thought. Another thought rushed in on his excited mind: "At any rate this disposes of the notion that Tom was mixed up with the woman."

"Not necessarily. Harley could have been using her as bait."

"But that's fantastic. The woman must be—have been old enough to be his mother."

"Still, she wasn't an old woman. She was born about 1930."

"And you're seriously suggesting that Tom had an affair with her?"

"It's an academic question under the circumstances, Mr. Hillman."

His patrician head turned slowly toward me, catching the light on its flat handsome planes. The days were carving him like sculpture. "You mean the fact that Tom is dead."

"It isn't a fact yet. It is a strong possibility."

"If my boy were alive, wouldn't he have come home by now?"

"Not if he's deliberately staying away."

"Do you have reason to believe that he is?"

"Nothing conclusive, but several facts suggest the possibility. He was seen with the woman on Sunday, under his own power. And he did run away in the first place."

"From Laguna Perdida School. Not from us."

"He may expect to be clapped back into the school if he returns."

"Good Lord, I'd never do that."

"You did it once."

"I was forced to by circumstances."

"What were the circumstances, Mr. Hillman?"

"There's no need to go into them. As you would say, the question is academic."

"Did he attempt suicide?"

"No."

"Homicide?"

His eyes flickered. "Certainly not." He changed the subject hurriedly: "We shouldn't be standing here talking. If Thomas is alive, he's got to be found. Harley is the one man who must know where he is, and you tell me Harley is probably on his way to Nevada."

"He's probably there by now."

"Why aren't you? I'd fly you myself if I could leave my wife. But you can charter a plane."

I explained that this took money, of which I'd already spent a fair amount in his behalf.

"I'm sorry, I didn't realize."

He produced the two-thousand-dollar check that Dr. Sponti and Mr. Squerry had given him on Monday, and endorsed it to me. I was back in business.

15

Stella, in her hooded blue jacket, was waiting for me part way down the driveway. The girl had a heavy pair of binoculars hung around her neck on a strap. Her face was bloodless and thin, as if it had provided sustenance for her eyes.

When I stopped the car, she climbed uninvited into the seat beside me. "I've been watching for you."

"Is that what the field glasses are for?"

She nodded gravely. "I watch everybody who comes in or goes out of Tommy's house. Mother thinks I'm bird-watching, which she lets me do because it's a status-symbol activity. Actually I am doing a bird study for next year's biology class, on the nesting habits of the acorn woodpeckers. Only they all look so much alike they're hard to keep track of."

"So are people."

"I'm finding that out." She leaned toward me. Her small breast brushed my shoulder like a gift of trust. "But you know what, Mr. Archer? Tommy tried to call me this morning, I'm almost certain."

"Tell me about it."

"There isn't much to tell, really. It was one of those calls with nobody on the other end of the line. My mother answered the phone, and that's why Tommy didn't speak. He wanted me to answer it." Her eyes were luminous with hope.

"What makes you think it was Tommy?"

"I just know it was. Besides, he called at five to eight, which is the exact same time he always used to call me in the morning. He used to pick me up and drive me to school."

"That isn't too much to go on, Stella. More likely it was a wrong number."

"No. I believe it was Tommy. And he'll be trying again."

"Why would he call you instead of his parents?"

"He's probably afraid to call them. He must be in serious trouble."

"You can be sure of that, one way or another."

I was only trying to moderate her hopefulness, but I frightened her. She said in a hushed voice: "You've found out something."

"Nothing definite. We're on the track of the kidnapper. And incidentally, I have to be on my way."

She held me with her eyes. "He really was kidnapped then? He didn't go to them of his own accord or anything like that?"

"He may have in the first place. After that, I don't know. Did Tommy ever mention a woman named Carol?"

"The woman who was killed?"

"Yes."

"He never did. Why? Did he know her?"

"He knew her very well."

She caught my implication and shook her head. "I don't believe it."

"That doesn't prevent it from being true, Stella. Didn't you ever see them together?"

I got out my collection of pictures and selected the one that Harold Harley had taken of Carol in 1945. The girl studied it. She said with something like awe in her voice:

"She's—she was very beautiful. She couldn't have been much older than I am."

"She wasn't, when the picture was taken. But that was a long time ago, and you should make allowances for that."

"I've never seen her. I'm sure. And Tommy never said a word about her." She looked at me glumly. "People *are* hard to keep track of." She handed me the picture as if it was heavy and hot and would spill if it was tilted.

At this point a female moose deprived of her calf, or something closely resembling her, came crashing through the oak woods. It was Stella's mother. Her handsome red head was tousled and her face was brutalized by anxiety. She spotted Stella and charged around to her side of the car. Stella turned up the window and snapped the lock.

Rhea Carlson rapped on the glass with her fist. "Come out of there. What do you think you're doing?"

"Talking to Mr. Archer."

"You must be crazy. Are you trying to ruin yourself?"

"I don't care what happens to me, that's true."

"You have no right to talk like that. You're ungrateful!"

"Ungrateful for what?"

"I gave you life, didn't I? Your father and I have given you everything."

"I don't want everything. I just want to be let alone, Mother."

"No! You come out of there."

"I don't have to."

"Yes you do," I said.

Stella looked at me as if I had betrayed her to the enemy.

"She's your mother," I said, "and you're a minor, and if you don't obey her you're out of control, and I'm contributing to the delinquency of a minor."

"*You* are?"

"Reluctantly," I said.

The word persuaded her. She even gave me a little half-smile. Then she unlocked the door and climbed out of the car. I got out and walked around to their side. Rhea Carlson looked at me as if I might be on the point of assaulting her.

"Calm down, Mrs. Carlson. Nothing's happened."

"Oh? Would you know?"

"I know that no harm will ever come to Stella if I'm around. May I ask you a question?"

She hesitated. "I won't promise to answer it."

"You received a phone call this morning at five to eight. Was it local or long distance?"

"I don't know. Most of our long-distance calls are dialed direct."

"Was anything said?"

"I said hello."

"I mean on the other end of the line."

"No. Not a word."

"Did whoever it was hang up?"

"Yes, and I'm sure it wasn't the Hillman boy. It was just another stupid mistake in dialing. We get them all the time."

"It was so Tommy," Stella said. "I *know* it."

"Don't believe her. She's always making things up."

"I am not." Stella looked ready to cry.

"Don't contradict me, Stella. Why do you always have to contradict me?"

"I don't."

"You do."

I stepped between them. "Your daughter's a good girl, and she's almost a woman. Please try to bear that in mind, and treat her gently."

Mrs. Carlson said in scornful desperation: "What do you know about mothers and daughters? Who are you, anyway?"

"I've been a private detective since the war. In the course of time you pick up a few primitive ideas about people, and you develop an instinct for the good ones. Like Stella."

Stella blushed. Her mother peered at me without understanding. In my rear-view mirror, as I started away, I saw them walking down the driveway, far apart. It seemed a pity. For all I knew, Rhea Carlson was a good girl, too.

I drove downtown and took Sponti's two-thousand-dollar check to the bank it was drawn on. I endorsed it, under Ralph Hillman's signature: "With many thanks, Lew Archer." It was a weak riposte for being fired, but it gave me some satisfaction to think that it might bring out the purple in Dr. Sponti's face.

The transfusion of cash made me feel mobile and imaginative. Just on a hunch, I drove back to Harold Harley's place in Long Beach. It was a good hunch. Lila answered the door.

She had on an apron and a dusting cap, and she pushed a strand of black hair up under the cap. Her breast rose with the gesture. Lila wasn't a pretty woman, but she had vitality.

"Are you another one of them?" she said.

"Yes. I thought you left Harold."

"So did I. But I decided to come back."

"I'm glad you did. He needs your support."

"Yeah." Her voice softened. "What's going to happen to Harold? Are they going to lock him up and throw the key away?"

"Not if I can help it."

"Are you with the FBI?"

"I'm more of a free lance."

"I was wondering. They came this morning and took the car away. No Harold. Now no car. Next they'll be taking the house from over my head. All on account of that lousy brother of his. It isn't fair."

"It'll be straightened out. I'll tell you the same thing I told Harold. His best chance of getting free and clear is to tell the truth."

"The truth is, he let his brother take advantage of him. He always has. Mike is still—" She clapped her hand to her mouth and looked at me over it with alarm in her brown eyes.

"What is Mike still doing, Mrs. Harley?"

She glanced up and down the dingy street. A few young children were playing in the yards, with their mothers watching them. Lila plucked at my sleeve.

"Come inside, will you? Maybe we can make some kind of a deal."

The front door opened directly into the living room. I stepped over a vacuum-cleaner hose just inside the door.

"I've been cleaning the house," she said. "I had to do something and that was all I could think of."

"I hope Harold will be coming home to appreciate it soon."

"Yeah. It would help him, wouldn't it, if I helped you to nail his brother?"

"It certainly would."

"Would you let him go if you got Mike in his place?"

"I can't promise that. I think it would probably happen."

"Why can't you promise?"

"I'm just a local investigator. But Mike is the one we really want. Do you know where he is, Mrs. Harley?"

For a long moment she stood perfectly still, her face as unchanging as one of her photographs hanging on the wall. Then she nodded slightly.

"I know where he was at three a.m. this morning." She jabbed a thumb toward the telephone. "He called here from Las Vegas at three a.m. He wanted Harold. I told him I didn't know where Harold was—he was gone when I came home last night."

"You're sure it was Mike who called?"

"It couldn't have been anybody else. I know his voice. And it isn't the first time he called here, whining and wheedling for some of our hard-earned money."

"He wanted money?"

"That's right. I was to wire him five hundred dollars to the Western Union office in Las Vegas."

"But he was carrying over twenty thousand."

Her face closed, and became impassive. "I wouldn't know about that. All I know is what he said. He needed money bad, and I was to wire him five hundred, which he would pay back double in twenty-four hours. I told him I'd see him in the hot place first. He was gambling."

"It sounds like it, doesn't it?"

"He's a crazy gambler," she said. "I hate a gambler."

I called the Walters Agency in Reno. Arnie's wife and partner Phyllis told me that Arnie had taken an early plane to Vegas. Harold Harley's two-tone Plymouth had been spotted at a motel on the Vegas Strip.

Not more than two hours later, after a plane ride of my own, I was sitting in a room of the motel talking with Arnie and the Plymouth's new owner. He was a man named Fletcher who said he was from Phoenix, Arizona, although his accent sounded more like Texas. He was dressed up in a western dude costume, with high-heeled boots, a matching belt with a fancy silver buckle, and an amethyst instead of a tie. His Stetson lay on one of the twin beds, some women's clothes on the other. The woman was in the bathroom taking a bath, Arnie told me, and I never did see her.

Mr. Fletcher was large and self-assured and very rough-looking. His face had been chopped rather carelessly from granite, then put out to weather for fifty or fifty-five years.

"I didn't want to buy his heap," he said. "I have a new Cadillac in Phoenix, you can check that. He didn't even have a pink slip for it. I paid him five hundred for the heap because he was broke, desperate to stay in the game."

"What game was that?" I asked him.

"Poker."

"It was a floating game," Arnie said, "in one of the big hotels. Mr. Fletcher refuses to name the hotel, or the other players. It went on all day yesterday and most of last night. There's no telling how much Harley lost, but he lost everything he had."

"Over twenty thousand, probably. Was the game rigged?"

Fletcher turned his head and looked at me the way a statue looks at a man. "It was an honest game, friend. It had to be. I was the big winner."

"I wasn't questioning your honesty."

"No sir. Some of the finest people in Phoenix visit the little woman and I in our residence and we visit them in their residences. Honest Jack Fletcher, they call me."

There was a silence in which the three of us sat and listened to the air-conditioner. I said: "That's fine, Mr. Fletcher. How much did you win?"

"That's between I and the tax collector, friend. I won a bundle. Which is why I gave him five hundred for his heap. I have no use for the heap. You can take it away." He lifted his arm in an imperial gesture.

"We'll be doing just that," Arnie said.

"You're welcome to it. Anything I can do to cooperate."

"You can answer a few more questions, Mr. Fletcher." I got out my picture of Tom. "Did you see this boy with Harley at any time?"

He examined the picture as if it was a card he had drawn, then passed it back to me. "I did not."

"Hear any mention of him?"

"I never did. Harley came and went by himself and he didn't talk. You could see he didn't belong in a high-stakes game, but he had the money, and he wanted to lose it."

"He wanted to lose it?" Arnie said.

"That's right, the same way I wanted to win. He's a born loser, I'm a born winner."

Fletcher got up and strutted back and forth across the room. He lit a Brazilian cigar, not offering any around. As fast as he blew it out, the smoke disappeared in the draft from the air conditioner. "What time did the game break up this morning?" I said.

"Around three, when I took my last big pot." His mouth savored the recollection. "I was willing to stay, but the other people weren't. Harley wanted to stay, naturally, but he didn't have the money to back it up. He isn't much of a poker player, frankly."

"Did he give you any trouble?"

"No sir. The gentleman who runs the game discourages that sort of thing. No trouble. Harley did put the bite on me at the end. I gave him a hundred dollars ding money to get home."

"Home where?"

"He said he came from Idaho."

I took a taxi back to the airport and made a reservation on a plane that stopped in Pocatello. Before sundown I was driving a rented car out of Pocatello along Rural Route Seven, where the elder Harleys lived.

16

Their farm, green and golden in the slanting light, lay in a curve of the river. I drove down a dusty lane to the farmhouse. It was built of white brick, without ornament of any kind. The barn, unpainted, was weathered gray and in poor repair.

The late afternoon was windless. The trees surrounding the fenced yard were as still as watercolors. The heat was oppressive, in spite of the river nearby, even worse than it had been in Vegas.

It was a far cry from Vegas to here, and difficult to believe that Harley had come home, or ever would. But the possibility had to be checked out.

A black and white farm collie with just one eye barked at me through the yard fence when I stepped out of the car. I tried to calm him down by talking to him, but he was afraid of me and he wouldn't be calmed. Eventually an old woman wearing an apron came out of the house and silenced the dog with a word. She called to me:

"Mr. Harley's in the barn."

I let myself in through the wire gate. "May I talk to you?"

"That depends what the talk's about."

"Family matters."

"If that's another way to sell insurance, Mr. Harley doesn't believe in insurance."

"I'm not selling anything. Are you Mrs. Harley?"

"I am."

She was a gaunt woman of seventy, square-shouldered in a long-sleeved, striped shirtwaist. Her gray hair was drawn back severely from her face. I liked her face, in spite of the brokenness in and around her eyes. There was humor in it, and suffering half transformed into understanding.

"Who are you?" she said.

"A friend of your son Harold's. My name is Archer."

"Isn't that nice? We're going to sit down to supper as soon as Mr. Harley finishes up the milking. Why don't you stay and have some supper with us?"

"You're very kind." But I didn't want to eat with them.

"How is Harold?" she said. "We don't hear from him so often since he married his wife. Lila."

Evidently she hadn't heard the trouble her sons were in. I hesitated to tell her, and she noticed my hesitation.

"Is something the matter with Harold?" she said sharply.

"The matter is with Mike. Have you seen him?"

Her large rough hands began to wipe themselves over and

over on the front of her apron. "We haven't seen Mike in twenty years. We don't expect to see him again in this life."

"You may, though. He told a man he was coming home."

"This is not his home. It hasn't been since he was a boy. He turned his back on us then. He went off to Pocatello to live with a man named Brown, and that was his downfall."

"How so?"

"That daughter of Brown was a Jezebel. She ruined my son. She taught him all the filthy ways of the world."

Her voice had changed. It sounded as if the voice of somebody slightly crazy was ranting ventriloquially through her. I said with deliberate intent to stop it:

"Carol's been paid back for whatever she did to him. She was murdered in California on Monday."

Her hands stopped wiping themselves and flew up in front of her. She looked at their raw ugliness with her broken eyes.

"Did Mike do it to her?"

"We think so. We're not sure."

"And you're a policeman," she stated.

"More or less."

"Why do you come to us? We did our best, but we couldn't control him. He passed out of our control long ago." Her hands dropped to her sides.

"If he gets desperate enough, he may head this way."

"No, he never will. Mr. Harley said he would kill him if he ever set foot on our property again. That was twenty years ago, when he ran away from the Navy. Mr. Harley meant it, too. Mr. Harley never could abide a lawbreaker. It isn't true that Mr. Harley treated him cruelly. Mr. Harley was only trying to save him from the Devil."

The ranting, ventriloquial note had entered her voice again. Apparently she knew nothing about her son, and if she did she couldn't talk about him in realistic terms. It was beginning to look like a dry run.

I left her and went to the barn to find her husband. He was in the stable under the barn, sitting on a milking stool with his forehead against the black and white flank of a Holstein cow. His hands were busy at her teats, and her milk surged in the pail between his knees. Its sweet fresh smell penetrated the smell of dung that hung like corruption in the heated air.

"Mr. Harley?"

"I'm busy," he said morosely. "This is the last one, if you want to wait."

I backed away and looked at the other cows. There were ten or twelve of them, moving uneasily in their stanchions as I moved. Somewhere out of sight a horse blew and stamped.

"You're disturbing the livestock," Mr. Harley said. "Stand still if you want to stay."

I stood still for about five minutes. The one-eyed collie drifted into the stable and did a thorough job of smelling my shoes. But he still wouldn't let me touch him. When I reached down, he moved back.

Mr. Harley got up and emptied his pail into a ten-gallon can; the foaming milk almost overflowed. He was a tall old man wearing overalls and a straw hat which almost brushed the low rafters. His eyes were as flat and angry and his mouth as sternly righteous as in Harold's portrait of him. The dog retreated whining as he came near.

"You're not from around here. Are you on the road?"

"No." I told him who I was. "And I'll get to the point right away. Your son Mike's in very serious trouble."

"Mike is not my son," he intoned solemnly, "and I have no wish to hear about him or his trouble."

"But he may be coming here. He said he was. If he does, you'll have to inform the police."

"You don't have to instruct me in what I ought to do. I get my instructions from a higher power. He gives me my instructions direct in my heart." He thumped his chest with a gnarled fist.

"That must be convenient."

"Don't blaspheme or make mock, or you'll regret it. I can call down the punishment."

He reached for a pitchfork leaning against the wall. The dog ran out of the stable with his tail down. I became aware suddenly that my shirt was sticking to my back and I was intensely uncomfortable. The three tines of the pitchfork were sharp and gleaming, and they were pointed at my stomach.

"Get out of here," the old man said. "I've been fighting the Devil all my life, and I know one of his cohorts when I see one."

So do I, I said, but not out loud. I backed as far as the door, stumbled on the high threshold, and went out. Mrs. Harley was standing near my car, just inside the wire gate. Her hands were quiet on her meager breast.

"I'm sorry," she said to me. "I'm sorry for Carol Brown. She wasn't a bad little girl, but I hardened my heart against her."

"It doesn't matter now. She's dead."

"It matters in the sight of heaven."

She raised her eyes to the arching sky as if she imagined a literal heaven like a second story above it. Just now it was easier for me to imagine a literal hell, just over the horizon, where the sunset fires were burning.

"I've done so many wrong things," she said, "and closed my eyes to so many others. But don't you see, I had to make a choice."

"I don't understand you."

"A choice between Mr. Harley and my sons. I knew that he was a hard man. A cruel man, maybe not quite right in the head. But what could I do? I had to stick with my husband. And I wasn't strong enough to stand up to him. Nobody is. I had to stand by while he drove our sons out of our home. Harold was the soft one, he forgave us in the end. But Mike never did. He's like his father. I never even got to see my grandson."

Tears ran in the gullies of her face. Her husband came out of the barn carrying his ten-gallon can in his left hand and the pitchfork in his right.

"Go in the house, Martha. This man is a cohort of the Devil. I won't allow you to talk to him."

"Don't hurt him. Please."

"Go in the house," he repeated.

She went, with her gray head down and her feet dragging.

"As for you, cohort," he said, "you get off my farm or I'll call down the punishment on you."

He shook his pitchfork at the reddening sky. I was already in the car and turning up the windows.

I turned them down again as soon as I got a few hundred yards up the lane. My shirt was wet through now, and I could feel sweat running down my legs. Looking back, I caught a glimpse of the river, flowing sleek and solid in the failing light, and it refreshed me.

17

Before driving out to the Harley farm, I had made an evening appointment with Robert Brown and his wife. They already knew what had happened to their daughter. I didn't have to tell them.

I found their house in the north end of the city, on a pleasant, tree-lined street parallel to Arthur Street. Night had fallen almost completely, and the street lights were shining under the clotted masses of the trees. It was still very warm. The earth itself seemed to exude heat like a hot-blooded animal.

Robert Brown had been watching for me. He hailed me from his front porch and came out to the curb. A big man with short gray hair, vigorous in his movements, he still seemed to be wading in some invisible substance, age or sorrow. We shook hands solemnly.

He spoke with more apparent gentleness than force: "I was planning to fly out to California tomorrow. It might have saved you a trip if you had known."

"I wanted to talk to the Harleys, anyway."

"I see." He cocked his head on one side in a birdlike movement which seemed odd in such a big man. "Did you get any sense out of them?"

"Mrs. Harley made a good deal of sense. Harley didn't."

"I'm not surprised. He's a pretty good farmer, they say, but he's been in and out of the mental hospital. I took—my wife and I took care of his son Mike during one of his bouts. We took him into our home." He sounded ashamed of the act.

"That was a generous thing to do."

"I'm afraid it was misguided generosity. But who can prophesy the future? Anyway, it's over now. All over." He forgot about me completely for a moment, then came to himself with a start. "Come in, Mr. Archer. My wife will want to talk to you."

He took me into the living room. It had group and family photos on the walls, and a claustrophobic wallpaper, which lent it some of the stuffiness of an old-fashioned country parlor. The room was sedately furnished with well-cared-for maple pieces. Across the mantel marched a phalanx of sports trophies gleaming gold and silver in the harsh overhead light.

Mrs. Brown was sitting in an armchair under the light. She was a strikingly handsome woman a few years younger than her husband, maybe fifty-five. She had chosen to disguise herself in a stiff and rather dowdy black dress. Her too precisely marcelled brown hair had specks of gray in it. Her fine eyes were confused, and surrounded by dark patches. When she gave me her hand, the gesture seemed less like a greeting than a bid for help.

She made me sit down on a footstool near her. "Tell us all about poor Carol, Mr. Archer."

All about Carol. I glanced around the safe, middle-class room, with the pictures of Carol's ancestors on the walls, and back at her parents' living faces. Where did Carol come in? I could see the source of her beauty in her mother's undisguisable good looks. But I couldn't see how one life led to the other, or why Carol's life had ended as it had.

Brown said: "We know she's dead, murdered, and that Mike probably did it, and that's about all." His face was like a Roman general's, a late Roman general's, after a long series of defeats by barbarian hordes.

"It's about all I know. Mike seems to have been using her as a decoy in an extortion attempt. You know about the Hillman boy?"

He nodded. "I read about it before I knew that my daughter—" His voice receded.

"They say he may be dead, too," his wife said.

"He may be, Mrs. Brown."

"And Mike did these things? I knew he was far gone, but I didn't know he was a monster."

"He's not a monster," Brown said wearily. "He's a sick man. His father was a sick man. He still is, after all the mental hospital could do for him."

"If Mike was so sick, why did you bring him into this house and expose your daughter to him?"

"She's your daughter, too."

"I know that. I'm not allowed to forget it. But I'm not the one that ruined her for life."

"You certainly had a hand in it. You were the one, for instance, who encouraged her to enter that beauty contest."

"She didn't win, did she?"

"That was the trouble."

"Was it? The trouble was the way you felt about the Harley boy."

"I wanted to help him. He needed help, and he had talent."

"Talent?"

"As an athlete. I thought I could develop him."

"You developed him all right."

They were talking across me, not really oblivious of me, using me as a fulcrum for leverage, or a kind of stand-in for reality. I guessed that the argument had been going on for twenty years.

"I wanted a son," Brown said.

"Well, you got a son. A fine upstanding son."

He looked as if he was about to strike her. He didn't, though. He turned to me:

"Forgive us. We shouldn't do this. It's embarrassing."

His wife stared at him in unforgiving silence. I tried to think of something that would break or at least soften the tension between them:

"I didn't come here to start a quarrel."

"You didn't start it, let me assure you." Brown snickered remorsefully. "It started the day Carol ran off with Mike. It was something I didn't foresee—"

His wife's bitter voice cut in: "It started when she was born, Rob. You wanted a son. You didn't want a daughter. You rejected her and you rejected me."

"I did nothing of the sort."

"He doesn't remember," she said to me. "He has one of these convenient memories that men have. You blot out anything that doesn't suit your upright idea of yourself. My husband is a very dishonest man." She had a peculiar angry gnawing smile.

"That's nonsense," he protested. "I've been faithful to you all my life."

"Except in ways I couldn't cope with. Like when you brought the Harley boy into our home. The great altruist. The noble counselor."

"You have no right to jeer at me," he said. "I wanted to help him. I had no way of knowing that he couldn't be reached."

"Go on. You wanted a son any way you could get one."

He said stubbornly: "You don't understand. A man gets natural pleasure from raising a boy, teaching him what he knows."

"All you succeeded in teaching Mike was your dishonesty."

He turned to me with a helpless gesture, his hands swinging out. "She blames me for everything." Walking rather aimlessly, he went out to the back part of the house.

I felt as if I'd been left alone with a far from toothless lioness. She stirred in her chair:

"I blame myself as well for being a fool. I married a man who has the feelings of a little boy. He still gets excited about his high-school football teams. The boys adore him. Everybody adores him. They talk about him as if he was some kind of a plaster saint. And he couldn't even keep his own daughter out of trouble."

"You and your husband should be pulling together."

"It's a little late to start, isn't it?"

Her glance came up to my face, probed at it for a moment, moved restlessly from side to side.

"It may be that you'll kill him if you go on like this."

"No. He'll live to be eighty, like his father."

She jerked her marcelled head toward one of the pictures on the wall. Seen from varying angles, her head was such a handsome object I could hardly take my eyes off it. It was hard to believe that such a finely shaped container could be full of cold boiling trouble.

I said, partly because I wanted to, and partly to appease her: "You must have been a very beautiful girl."

"Yes. I was."

She seemed to take no pleasure even from her vanity. I began to suspect that she didn't relate to men. It happened sometimes to girls who were too good-looking. They were treated as beautiful objects until they felt like that and nothing more.

"I could have married anybody," she said, "any man I went to college with. Some of them are bank presidents and big corporation executives now. But I had to fall in love with a football player."

"Your husband is a little more than that."

"Don't *sell* him to me," she said. "I know what he is, and I know what my life has been. I've been defrauded. I gave everything I had to marriage and motherhood, and what have I got to show for it? Do you know I never even saw my grandson?"

Mrs. Harley had said the same thing. I didn't mention the coincidence.

"What happened to your grandson?"

"Carol put him out for adoption, can you imagine? Actually I know why she did it. She didn't trust her husband not to harm the baby. That's the kind of man she married."

"Did she tell you this?"

"More or less. Mike is a sadist, among other things. He used to swing cats by their tails. He lived in this house for over a year and all the time I was afraid of him. He was terribly strong, and I never was certain what he was going to do."

"Did he ever attack you?"

"No. He never dared to."

"How old was he when he left?"

"Let me see, Carol was fifteen at the time. That would make him seventeen or eighteen."

"And he left to join the Navy, is that correct?"

"He didn't go into the Navy right away. He left town with an older man, a policeman who used to be on the local force. I forgot his name. Anyway, this man lost his position on the force through bribery, and left town, taking Mike with him. He said he was going to make a boxer out of him. They went out to the west coast. I think Mike joined the Navy a few months later. Carol could—" She stopped in dismay.

"What about Carol?"

"I was going to say that Carol could tell you." The angry smile twisted and insulted her mouth. "I must be losing my mind."

"I doubt that, Mrs. Brown. It takes time to get used to these shocks and changes."

"More time than I have. More time than I'll ever have." She rose impatiently and went to the mantelpiece. One of the trophies standing on it was out of line with the others. She reached up and adjusted its position. "I wonder what Rob thinks he's doing in the kitchen."

She didn't go and find out what he was doing. She stood in an awkward position, one hip out, in front of the empty fireplace. Under her dowdy black dress, the slopes and masses of her body were angry. But nothing that she could do with her body, or her face, could change the essential beauty of the structure. She was trapped in it, as her daughter had been.

"I wish you'd go on with your story, Mrs. Brown."

"It hardly qualifies as a story."

"Whatever you want to call it, then. I'm very grateful for

the chance to talk to you. It's the first decent chance I've had to get any information about the background of this case."

"The background hardly matters now, or the foreground either."

"It does, though. You may tell me something that will help me to find Harley. I take it you've seen him and Carol from time to time over the years."

"I saw *him* just once more—after that, I wouldn't give him house room—when he came home from the Navy in the winter of 1944–45. He claimed to be on leave. Actually he was absent without leave. He talked himself back into Rob's good graces. Rob had been terribly let down when he left town with that ex-policeman, the bribery artist. But my gullible husband fell for his line all over again. He even gave him money. Which Mike used to elope with my only daughter."

"Why did Carol go with him?"

She scratched at her forehead, leaving faint weals in the clear skin. "I asked her that, the last time she was home, just a couple of months ago. I asked her why she went and why she stuck with him. She didn't really know. Of course she wanted to get out of Pocatello. She hated Pocatello. She wanted to go out to the coast and break into the movies. I'm afraid my daughter had very childish dreams."

"Girls of fifteen do." With a pang, I thought of Stella. The pang became a vaguely formed idea of an unattended area of my mind. Generation after generation had to start from scratch and learn the world over again. It changed so rapidly that children couldn't learn from their parents or parents from their children. The generations were like alien tribes islanded in time.

"The fact is," I said, "Carol did make it into the movies."

"Really? She told me that once, but I didn't believe her."

"Was she a chronic liar?"

"No. Mike was the chronic liar. I simply didn't believe that she could succeed at anything. She never had."

The woman's bitterness was getting me down. She seemed to have an inexhaustible reservoir of the stuff. If she had been like this twenty years before, I could understand why Carol had left home at the first opportunity, and stayed away.

"You say you saw Carol just a couple of months ago."

"Yes. She rode the bus from Lake Tahoe in June. I hadn't seen her for quite a long time. She was looking pretty bedraggled. God knows what kind of a life he was leading her. She didn't talk much.''

"It was a chancy life. Harley seems to have lost his job, and they were on their uppers.''

"So she told me. There was the usual plea for money. I guess Rob gave her money. He always did. He tried to pretend afterwards, to me, that he gave her the car, too, but I know better. She took it. Apparently their old car had broken down, and they couldn't live at Tahoe without a car.''

"How do you know she took it if your husband says she didn't?''

She showed signs of embarrassment. "It doesn't matter. They were welcome to the car.'' It was her first generous word. She half-spoiled it: "We needed a new one, anyway, and I'm sure she did it on the spur of the moment. Carol always was a very impulsive girl.

"The point is,'' she said, "she left without saying goodbye. She took the car to go downtown to the movies and simply never came back. She even left her suitcase in her room.''

"Had there been trouble?''

"No more than the usual trouble. We did have an argument at supper.''

"What about?''

"My grandson. She had no right to put him out for adoption. She said he was her baby to do with as she pleased. But she had no right. If she couldn't keep him, she should have brought him to us. We could have given him opportunities, an education.'' She breathed heavily and audibly. "She said an unforgivable thing to me that evening. She said, did I mean the kind of opportunities she had? And she walked out. I never saw her again. Neither did her father.'' Her head jerked forward in emphatic affirmation: "We *did* give her opportunities. It's not our fault if she didn't take advantage of them. It isn't fair to blame us.''

"You blame each other,'' I said. "You're tearing each other to pieces.''

"Don't give me that sort of talk. I've had enough of it from my husband.''

"I'm merely calling your attention to an obvious fact. You need some kind of an intermediary, a third party, to help straighten out your thinking.''

"And you're electing yourself, are you?''

"Far from it. You need an expert counselor."

"My husband *is* a counselor," she said. "What good has it done him? Anyway, I don't believe in seeking that kind of help. People should be able to handle their own problems."

She composed her face and sat down in the armchair again, with great calm, to show me how well she was handling hers.

"But what if they can't, Mrs. Brown?"

"Then they can't, that's all."

I made one more attempt. "Do you go to church?"

"Naturally I do."

"You could talk these problems over with your minister."

"What problems? I'm not aware of any outstanding problems." She was in despair so deep that she wouldn't even look up toward the light. I think she was afraid it would reveal her to herself.

I turned to other matters. "You mentioned a suitcase that your daughter left behind. Is it still here in the house?"

"It's up in her room. There isn't much in it. I almost threw it out with the trash, but there was always the chance that she would come back for it."

"May I see it?"

"I'll go and get it."

"If you don't mind, I'd sooner go up to her room."

"I don't mind."

We went upstairs together, with Mrs. Brown leading the way. She turned on the light in a rear bedroom and stood back to let me enter.

The room provided the first clear evidence that she had been hit very hard by Carol's running away. It was the bedroom of a high-school girl. The flouncy yellow cover on the French provincial bed matched the yellow flounces on the dressing table, where a pair of Kewpie-doll lamps smiled vacantly at each other. A floppy cloth dog with his red felt tongue hanging out watched me from the yellow lamb's wool rug. A little bookcase, painted white like the bed, was filled with high-school texts and hospital novels and juvenile mysteries. There were college pennants tacked around the walls.

"I kept her room as she left it," Mrs. Brown said behind me. "Why?"

"I don't know. I guess I always thought that she'd come home in the end. Well, she did a few times. The suitcase is in the closet."

The closet smelled faintly of sachet. It was full of skirts and dresses, the kind girls wore in high school a half-generation before. I began to suspect that the room and its contents had less to do with Carol than with some secret fantasy of her mother's. Her mother said, as if in answer to my thought:

"I spend a lot of time here in this room. I feel very close to her here. We really were quite close at one time. She used to tell me everything, all about the boys she dated and so on. It was like living my own high school days over again."

"Is that good?"

"I don't know." Her lips gnawed at each other. "I guess not, because she suddenly turned against me. Suddenly she closed up completely. I didn't know what went on in her life, but I could see her changing, coarsening. She was such a pretty girl, such a pure-looking girl." Her mouth was wrenched far off center and it remained that way, as if the knowledge of her loss had fallen on her like a cerebral stroke.

The suitcase was an old scuffed cowhide one with Rob Brown's initials on it. I pulled it out into the middle of the floor and opened it. Suddenly I was back in Dack's Auto Court opening Carol's other suitcase. The same sour odor of regret rose from the contents of this one and seemed to permeate the room.

There was the same tangle of clothes, this time all of them women's, skirts and dresses and underthings and stockings, a few cosmetics, a paperback book on the divination of dreams. A hand-scrawled piece of paper was stuck in this as a bookmark. I pulled it out and looked at it. It was signed "Your Brother 'Har.'"

DEAR MIKE:

I'm sorry you and Carole are haveing a "tough time" and I enclose a money order for fifty which I hope will help out you have to cash it at a postoffice. I would send more but things are a little "tight" since I got married to Lila shes a good girl but does not believe that blood· is thicker than water which it is. You asked me do I bing married well in some ways I really like it in other ways I dont Lila has very strong ideas of her own. Shes no "sinsational" beauty like Carole is but we get long.

Im sorry you lost your job Mike unskilled jobs are hard to come by in these times I know you are a good bartender

and that is a skill you should be able to pick up something
in that line even if they are prejudiced like you say. I did
look up Mr. Sipe like you asked me to but he is in no
position to do anything for anybody hes on the skids
himself the Barcelona went bankrupt last winter and now
old Sipe is just watchman on the place but he sent his best
regards for old time sake he wanted to know if you ever
developed a left.

I saw another "freind" of yours last week I mean
Captain Hillman I know you bear a grudge there but after
all he treated you pretty good he could have sent you to
prison for ten years. No Im not rakeing up old recriminations
because Hillman could do something for you if he wanted
you ought to see the raceing yacht he has thats how I saw
him went down to Newport to take some sailing pictures.
I bet he has twenty-five thousand in that yacht the guy is
loaded. I found out he lives with his wife and boy in
Pacific Point if you want to try him for a job hes head of
some kind of "smogless industry."

Well thats about all for now if you deside to come out
to "sunny Cal" you know where we live and dont worry
Lila will make you welcome shes a good soul "at heart."

SINCERELY YOURS

Mrs. Brown had come out of her trance and moved toward
me with a curious look. "What is that?"

"A letter to Mike from his brother Harold. May I have it?"

"You're welcome to it."

"Thank you. I believe it's evidence. It seems to have started
Mike thinking about the possibility of bleeding the Hillmans for
money." And it explained, I thought, why Harold had blamed
himself for instigating the crime.

"May I read it?"

I handed it to her. She held it at arm's length, squinting.

"I'm afraid I need my glasses."

We went downstairs to the living room, where she put on
horn-rimmed reading glasses and sat in her armchair with the
letter. "Sipe," she said when she finished reading it. "That's
the name I was trying to think of before." She raised her voice
and called: "Robert! Come in here."

Rob Brown answered from the back of the house: "I was just
coming."

He appeared in the doorway carrying a clinking pitcher and three glasses on a tray. He said with a placatory look at his wife: "I thought I'd make some fresh lemonade for the three of us. It's a warm night."

"That was thoughtful, Robert. Put it down on the coffee table. Now, what was the name of the ex-policeman that Mike left town with, the first time?"

"Sipe. Otto Sipe." He flushed slightly. "That man was a bad influence, I can tell you."

I wondered if he still was. The question seemed so urgent that I drove right back to the airport and caught the first plane out, to Salt Lake City. A late jet from Minneapolis rescued me from a night in the Salt Lake City airport and deposited me at Los Angeles International, not many miles from the Barcelona Hotel, where a man named Sipe was watchman.

18

I had a gun in a locked desk drawer in my apartment, and one in my office. The apartment in West Los Angeles was nearer. I went there.

It was in a fairly new, two-story building with a long roofed gallery on which the second-floor apartments opened directly. Mine was the second-floor back. I parked in the street and climbed the outside stairs.

It was the dead dull middle of the night, the static hour when yesterday ended and tomorrow gathered its forces to begin. My own forces were running rather low, but I wasn't tired. I had slept on the planes. And my case was breaking, my beautiful terrible mess of a case was breaking.

A light shone dimly behind my draped front window, and when I tried the door it was unlocked. I had no family, no wife, no girl. I turned the knob quietly, and slowly and tentatively opened the door.

It seemed I had a girl after all. She was curled up on the studio couch under a blanket which came from my bed. The light from a standing lamp shone down on her sleeping face. She looked so young I felt a hundred years old.

I closed the door. "Hey, Stella."

Her body jerked under the blanket. Throwing it off, she sat up. She was wearing a blue sweater and a skirt. "Oh," she said. "It's you."

"Who were you expecting?"

"I don't know. But don't be cross with me. I was just dreaming something, I forget what, but it was depressing." Her eyes were still dark with the dream.

"How in the world did you get in here?"

"The manager let me in. I told him I was a witness. He understood."

"I don't. A witness to what?"

"Quite a few things," she said with some spirit. "If you want me to tell you, you can stop treating me like a mentally retarded delinquent. Nobody else does, except my parents."

I sat on the edge of the studio couch beside her. I liked the girl but at the moment she was an obstruction, and could turn into a serious embarrassment. "Do your parents know you're here?"

"Of course not. How could I tell them? They wouldn't have let me come, and I had to come. You *ordered* me to get in touch with you if I ever heard from Tommy. Your answering service couldn't find you and finally they gave me your home address."

"Are you telling me you've heard from him?"

She nodded. Her eyes held steady on my face. They were brimming with complex feelings, more womanly than girlish. "He phoned around four o'clock this afternoon. Mother was at the store, and I had a chance to answer the phone myself."

"Where was he, did he say?"

"Here in—" She hesitated. "He made me promise not to tell anyone. And I've already broken my promise once."

"How did you do that?"

"I put a little note in Mr. Hillman's mailbox, before I left El Rancho. I couldn't just leave him dangling, when I *knew*."

"What did you tell him?"

"Just that I'd heard from Tommy, and he was alive."

"It was a kind thing to do."

"But it broke my promise. He said I wasn't to tell anyone, especially not his parents."

"Promises have to be broken sometimes, when there are higher considerations."

"What do you mean?"

"His safety. I've been afraid that Tom was dead. Are you absolutely certain you talked to him?"

"I'm not telling a lie."

"I mean, you're sure it wasn't an impostor, or a tape recording?"

"I'm sure. We talked back and forth."

"Where was he calling from?"

"I don't know, but I think it was long distance."

"What did he say?"

She hesitated again, with her finger raised. "Is it all right for me to tell you, even after I promised?"

"It would be all wrong if you didn't. You know that, don't you? You didn't come all the way here to hold it back."

"No." She smiled a little. "He didn't tell me too much. He didn't say a word about the kidnappers. Anyway, the fact that he's alive is the important thing. He said he was sorry I'd been worried about him, but he couldn't help it. Then he asked me to meet him and bring some money."

I was relieved. Tom's need for money implied that he had no part of the payoff. "How much money?"

"As much as I could get hold of in a hurry. He knew it wouldn't amount to a great deal. I borrowed some from the people at the beach club. The secretary of the club gave me a hundred dollars of her own money—she knows I'm honest. I took a taxi to the bus station. You know, I never rode on a bus before, except the school bus."

I cut in impatiently: "Did you meet him here in Los Angeles?"

"No. I was supposed to meet him in the Santa Monica bus station at nine o'clock. The bus was a few minutes late, and I may have missed him. He did say on the phone that he mightn't be able to make it tonight. In which case I was to meet him tomorrow night. He said he generally only goes out at night."

"Did he tell you where he's staying?"

"No. That's the trouble. I hung around the bus station for about an hour and then I tried to phone you and when I couldn't I took a taxi here. I had to spend the night somewhere."

"So you did. It's too bad Tom didn't think of that."

"He probably has other things on his mind," she said in a defensive tone. "He's been having a terrible time."

"Did he say so?"

"I could tell by the way he talked to me. He sounded—I don't know—so upset."

"Emotionally upset, or just plain scared?"

Her brow knit. "More worried than scared. But he wouldn't say what about. He wouldn't tell me anything that happened. I asked him if he was okay, you know, physically okay, and he said he was. So I asked him why he didn't come home. He said on account of his parents, only he didn't call them his parents. He called them his anti-parents. He said they could probably hardly wait to put him back in Laguna Perdida School."

Her eyes were very dark. "I remember now what I was dreaming before you woke me up. Tommy was in that school and they wouldn't let him out and they wouldn't let me see him. I went around to all the doors and windows, trying to get in. All I could see was the terrible faces leering at me through the windows."

"The faces aren't so terrible. I was there."

"Yes, but you weren't locked up there. Tommy says it's a terrible place. His parents had no right to put him there. I don't blame him for staying away."

"Neither do I, Stella. But, under the circumstances, he has to be brought in. You understand that, don't you?"

"I guess I do."

"It would be a rotten anticlimax if something happened to him now. You don't want that."

She shook her head.

"Then will you help me get him?"

"It's why I came here, really. I couldn't sic the police on him. But you're different." She touched the back of my hand. "You won't let them put him back in Laguna Perdida."

"It won't happen if I can possibly help it. I think I can. If Tom needs treatment, he should be able to get it as an outpatient."

"He isn't sick!"

"His father must have had a reason for putting him there. Something happened that Sunday, he wouldn't tell me what."

"It happened long before that Sunday," she said. "His father turned against him, that's what happened. Tommy isn't the hairy-chested type, and he preferred music to trap-shooting and sailing and such things. So his father turned against him. It's as simple as that."

"Nothing ever is, but we won't argue. If you'll excuse me for a minute, Stella, I have to make a phone call."

The phone was on the desk under the window. I sat down there and dialed Susanna Drew's unlisted number. She answered on the first ring.

"Hello."

"Lew Archer. You sound very alert for three o'clock in the morning."

"I've been lying awake thinking, about you among other things and people. Somebody said—I think it was Scott Fitzgerald—something to the effect that in the real dark night of the soul it's always three o'clock in the morning. I have a reverse twist on that. At three o'clock in the morning it's always the real dark night of the soul."

"The thought of me depresses you?"

"In certain contexts it does. In others, not."

"You're talking in riddles, Sphinx."

"I mean to be, Oedipus. But you're not the source of my depression. That goes back a long way."

"Do you want to tell me about it?"

"Another time, doctor." Her footwork was very skittish. "You didn't call me at this hour for snatches of autobiography."

"No, though I'd still like to know who that telephone call was from the other day."

"And that's why you called me?" There was disappointment in her voice, ready to turn into anger.

"It isn't why I called you. I need your help."

"Really?" She sounded surprised, and rather pleased. But she said guardedly: "You mean by telling you all I know and like that?"

"We don't have time. I think this case is breaking. Anyway I have to make a move, now. A very nice high-school girl named Stella has turned up on my doorstep." I was speaking to the girl in the room as well as to the woman on the line; as I did so, I realized that they were rapidly becoming my favorite girl and woman. "I need a safe place to keep her for the rest of the night."

"I'm not that safe." A rough note in her voice suggested that she meant it.

Stella said quickly behind me: "I could stay here."

"She can't stay here. Her parents would probably try to hang a child-stealing rap on me."

"Are you serious?"

"The situation is serious, yes."

"All right. Where do you live?"

"Stella and I will come there. We're less than half an hour from you at this time of night."

Stella said when I hung up: "You didn't have to do it behind my back."

"I did it right in front of your face. And I don't have time to argue."

To underline the urgency I took off my jacket, got my gun and its harness out of the drawer, and put it on in front of her. She watched me with wide eyes. The ugly ritual didn't quite silence her.

"But I didn't want to *meet* anybody tonight."

"You'll like Susanna Drew. She's very stylish and hep."

"But I never *do* like people when adults tell me I will."

After the big effort of the night, she was relapsing into childishness. I said, to buck her up:

"Forget your war with the adults. You're going to be an adult pretty soon yourself. Then who will you have to blame for everything?"

"That isn't fair."

It wasn't, but it held her all the way to the apartment house on Beverly Glen. Susanna came to the door in silk pajamas, not the kind anyone slept in. Her hair was brushed. She hadn't bothered with makeup. Her face was extraordinarily and nakedly handsome, with eyes as real and dark as any night.

"Come in, Lew. It's nice to see you, Stella. I'm Susanna. I have a bed made up for you upstairs." She indicated the indoor balcony which hung halfway up the wall of the big central studio, and on which an upstairs room opened. "Do you want something to eat?"

"No, thank you," Stella said. "I had a hamburger at the bus station."

"I'll be glad to make you a sandwich."

"No. Really. I'm not hungry." The girl looked pale and a little sick.

"Would you like to go to bed then?"

"I have no choice." Stella heard herself, and added: "That

was rude, wasn't it? I didn't mean it to be. It's awfully kind of you to take me in. It was Mr. Archer who gave me no choice."

"I had no choice, either," I said. "What would you do if you had one?"

"I'd be with Tommy, wherever he is."

Her mouth began to work, and so did the delicate flesh around her eyes and mouth. The mask of a crying child seemed to be struggling for possession of her face. She ran away from it, or from our eyes, up the circular stairs to the balcony.

Susanna called after her before she closed the door: "Pajamas on the bed, new toothbrush in the bathroom."

"You're an efficient hostess," I said.

"Thank you. Have a drink before you go."

"It wouldn't do anything for me."

"Do you want to go into where you're going and what you have to do?"

"I'm on my way to the Barcelona Hotel, but I keep running into detours."

She reacted more sharply than she had any apparent reason to. "Is that what I am, a detour?"

"Stella was the detour. You're the United States Cavalry."

"I love your imagery." She made a face. "What on earth are you planning to do at the old Barcelona? Isn't it closed down?"

"There's at least one man living there, a watchman who used to be the hotel detective, named Otto Sipe."

"Good Lord, I think I know him. Is he a big red-faced character with a whisky breath?"

"That's probably the man. How do you happen to know him?"

She hesitated before she answered, in a careful voice: "I sort of frequented the Barcelona at one time, way back at the end of the war. That was where I met Carol."

"And Mr. Sipe."

"And Mr. Sipe."

She wouldn't tell me more.

"You have no right to cross-question me," she said finally. "Leave me alone."

"I'll be glad to."

She followed me to the door. "Don't leave on that note. Please. I'm not holding back for the fun of it. Why do you think I've been lying awake all night?"

"Guilt?"

"Nonsense. I'm not ashamed of anything." But there was shame in her eyes, deeper than the knowledge of herself. "Anyway, the little I know can't be of any importance."

"You're not being fair. You're trying to use my personal feeling for you—"

"I didn't know it existed. If it does, I ought to have a right to use it any way I need to."

"You don't have that right, though. My privacy is a very precious thing to me, and you have no right to violate it."

"Even to save a life?"

Stella opened her door and came out on the balcony. She looked like a young, pajamaed saint in a very large niche.

"If you *adults*," she said, "will lower your voices a few decibels, it might be possible to get a little sleep."

"Sorry," I said to both of them.

Stella retreated. Susanna said: "Whose life is in danger, Lew?"

"Tom Hillman's for one. Possibly others, including mine."

She touched the front of my jacket. "You're wearing a shoulder holster. Is Otto Sipe one of the kidnappers?"

I countered with a question: "Was he a man in your life?"

She was offended. "Of course not. Go away now." She pushed me out. "Take care."

The night air was chilly on my face.

19

Traffic was sparse on the coastal highway. Occasional night-crawling trucks went by, blazing with red and yellow lights. This stretch of highway was an ugly oil-stained place, fouled by petroleum fumes and rubbed barren by tires. Even the sea below it had a used-dishwater odor.

Ben Daly's service station was dark, except for an inside bulb left on to discourage burglars. I left my car in his lot, beside an outside telephone booth, and crossed the highway to the Barcelona Hotel.

It was as dead as Nineveh. In the gardens behind the main building a mockingbird tried a few throbbing notes, like a tiny heart of sound attempting to beat, and then subsided. The intermittent mechanical movement of the highway was the only life in the inert black night.

I went up to the front door where the bankruptcy notice was posted and knocked on the glass with my flashlight. I knocked repeatedly, and got no answer. I was about to punch out a pane of glass and let myself in. Then I noticed that the door was unlocked. It opened under my hand.

I entered the lobby, jostling a couple of ghosts. They were Susanna, twenty years old, and a man without a face. I told them to get the hell out of my way.

I went down the corridor where Mr. Sipe had first appeared with his light, past the closed, numbered doors, to a door at the end which was standing slightly ajar. I could hear breathing inside the dark room, the heavy sighing breathing of a man in sleep or stupor. The odor of whisky was strong.

I reached inside the door and found the light switch with my right hand. I turned it on and shifted my hand to my gun butt. There was no need. Sipe was lying on the bed, fully clothed, with his ugly nostrils glaring and his loose mouth sighing at the ceiling. He was alone.

There was hardly space for anyone else. The room had never been large, and it was jammed with stuff which looked as if it had been accumulating for decades. Cartons and packing cases, piles of rugs, magazines and newspapers, suitcases and foot lockers, were heaped at the back of the room almost to the ceiling. On the visible parts of the walls were pictures of young men in boxing stance, interspersed with a few girlie pictures.

Empty whisky bottles were ranged along the wall beside the door. A half-full bottle stood by the bed where Sipe was lying. I turned the key that was in the lock of the door and took a closer look at the sleeping man.

He wasn't just sleeping. He was out, far out and possibly far gone. If I had put a match to his lips, his breath would have ignited like an alcohol burner. Even the front of his shirt seemed to be saturated with whisky, as though he'd poured it over himself in one last wild libation before he passed out.

His gun was stuck in the greasy waistband of his trousers. I transferred it to my jacket pocket before I tried to rouse him. He wouldn't wake up. I shook him. He was inert as a side of beef, and his big head rolled loosely on the pillow. I slapped his pitted red cheeks. He didn't even groan.

I went into the adjoining bathroom—it was also a kind of kitchen fitted out with an electric plate and a percolator that smelled of burned coffee—and filled the percolator with cold water from the bathtub faucet. This I poured over Sipe's head and face, being careful not to drown him. He didn't wake up.

I was getting a little worried, not so much about Sipe as about the possibility that he might never be able to give me his story. There was no way of telling how many of the bottles in the room had been emptied recently. I felt his pulse: laboriously slow. I lifted one of his eyelids. It was like looking down into a red oyster.

I had noticed that the bathroom was one of those with two doors, serving two rooms, that you find in older hotels. I went through it into the adjoining bedroom and shone my light around. It was a room similar in shape and size to the other, but almost bare. A brass double bed with a single blanket covering the mattress was just about the only furniture. The blanket lay in the tumbled folds that a man, or a boy, leaves behind when he gets up.

Hung over the head of the bed, like a limp truncated shadow of a boy, was a black sweater. It was a knitted sweater, and it had a raveled sleeve. Where the yarn was snarled and broken I could see traces of light-colored grease, the kind they use on the locks of automobile trunks. In the wastebasket I found several cardboard baskets containing the remains of hamburgers and french fries.

My heart was beating in my ears. The sweater was pretty good physical evidence that Stella had not been conned. Tom was alive.

I found Sipe's keys and locked him in his room and went through every other room in the building. There were nearly a hundred guest and service rooms, and it took a long time. I felt like an archaeologist exploring the interior of a pyramid. The Barcelona's palmy days seemed that long ago.

All I got for my efforts was a noseful of dust. If Tom was in the building, he was hiding. I had a feeling that he wasn't there, that he had left the Barcelona for good. Anybody would if he had the chance.

I went back across the highway to Daly's station. My flashlight found a notice pasted to the lower righthand corner of the front door: "In case of emergency call owner," with Daly's home number. I called it from the outside booth, and after a while got an answer:

"Daly here."

"Lew Archer. I'm the detective who was looking for Harold Harley."

"This is a heck of a time to be looking for anybody."

"I found Harley, thanks to you. Now I need your help in some more important business."

"What's the business?"

"I'll tell you when you get here. I'm at your station."

Daly had the habit of serviceability. "Okay. I'll be there in fifteen minutes."

I waited for him in my car, trying to put the case together in my mind. It was fairly clear that Sipe and Mike Harley had been working together, and had used the Barcelona as a hideout. It didn't look as if Tom had been a prisoner; more likely a willing guest, as Harley had said from the start. Even with Laguna Perdida School in the background, it was hard to figure out why a boy would do this to his parents and himself.

Daly came off the highway with a flourish and parked his pickup beside me. He got out and slammed the door, which had his name on it. He gave me a frowzy sardonic pre-dawn look.

"What's on your mind, Mr. Archer?"

"Get in. I'll show you a picture."

He climbed in beside me. I turned on the dome light and got out Tom's photograph. Every time I looked at it it had changed, gathering ambiguities on the mouth and in the eyes.

I put it in Daly's oil-grained hands. "Have you seen him?"

"Yeah. I have. I saw him two or three times over the last couple of days. He made some telephone calls from the booth there. He made one yesterday afternoon."

"What time?"

"I didn't notice, I was busy. It was along toward the end of the afternoon. Then I saw him again last night waiting for the bus." He pointed down the road toward Santa Monica. "The bus stops at the intersection if you flag it down. Otherwise it don't."

"Which bus is that?"

"Any of the intercity buses, excepting the express ones."

"Did you see him get on a bus?"

"No. I was getting ready to close up. Next time I looked he was gone."

"What time was this?"

"Around eight-thirty last night."

"What was he wearing?"

"White shirt, dark slacks."

"What made you interested enough to watch him?"

Daly fidgeted. "I dunno. I didn't *watch* him exactly. I saw him come out of the grounds of the Barcelona and I wondered what he was doing there, naturally. I'd hate to see such a nice-looking boy mixed up with a man like Sipe." He glanced at the photograph and handed it back to me, as if to relieve himself of the responsibility of explaining Tom.

"What's the matter with Sipe?"

"What isn't? I've got boys of my own, and I hate to see a man like Sipe teaching boys to drink and—other things. He ought to be in jail, if you want my opinion."

"I agree. Let's put him there."

"You're kidding."

"I'm serious, Ben. Right now Sipe is in his hotel room, passed out. He probably won't wake up for a long time. Just in case he does, will you stay here and watch for him to come out?"

"What do I do if he *comes* out?"

"Call the police and tell them to arrest him."

"I can't do that," he said uneasily. "I know he's a bad actor, but I got nothing definite to go on."

"I have. If you're forced to call the police, tell them Sipe is wanted in Pacific Point on suspicion of kidnapping. But don't call them unless you have to. Sipe is my best witness, and once he's arrested I'll never see him again."

"Where are you going?"

"To see if I can trace the boy."

His eyes brightened. "Is he the one that's been in all the papers? What's his name? Hillman?"

"He's the one."

"I should have recognized him. I dunno. I don't pay too much attention to people's faces. But I can tell you what kind of a car they drive."

"Does Sipe have a car?"

"Yeah. It's a '53 Ford with a cracked engine. I put some goop in it for him, but it's due to die any day."

Before I left, I asked Daly if he had seen anyone else around the hotel. He had, and he remembered. Mike Harley had been there Monday morning, driving the car with the Idaho license. I guess that Tom had been riding in the trunk.

"And just last night," he said, "there was this other young fellow driving a brand-new Chevvy. I think he had a girl with him, or maybe a smaller fellow. I was just closed up, and my bright lights were off."

"Did you get a good look at the driver?"

"Not so good, no. I think he was dark-haired, a nice-looking boy. What he was doing with that crumb-bum—" Shaking his head some more, Ben started to get out of my car. He froze in mid-action: "Come to think of it, what's the Hillman boy been doing walking around? I thought he was a prisoner and everybody in Southern California was looking for him."

"We are."

It took me a couple of hours, with the help of several bus-company employees, to sort out the driver who had picked Tom up last night. His name was Albertson and he lived far out on La Cienaga in an apartment over a bakery. The sweet yeasty smell of freshly made bread permeated his small front room.

It was still very early in the morning. Albertson had pulled on trousers over his pajamas. He was a square-shouldered man of about forty, with alert eyes. He nodded briskly over the picture:

"Yessir. I remember him. He got on my bus at the Barcelona intersection and bought a ticket into Santa Monica. He didn't get off at Santa Monica, though."

"Why not?"

He rubbed his heavily bearded chin. The sound rasped on my nerves. "Would he be wanted for something?" Albertson said.

"He would."

"That's what I thought at the time. He started to get off and then he saw somebody inside the station and the kid went back to his seat. I got off for a rest stop and it turned out there was a cop inside. When I came back the boy was still on the bus. I told him this was as far as his fare would take him. So he asked me to sell him a ticket to L. A. I was all set to go and I didn't make an issue. If the kid was in trouble, it wasn't up to me to turn him in. I've been in trouble myself. Did I do wrong?"

"You'll find out on Judgment Day."

He smiled. "That's a long time to wait. What's the pitch on the kid?"

"Read it in the papers, Mr. Albertson. Did he ride all the way downtown?"

"Yeah. I'm sure he did. He was one of the last ones to get off the bus."

I went downtown and did some bird-dogging in and around the bus station. Nobody remembered seeing the boy. Of course, the wrong people were on duty at this time in the morning. I'd stand a better chance if I tried again in the evening. And it was time I got back to Otto Sipe.

Ben Daly said he hadn't come out of the hotel. But when we went to Sipe's room the door was standing open and he was gone. Before he left he had finished the bottle of whisky by his bed.

"He must have had a master key, Ben. Is there any way out of here except the front?"

"No sir. He has to be on the grounds some place."

We went around to the back of the sprawling building, past a dry swimming pool with a drift of brown leaves in the deep end. Under the raw bluff which rose a couple of hundred feet behind the hotel were the employees' dormitories, garages, and other outbuildings. The two rear wings of the hotel contained a formal garden whose clipped shrubs and box hedges were growing back into natural shapes. Swaying on the topmost spray of a blue plumbago bush, a mockingbird was scolding like a jay.

I stood still and made a silencing gesture to Daly. Someone was digging on the far side of the bush. I could see some of his movements and hear the scrape of the spade, the thump of earth. I took out my gun and showed myself.

Otto Sipe looked up from his work. He was standing in a shallow hole about five feet long and two feet wide. There was dirt on his clothes. His face was muddy with sweat.

In the grass beside the hole a man in a gray jacket was lying on his back. The striped handle of a knife protruded from his chest. The man looked like Mike Harley, and he lay as if the knife had nailed him permanently to the earth.

"What are you doing, Otto?"

"Planting petunias." He bared his teeth in a doggish grin.

The man seemed to be in that detached state of drunkenness where everything appears surreal or funny.

"Planting dead men, you mean."

He turned and looked at Harley's body as if it had just fallen from the sky. "Did he come with you?"

"You know who he is. You and Mike have been buddies ever since he left Pocatello with you in the early forties."

"All right, I got a right to give a buddy a decent burial. You just can't leave them lying around in the open for the vultures."

"The only vultures I see around here are human ones. Did you kill him?"

"Naw. Why would I kill my buddy?"

"Who did?"

Leaning on his spade, he gave me a queer cunning look.

"Where's Tom Hillman, Otto?"

"I'm gonna save my talk for when it counts."

I turned to Ben Daly. "Can you handle a gun?"

"Hell no, I was only at Guadal."

"Hold this on him."

I handed him my revolver and went to look at Harley. His face when I touched it was cold as the night had been. This and the advance coagulation of the blood that stained his shirt front told me he had been dead for many hours, probably all night.

I didn't try to pull the knife out of his ribs. I examined it closely without touching it. The handle was padded with rubber, striped black and white, and moulded to fit the hand. It looked new and fairly expensive.

The knife was the only thing of any value that had attached itself to Mike Harley. I went through his pockets and found the stub of a Las Vegas to Los Angeles plane ticket issued the day before, and three dollars and forty-two cents.

Ben Daly let out a yell. Several things happened at once. At the edge of my vision metal flashed and the mockingbird flew up out of the bush. The gun went off. A gash opened in the side of Daly's head where Otto Sipe had hit him with the spade. Otto Sipe's face became contorted. He clutched at his abdomen and fell forward, with the lower part of his body in the grave.

Ben Daly said: "I didn't mean to shoot him. The gun went off when he swung the spade at me. After the war I never wanted to shoot anything."

The gash in the side of his head was beginning to bleed. I

tied my handkerchief around it and told him to go and call the police and an ambulance. He ran. He was surprisingly light on his feet for a man of middle age.

I was feeling surprisingly heavy on mine. I went to Sipe and turned him onto his back and opened his clothes. The wound in his belly was just below the umbilicus. It wasn't bleeding much, externally, but he must have been bleeding inside. The life was draining visibly from his face.

It was Archer I mourned for. It had been a hard three days. All I had to show for them was a dead man and a man who was probably dying. The fact that the bullet in Sipe had come from my gun made it worse.

Compunction didn't prevent me from going through Sipe's pockets. His wallet was fat with bills, all of them twenties. But his share of the Hillman payoff wasn't going to do him any good. He was dead before the ambulance came shrieking down the highway.

20

A lot of talking was done, some on the scene and some in the sheriff's office. With my support, and a phone call from Lieutenant Bastian, and the fairly nasty cut in the side of his head, Ben was able to convince the sheriff's and the D. A.'s men that he had committed justifiable homicide. But they weren't happy about it. Neither was I. I had let him kill my witness.

There was still another witness, if she would talk. By the middle of the morning I was back at the door of Susanna Drew's apartment. Stella said through the door:

"Who is it, please?"

"Lew Archer."

She let me in. The girl had bluish patches under her eyes, as if their color had run. There was hardly any other color in her face.

"You look scared," I said. "Has anything happened?"

"No. It's one of the things that scares me. And I have to call my parents and I don't want to. They'll make me go home."

"You have to go home."

"No."

"Yes. Think of them for a minute. You're putting them through a bad time for no good reason."

"But I do have a good reason. I want to try and meet Tommy again tonight. He said if he didn't make it last night he'd be at the bus station tonight."

"What time?"

"The same time. Nine o'clock."

"I'll meet him for you."

She didn't argue, but her look was evasive.

"Where's Miss Drew, Stella?"

"She went out for breakfast. I was still in bed, and she left me a note. She said she'd be back soon, but she's been gone for at least two hours." She clenched her fists and rapped her knuckles together in front of her. "I'm worried."

"About Susanna Drew?"

"About everything. About me. Things keep getting worse. I keep expecting it to end, but it keeps getting worse. I'm changing, too. There's hardly anybody I like any more."

"The thing will end, Stella, and you'll change back."

"Will I? It doesn't feel like a reversible change. I don't see how Tommy and I are ever going to be happy."

"Survival is the main thing." It was a hard saying to offer a young girl. "Happiness comes in fits and snatches. I'm having more of it as I get older. The teens were my worst time."

"Really?" Her brow puckered. "Do you mind if I ask you a personal question, Mr. Archer?"

"Go ahead."

"Are you interested in Miss Drew? You know what I mean. Seriously."

"I think I am. Why?"

"I don't know whether I should tell you this or not. She went out for breakfast with another man."

"That's legitimate."

"I don't know. I didn't actually see him but I heard his voice and I'm very good on voices. I think it was a married man."

"How can you tell that from a man's voice?"

"It was Tommy's father," she said. "Mr. Hillman."

I sat down. For a minute I couldn't think of anything to say. The African masks on the sunlit wall seemed to be making faces at me.

Stella approached me with an anxious expression. "Shouldn't I have told you? Ordinarily I'm not a tattletale. I feel like a spy in her house."

"You should have told me. But don't tell anyone else, please."

"I won't." Having passed the information on to me, she seemed relieved.

"Did the two of them seem friendly, Stella?"

"Not exactly. I didn't see them together. I stayed in my room because I didn't want him to see *me*. She wasn't glad to have him come here, I could tell. But they did sound kind of—intimate."

"Just what do you mean by 'intimate'?"

She thought about her answer. "It was something about the way they talked, as if they were used to talking back and forth. There wasn't any politeness or formality."

"What did they say to each other?"

"Do you want me to try and tell you word for word?"

"Exactly, from the moment he came to the door."

"I didn't hear all of it. Anyway, when he came in, she said: 'I thought you had more discretion than this, Ralph.' She called him Ralph. He said: 'Don't give me that. The situation is getting desperate.' I don't know what he meant by that."

"What do you think he meant?"

"Tommy and all, but there may have been more to it. They didn't say. He said: 'I thought I could expect a little sympathy from you.' She said she was all out of sympathy, and he said she was a hard woman and then he did something—I think he tried to kiss her—and she said: 'Don't do that!' "

"Did she sound angry?"

Stella assumed a listening attitude and looked at the high ceiling. "Not so very. Just not interested. He said: 'You don't seem to like me very much.' She said that the question was a complicated one and she didn't think now was the time to go into it, especially with somebody in the guest room, meaning me. He said: 'Why didn't you say so in the first place? Is it a man?" After that they lowered their voices. I don't know what she told him. They went out for breakfast in a few minutes."

"You have a very good memory," I said.

She nodded, without self-consciousness. "It helps me in school, but in other ways it isn't so fabulous. I remember all the bad things along with the good things."

"And the conversation you heard this morning was one of the bad things?"

"Yes, it was. It frightened me. I don't know why."

It frightened me, too, to learn that Hillman might have been the faceless man with Susanna when she was twenty. In different degrees I cared about them both. They were people with enough feeling to be hurt, and enough complexity to do wrong. Susanna I cared about in ways I hadn't even begun to explore.

Now the case was taking hold of her skirt like the cogs of an automated machine that nobody knew how to stop. I have to admit that I wouldn't have stopped it even if I knew how. Which is the peculiar hell of being a pro.

"Let's see the note she left you."

Stella fetched it from the kitchen, a penciled note scrawled on an interoffice memo form: "Dear Stella: I am going out for breakfast and will be back soon. Help yourself to the contents of the refrig. S. Drew."

"Did you have anything to eat?" I said to Stella.

"I drank a glass of milk."

"And a hamburger last night for dinner. No wonder you look pinched. Come on, I'll take you out for breakfast. It's the going thing."

"All right. Thank you. But then what?"

"I drive you home."

She turned and walked to the sliding glass doors that opened onto the patio, as far away in the room as she could get from me. A little wind was blowing, and I could hear it rustling in the fronds of a miniature palm. Stella turned back to me decisively, as if the wind and the sunlight had influenced her through the glass.

"I guess I have to go home. I can't go on *scaring* my mother."

"Good girl. Now call her and tell her you're on your way."

She considered my suggestion, standing in the sunlight with

her head down, the white straight part of her hair bisecting her brown head. "I will if you won't listen."

"How will I know you've done it?"

"I never lied to you yet," she said with feeling. "That's because you don't tell lies to me. Not even for my own good." She produced her first smile of the morning.

I think I produced mine. It had been a bad morning.

I immured myself in a large elaborate bathroom with fuzzy blue carpeting and did some washing, ritual and otherwise. I found a safety razor among the cosmetics and sleeping pills in the medicine cabinet, and used it to shave with. I was planning an important interview, a series of them if I could set them up.

Stella's cheeks were flushed when I came out. "I called home. We better not stop for breakfast on the way."

"Your mother's pretty excited, is she?"

"Dad was the one I talked to. He blames you. I'm sorry."

"It was my bad judgment," I said. "I should have taken you home last night. But I had something else to do." Get a man killed.

"It was *my* bad judgment," she said. "I was *punishing* them for lying about Tommy and me and the car."

"I'm glad you know that. How upset is your father?"

"Very upset. He even said something about Laguna Perdida School. He didn't really mean it, though." But a shadow crossed her face.

About an hour later, driving south with Stella toward El Rancho, I caught a distant glimpse of the school. The rising wind had blown away all trace of the overcast, but even in unobstructed sunlight its buildings had a desolate look about them. I found myself straining my eyes for the lonely blue heron. He wasn't on the water or in the sky.

On impulse, I turned off the highway and took the access road to Laguna Perdida. My car passed over the treadle. The automatic gates rose.

Stella said in a tiny voice: "You're not going to put me in here?"

"Of course not. I want to ask a certain person a question. I won't be long."

"They better not try to put me in here," she said. "I'll run away for good."

"You've had more mature ideas."

"What else can I do?" she said a little wildly.

"Stay inside the safety ropes, with your own kind of people. You're much too young to step outside, and I don't think your parents are so bad. They're probably better than average."

"You don't know them."

"I know you. You didn't just happen."

The old guard came out of his kiosk and limped up to my side of the car. "Dr. Sponti isn't here just now."

"How about Mrs. Mallow?"

"Yeah. You'll find her down the line in East Hall." He pointed toward the building with the ungenerous windows.

Leaving Stella in the car, I knocked on the front door of East Hall. After what seemed a long time, Mrs. Mallow answered. She was wearing the same dark formal costume that she had been wearing on Monday, and the same rather informal smell of gin.

She smiled at me, at the same time flinching away from the daylight. "Mr. Archer, isn't it?"

"How are you, Mrs. Mallow?"

"Don't ever ask me that question in the morning. Or any other time, now that I come to think of it. I'm surviving."

"Good."

"But you didn't come here to inquire after my health."

"I'd like to have a few minutes with Fred Tyndal."

"I'm sorry," she said, "the boys are all in class."

"It could be important."

"You want to ask Fred some questions, is that it?"

"Just one, really. It wouldn't have to take long."

"And it won't be anything disturbing?"

"I don't think so."

She left me in the lounge and went into Patch's office to make a telephone call. I wandered around the big battered homeless room, imagining how it would feel to be a boy whose parents had left him here. Mrs. Mallow came back into the room:

"Fred will be right over."

While I was waiting, I listened to the story of her marriages, including the one that had lasted, her marriage to the bottle. Then Fred came in out of the sunlight, none of which adhered to him. He sort of loitered just inside the door, pulling at the hairs on his chin and waiting to be told what he had done wrong this time.

I got up and moved toward him, not too quickly. "Hello, Fred."

"Hello."

"You remember the talk we had the other day?"

"There's nothing the matter with my memory." He added with his quick evanescent smile: "You're Lew Archer the First. Did you find Tom yet?"

"Not yet. I think you can help me find him."

He scuffed the door frame with the side of his shoe. "I don't see how."

"By telling me everything you know. One thing I can promise—they won't put him back in here."

"What good will that do me?" he said forlornly.

I had no answer ready. After a moment the boy said, "What do you want me to tell you?"

"I think you were holding back a little the other day. I don't blame you. You didn't know me from Adam. You still don't, but it's three days later now, and Tom is still missing."

His face reflected the seriousness of this. He couldn't stand such seriousness for very long. He said with a touch of parody:

"Okay, I'll talk, I'll spill everything."

"I want to ask you this. When Tom broke out of here Saturday night, did he have any definite person or place in mind that he intended to go to?"

He ducked his head quickly in the affirmative. "Yeah, I think so."

"Do you know where he was going?"

"Tom didn't say. He did say something else, though, something about finding his true father." The boy's voice broke through into feeling he couldn't handle. He said: "Big deal."

"What did he mean by that, Fred?"

"He said he was adopted."

"Was he really?"

"I don't know. A lot of kids here want to think they're adopted. My therapist calls it a typical Freudian family romance."

"Do you think Tom was serious?"

"Sure he was." Once again the boy's face reflected seriousness, and I caught a glimpse there of the maturity that he might reach yet. "He said he couldn't know who he was until he knew for sure who his father was." He grinned wryly. "I'm trying to forget who my father is."

"You can't."

"I can try."

"Get interested in something else."

"There isn't anything else."

"There will be."

"When?" he said.

Mrs. Mallow interrupted us. "Have you found out what you need to know, Mr. Archer? Fred really should be going back to class now."

I said to him: "Is there anything else you can tell me?"

"No, sir. Honestly. We didn't talk much."

The boy started out. He turned in the doorway suddenly, and spoke to me in a voice different from the one he had been using, a voice more deep and measured:

"I wish you were my father."

He turned away into the bleak sunlight.

Back in the car, I said to Stella: "Did Tom ever tell you that he was adopted?"

"Adopted? He can't be."

"Why not?"

"He can't be, that's all." The road curved around a reedy marsh where the red-winged blackbirds sounded like woodwinds tuning up, and violins. Stella added after a while: "For one thing, he looks like his father."

"Adopted children often do. They're picked to match the parents."

"How awful. How *commercial*. Who *told* you he was adopted?"

"He told a friend at the school."

"A girl?"

"A boy."

"I'm sure he was making it up."

"Did he often make things up?"

"Not often. But he did—he does have some funny ideas about some things. He told me just this summer that he was probably a changeling, you know? That they got him mixed up with some other baby in the hospital, and Mr. and Mrs. Hillman weren't his real parents." She turned toward me, crouching on the seat with her legs under her. "Do you think that could be true?"

"It could be. Almost anything can happen."

"But you don't believe it."

"I don't know what I believe, Stella."

"You're an adult," she said with a hint of mockery. "You're supposed to know."

I let it drop. We rode in silence to the gate of El Rancho. Stella said:

"I wonder what my father is going to do to me." She hesitated. "I apologize for getting you into this."

"It's all right. You've been the best help I've had."

Jay Carlson, whom I hadn't met and wasn't looking forward to meeting, was standing out in front of his house when we got there. He was a well-fed, youngish man with sensitive blue eyes resembling Stella's. At the moment he looked sick with anger, gray and shuddering with it.

Rhea Carlson, her red hair flaring like a danger signal, came out of the house and rushed up to the car, with her husband trudging behind her. He acted like a man who disliked trouble and couldn't handle it well. The woman spoke first:

"What have you been doing with my daughter?"

"Protecting her as well as I could. She spent the night with a woman friend of mine. This morning I talked her into coming home."

"I intend to check that story very carefully," Carlson said. "What was the name of this alleged woman friend?"

"Susanna Drew."

"Is he telling the truth, Stella?"

She nodded.

"Can't you talk?" he cried. "You've been gone all night and you won't even speak to us."

"Don't get so excited, Daddy. He's telling the truth. I'm sorry I went to Los Angeles but—"

He couldn't wait for her to finish. "I've got a right to get excited, after what you've done. We didn't even know if you were alive."

Stella bowed her head. "I'm sorry, Daddy."

"You're a cruel, unfeeling girl," her mother said. "And I'll never be able to believe you again. Never."

"You know better than that, Mrs. Carlson."

Her husband turned on me fiercely. "You stay out of it." He probably wanted to hit me. In lieu of this, he grasped Stella by the shoulders and shook her. "Are you out of your mind, to do a thing like this?"

"Lay off her, Carlson."

"She's my daughter!"

"Treat her like one. Stella's had a rough night—"

"She's had a rough night, has she? What happened?"

"She's been trying to grow up, under difficulties, and you're not giving her much help."

"What she needs is discipline. And I know where she can get it."

"If you're thinking of Laguna Perdida, your thinking is way out of line. Stella is one of the good ones, one of the best—"

"I'm not interested in your opinion. I suggest you get off my place before I call the police."

I left them together, three well-intentioned people who couldn't seem to stop hurting each other. Stella had the courage to lift her hand to me in farewell.

21

I went next door to the Hillmans'. Turning in past their mailbox, I heard the noise of a sports car coming down the driveway. I stopped in the middle of the narrow blacktop so that Dick Leandro had to stop, too.

He sat there looking at me rather sulkily from under his hair, as if I'd halted him in the middle of a Grand Prix. I got out and walked over to the side of his car and patted the hood.

"Nice car."

"I like it."

"You have any other cars?"

"Just this one," he said. "Listen, I hear they f-found Tom, is that the true word?"

"He hasn't been found yet, but he is running free."

"Hey, that's great," he said without enthusiasm. "Listen, do you know where Skipper is? Mrs. Hillman says he hasn't been home all night." He looked up at me with puzzled anxiety.

"I wouldn't worry about him. He can look after himself."

"Yeah, sure, but do you know where he *is?* I want to ta-talk to him."

"What about?"

"That's between him and I. It's a personal matter."

I said unpleasantly: "Do you and Mr. Hillman share a lot of secrets?"

"I w-wouldn't say that. He *advises* me. He gives me g-good advice."

The young man was almost babbling with fear and hostility. I let him go and drove up to the house. Elaine Hillman was the one I wanted to see, and she let me in herself.

She looked better than she had the last time I'd seen her. She was well groomed and well dressed, in a tailored sharkskin suit which concealed the shrinkage of her body. She was even able to smile at me.

"I got your good news, Mr. Archer."

"Good news?" I couldn't think of any.

"That Tom is definitely alive. Lieutenant Bastian passed the word to me. Come in and tell me more."

She led me across the reception hall, making a detour to avoid the area under the chandelier, and into the sitting room. She said almost brightly, as if she was determined to be cheerful:

"I call this the waiting room. It's like a dentist's waiting room. But the waiting is almost over, don't you think?" Her voice curled up thinly at the end, betraying her tension.

"Yes. I really think so."

"Good. I couldn't stand much more of this. None of us could. These days have been very difficult."

"I know. I'm sorry."

"Don't be sorry. You've brought us good news." She perched on the chesterfield. "Now sit down and tell me the rest of it."

I sat beside her. "There isn't much more, and not all of it is good. But Tom is alive, and free, and very likely still in Los Angeles. I traced him from the Barcelona Hotel, where he was hiding, to downtown Los Angeles. He was seen getting off a bus in the main station around ten o'clock last night. I'm going back there this afternoon to see if I can find him."

"I wish my husband was here to share this," she said. "I'm a little worried about him. He left the house early last evening and hasn't been back since." She looked around the room as if it felt strange without him.

I said: "He probably got word that Tom was alive."

"From whom?"

I left the question unanswered.

"But he wouldn't go without telling me."

"Not unless he had a reason."

"What possible reason could he have for keeping me in the dark?"

"I don't know, Mrs. Hillman."

"Is he going out of his mind, do you think?"

"I doubt it. He probably spent the night in Los Angeles searching for Tom. I know he had breakfast this morning with Susanna Drew."

I'd dropped the name deliberately, without preparation, and got the reaction I was looking for. Elaine's delicate blonde face crumpled like tissue paper. "Good Lord," she said, "is that still going on? Even in the midst of these horrors?"

"I don't know exactly what *is* going on."

"They're lovers," she said bitterly, "for twenty years. He swore to me it was over long ago. He begged me to stay with him, and gave me his word of honor that he would never go near her again. But he has no honor." She raised her eyes to mine. "My husband is a man without honor."

"He didn't strike me that way."

"Perhaps men can trust him. I know a woman can't. I'm rather an expert on the subject. I've been married to him for over twenty-five years. It wasn't loyalty that kept him with me. I know that. It was my family's money, which has been useful to him in his business, and in his hobbies. Including," she added in a disgusted tone, "his dirty little bed-hopping hobby."

She covered her mouth with her hand, as if to hide the anguish twisting it. "I shouldn't be talking this way. It isn't like me. It's very much against my New England grain. My mother, who had a similar problem with my father, taught me by precept and example always to suffer in silence. And I have. Except for Ralph himself, you're the only person I've spoken to about it."

"You haven't told me much. It might be a good idea to ventilate it."

"Do you believe it may be connected in some way with—all this?" She flung out her arm, with the fingers spread at the end of it.

"Very likely it is. I think that's why your husband and Miss

Drew got together this morning. He probably phoned her early in the week. Tuesday afternoon."

"He did! I remember now. He was phoning from the bar, and I came into the room. He cut it short. But I heard him say something to the effect that they must absolutely keep quiet. It must have been that Drew woman he was talking to."

The scornful phrase made me wince. It was a painful, strange colloquy, but we were both engrossed in it. The intimacy of the people we were talking about forced intimacy on us.

"It probably was her," I said. "I'd just told Lieutenant Bastian that she was a witness, and Bastian must have passed it on to your husband."

"You're right again, Mr. Archer. My husband had just heard from the lieutenant. How can you possibly know so much about the details of other people's lives?"

"Other people's lives are my business."

"And your passion?"

"And my passion. And my obsession, too, I guess. I've never been able to see much in the world besides the people in it."

"But how could you possibly find out about that phone call? You weren't here. My husband wouldn't tell you."

"I was in Miss Drew's apartment when the call came. I didn't heard what was said, but it shook her up."

"I hope so." She glanced at my face, and her eyes softened. She reached out and touched my arm with gentle fingers. "She isn't a friend of yours?"

"She is, in a way."

"You're not in love with her?"

"Not if I can help it."

"That's a puzzling answer."

"It puzzles me, too. If she's still in love with your husband it would tend to chill one's interest. But I don't think she is."

"Then what are they trying to conceal?"

"Something in the past." I hoped it was entirely in the past. Susanna, I had learned in the course of the morning, could still hurt me where I lived. "It would help if you'd go into it a little deeper. I know it will also hurt," I said to myself and her.

"I can stand pain if there's any purpose in it. It's the meaningless pain I can't stand. The pain for Tom, for instance." She didn't explain what she meant, but she touched her blue-veined temple with her fingertips.

"I'll try to make it short, Mrs. Hillman. You said the affair had been going on for twenty years. That would take it back to around the end of the war."

"Yes. The spring of 1945. I was living alone, or rather with a woman companion, in a house in Brentwood. My husband was in the Navy. He had been a squadron commander, but at the time I'm talking about he was executive officer of an escort carrier. Later they made him captain of the same ship." She spoke with a kind of forlorn pride, and very carefully, as if the precise facts of the past were all she had to hold on to.

"In January or February of 1945 my husband's ship was damaged by a kamikaze plane. They had to bring it back to San Diego for repairs. Ralph had some days of leave, of course, and of course he visited me. But I didn't see as much of him as I wanted to, or expected to. I found out later why. He was spending some of his nights, whole weekends, with Susanna Drew."

"In the Barcelona Hotel?"

"Did she tell you?"

"In a way." She had given me Harold Harley's picture of Carol, and the printing on the back of the picture had sent me to the Barcelona Hotel. "About herself she told me, not about your husband. She's a loyal girl, anyway."

"I don't want to hear her praised. She's caused me too much suffering."

"I'm sorry. But she was only twenty, remember."

"She's closer to forty now. The fact that she was twenty then only made it worse. I was still in my twenties myself, but my husband had already discarded me. Do you have any idea how a woman feels when her husband leaves her for a younger woman? Can you imagine the crawling of the flesh?"

She was suffering intense remembered pain. Her eyes were bright and dry, as if there was fire behind them. The cheerfullest thing I could think of to say was:

"But he didn't leave you."

"No. He came back. It wasn't me he cared for. There was the money, you see, and his postwar plans for his engineering firm. He was quite frank on the subject, and quite impenitent. In fact, he seemed to feel that he was doing me an enormous

favor. He felt that any couple who couldn't have a child—"
Her hand went to her mouth again.

I prompted her: "But you had Tom."

"Tom came later," she said, "too late to save us." Her
voice broke into a deeper range. "Too late to save my husband.
He's a tragically unhappy man. But I can't find it in my heart
to pity him." Her hand touched her thin breast and lingered
there.

"What's the source of the trouble between him and Tom?"

"The falsity," she said in her deeper voice.

"The falsity?"

"I might as well tell you, Mr. Archer. You're going to find
out about it sooner or later, anyway. And it may be important.
Certainly it's psychologically important."

"Was Tom—is Tom an adopted son?"

She nodded slowly. "It may have to come out publicly, I
don't know. For the present I'll ask you not to divulge it to
anyone. No one in town here knows it. Tom doesn't know it
himself. We adopted him in Los Angeles shortly after my
husband left the Navy and before we moved here."

"But he resembles your husband."

"Ralph chose him for that reason. He's a very vain man,
Mr. Archer. He's ashamed to admit even to our friends that we
were incapable of producing a child of our own. Actually
Ralph is the one who is sterile. I'm telling you this so you'll
understand why he has insisted from the beginning on the great
pretense. His desire to have a son was so powerful, I think he
has actually believed at times that Tom is his own flesh and
blood."

"And he hasn't told Tom he isn't?"

"No. Neither have I. Ralph wouldn't let me."

"Isn't that supposed to be a poor idea, with an adopted
child?"

"I told my husband that from the beginning. He had to be
honest with Tom, or Tom would not be honest with him. There
would be falsity at the center of the household." Her voice
trembled, and she looked down at the carpet as if there was no
floor under it. "Well, you see what the consequence has been.
A ruined boyhood for Tom and a breakdown of the family and
now this tragedy."

"This almost-tragedy. He's still alive and we're going to get
him back."

"But can we ever put the family back together?"

"That will depend on all three of you. I've seen worse fractures mended, but not without competent help. I don't mean Laguna Perdida. And I don't mean just help for Tom."

"I know. I've been wretchedly unhappy, and my husband has been quite—quite irrational on this subject for many years. Actually I think it goes back to Midway. Ralph's squadron was virtually massacred in that dreadful battle. Of course he blamed himself, since he was leading them. He felt as though he had lost a dozen sons."

"How do you know?"

"He was still writing to me then," she said, "freely and fully, as one human being to another. He wrote me a number of very poignant letters about our having children, sons of our own. I *know* the thought was connected with his lost fliers, although he never said so. And when he found out he couldn't have a son of his own, and decided to adopt Tom, well—" She dropped her hands in her lap. Her hands seemed restless without knitting to occupy them.

"What were you going to say, Mrs. Hillman?"

"I hardly know. I'm not a psychologist, though I once had some training in philosophy. I've felt that Ralph was trying to live out some sort of a fantasy with Tom—perhaps relive those terrible war years and make good his losses somehow. But you cant' use people in that way, as figures in a fantasy. The whole thing broke down between Tom and his father."

"And Tom caught on that your husband wasn't his father."

She looked at me nervously. "You think he did?"

"I'm reasonably certain of it," I said, remembering what Fred Tyndal had told me. "Mrs. Hillman, what happened on the Sunday morning that you put Tom in Laguna Perdida?"

She said quickly: "It was Ralph's doing, not mine."

"Had they quarreled?"

"Yes. Ralph was horribly angry with him."

"What about?"

She bowed her head. "My husband has forbidden me to speak of it."

"Did Tom say something or do something very wrong?"

She sat with her head bowed and wouldn't answer me. "I've told you more than I should have," she said eventually, "in the hope of getting to the bottom of this mess. Now will you tell me something? You mentioned a hotel called the Barcelona, and you said that Tom had been hiding there. You used the word 'hiding.' "

"Yes."

"Wasn't he being held?"

"I don't know. There may have been some duress, possibly psychological duress. But I doubt that he was held in the ordinary sense."

She looked at me with distaste. I'd brought her some very tough pieces of information to chew on, and probably this was the hardest one of all. "You've hinted from the beginning that Tom cooperated willingly with the kidnappers."

"It was a possibility that had to be considered. It still is."

"Please don't sidestep the question. I can stand a direct answer." She smiled dimly. "At this point I couldn't stand anything else."

"All right. I think Tom went with Harley of his own free will, rode in the trunk of Harley's car to the Barcelona Hotel, and stayed there without anybody having to hold a gun on him. I don't understand his reasons, and I won't until I talk to him. But he probably didn't know about the extortion angle. There's no evidence that he profited from it, anyway. He's broke."

"How do you know? Have you seen him?"

"I've talked to somebody who talked to him. Tom said he needed money."

"I suppose that's good news in a way."

"I thought it was."

I made a move to go, but she detained me. There was more on her mind:

"This Barcelona Hotel you speak of, is it the big old run-down place on the coast highway?"

"Yes. It's closed up now."

"And Tom hid, or was hidden, there?"

I nodded. "The watchman at the hotel, a man named Sipe, was a partner in the extortion. He may have been the brains behind it, to the extent that it took any brains. He was shot to death this morning. The other partner, Harley, was stabbed to death last night."

Her face was open, uncomprehending, as if she couldn't quite take in these terrible events.

"How extraordinary," she breathed.

"Not so very. They were heavy thieves, and they came to a heavy end."

"I don't mean those violent deaths, although they're part of it. I mean the deep connections you get in life, the coming together of the past and the present."

"What do you have in mind?"

She grimaced. "Something ugly, but I'm afraid it has to be said. You see, the Barcelona Hotel, where my son, my adopted son, has been staying with criminals, apparently"—she took a shuddering breath—"that very place was the scene of Ralph's affair with Susanna Drew. And did you say that the watchman's name was Sipe, the one who was shot?"

"Yes. Otto Sipe."

"Did he once work as a detective in the hotel?"

"Yes. He was the kind of detective who gives our trade a bad name."

"I have reason to know that," she said. "I knew Mr. Sipe. That is, I talked to him once, and he left an impression that I haven't been able to wipe out of my memory. He was a gross, corrupt man. He came to my house in Brentwood in the spring of 1945. He was the one who told me about Ralph's affair with Miss Drew."

"He wanted money, of course."

"Yes, and I gave him money. Two hundred dollars, he asked for, and when he saw that I was willing to pay he raised it to five hundred, all the cash I had on hand. Well, the money part is unimportant. It always is," she said, reminding me that she had never needed money.

"What did Sipe have to say to you?"

"That my husband was committing adultery—he had a snapshot to prove it—and it was his duty under the law to arrest him. I don't know now if there was ever such a law on the books—"

"There was. I don't think it's been enforced lately, or an awful lot of people would be in jail."

"He mentioned jail, and the effect it would have on my husband's reputation. This was just about the time when Ralph began to believe he could make Captain. I know from this height and distance it sounds childish, but it was the biggest thing in his life at that time. He came from an undistinguished family, you see—his father was just an unsuccessful small businessman—and he felt he had to shine in so many ways to match my family's distinction." She looked at me with sad intelligence. "We all need something to buttress our pride, don't we, fragments to shore against our ruins."

"You were telling me about your interview with Otto Sipe."

"So I was. My mind tends to veer away from scenes like that. In spite of the pain and shock I felt—it was my first inkling that Ralph was unfaithful to me—I didn't want to see all his bright ambitions wrecked. So I paid the dreadful man his dirty money—and he gave me his filthy snapshot."

"Did you hear from him again?"

"No."

"I'm surprised he didn't attach himself to you for life."

"Perhaps he intended to. But Ralph stopped him. I told Ralph about his visit, naturally." She added: "I didn't show him the snapshot. That I destroyed."

"How did Ralph stop him?"

"I believe he knocked him down and frightened him off. I didn't get a very clear account from Ralph. By then we weren't communicating freely. I went home to Boston and I didn't see Ralph again until the end of the year, when he brought his ship to Boston harbor. We had a reconciliation of sorts. It was then we decided to adopt a child."

I wasn't listening too closely. The meanings of the case were emerging. Ralph Hillman had had earlier transactions with both of the extortionists. He had been Mike Harley's superior officer, and had thrown him out of the Navy. He had knocked down Otto Sipe. And they had made him pay for his superiority and his power.

Elaine was thinking along the same lines. She said in a soft, despondent voice:

"Mr. Sipe would never have entered our lives if Ralph hadn't used that crummy hotel for his crummy little purposes."

"You mustn't blame your husband for everything. No doubt he did wrong. We all do. But the things he did nineteen or twenty years ago aren't solely responsible for this kidnapping, or whatever it was. It isn't that simple."

"I know. I don't blame him for everything."

"Sipe, for instance, would probably have been involved anyway. His partner Mike Harley knew your husband and had a grievance against him."

"But why did Tom, my poor dear Tom, end up at that same hotel? Isn't there fatality in it?"

"Maybe there is. To Sipe and Harley it was simply a convenient place to keep him."

"Why would Tom stay with them? They must be—have been outrageous creatures."

"Teen-age boys sometimes go for the outrageous."

"Do they not," she said. "But I can't really blame Tom for anything he's done. Ralph and I have given him little enough reality to hold on to. Tom's a sensitive, artistic, introverted boy. My husband didn't want him to be those things—perhaps they reminded Ralph that he wasn't our son, really. So he kept trying to change him. And when he couldn't, he withdrew his interest. Not his love, I'm sure. He's still profoundly concerned with Tom."

"But he spends his time with Dick Leandro."

One corner of her mouth lifted, wrinkling her cheek and eye, as if age and disillusion had taken sudden possession of that side of her face. "You're quite a noticer, Mr. Archer."

"You have to be, in my job. Not that Dick Leandro makes any secret of his role. I met him coming out of your driveway."

"Yes. He was looking for Ralph. He's very dependent on Ralph," she added dryly.

"How would you describe the relationship, Mrs. Hillman? Substitute son?"

"I suppose I would. Dick's mother and father broke up some years ago. His father left town, and of course his mother got custody of Dick. He needed a substitute father. And Ralph needed someone to crew for him on the sloop—I sometimes think it's the most urgent need he has, or had. Someone to share the lusty gusty things he likes to do, and would like a son to do."

"He could do better than Dick, couldn't he?"

She was silent for a while. "Perhaps he could. But when you have an urgent need, you tend to hook up with people who have urgent needs of their own. Poor Dick has a great many urgent needs."

"Some of which have been met. He told me that your husband put him through college."

"He did. But don't forget that Dick's father used to work for Ralph's firm. Ralph is very strong on loyalty up and down."

"Is Dick?"

"He's fanatically loyal to Ralph," she said with emphasis.

"Let me ask you a hypothetical question, without prejudice,

as they say in court. If your husband disinherited Tom, would Dick be a likely heir?"

"That's excessively hypothetical, isn't it?"

"But the answer might have practical consequences. What's your answer?"

"Dick might be left something. He probably will be in any case. But please don't imagine that poor stupid Dick, with his curly hair and his muscles, is capable of plotting—"

"I wasn't suggesting that."

"And you mustn't embarrass Dick. He's come through nobly in this crisis. Both of us have leaned on him."

"I know. I'll leave him alone." I got up to go. "Thank you for being frank with me."

"There's not much point in pretending at this late date. If there's anything else you need to know—"

"There is one thing that might help. If you could give me the name of the agency through which you adopted Tom?"

"It wasn't done through an agency. It was handled privately."

"Through a lawyer, or a doctor?"

"A doctor," she said. "I don't recall his name, but he delivered Tom at Cedars of Lebanon. We paid the expenses, you understand, as part of the bargain that we made with the mother."

"Who was she?"

"Some poor woman who'd got herself in trouble. I didn't actually meet her, nor did I want to. I wanted to feel that Tom was my own son."

"I understand."

"Does it matter who his parents were? I mean, in the current situation?"

"It does if he's wandering around Los Angeles looking for them. Which I have reason to think he may be doing. You should have a record somewhere of that doctor's name."

"My husband could tell you."

"But he isn't available."

"It may be in his desk in the library."

I followed her to the library and while she rummaged in the desk I looked at the pictures on the wall again. The group photo taken on the flight deck must have been Hillman's squadron. I looked closely at their faces, wondering which of the young men had died at Midway.

Next I studied the yachting picture of Dick Leandro. His

handsome, healthy, empty face told me nothing. Perhaps it would have meaning for somebody else. I took it off the wall and slipped it into the side pocket of my jacket.

Elaine Hillman didn't notice. She had found the name she was looking for.

"Elijah Weintraub," she said, "was the doctor's name."

22

I phoned Dr. Weintraub long-distance. He confirmed the fact that he had arranged for Thomas Hillman's adoption, but he refused to discuss it over the phone. I made an appointment to see him in his office that afternoon.

Before I drove back to Los Angeles I checked in with Lieutenant Bastian. He'd been working on the case for nearly three days, and the experience hadn't improved his disposition. The scarlike lines in his face seemed to have deepened. His voice was hoarse and harsh, made harsher by irony:

"It's nice of you to drop by every few days."

"I'm working for Ralph Hillman now."

"I know that, and it gives you certain advantages. Which you seize. But you and I are working on the same case, and we're supposed to be cooperating. That means periodic exchanges of information."

"Why do you think I'm here?"

His eyes flared down. "Fine. What have you found out about the Hillman boy?"

I told Bastian nearly all of it, enough to satisfy both him and my conscience. I left out the adoption and Dr. Weintraub, and the possibility that Tom might turn up at the Santa Monica bus station at nine that night. About his other movements, and the fact that he had probably been a voluntary captive in the Barcelona Hotel, I was quite frank.

"It's too bad Otto Sipe had to die," Bastian grumbled. "He could have cleared up a lot of things."

I agreed.

"Exactly what happened to Sipe? You were a witness."

"He attacked Ben Daly with a spade. Daly was holding my gun while I examined Harley's body. The gun went off."

Bastian made a disgusted noise with his lips. "What do you know about Daly?"

"Not much. He has a service station across from the Barcelona. He struck me as dependable. He's a war veteran—"

"So was Hitler. L. A. says Daly had previous dealings with Sipe. Sipe bought secondhand cars through him, for instance."

"That would be natural enough. Daly ran the nearest service station to where Sipe worked."

"So you don't think Daly killed him to shut him up?"

"No, but I'll bear it in mind. I'm more interested in the other killing. Have you seen the knife that Harley was stabbed with?"

"Not yet. I have a description." Bastian moved some papers around on top of his desk. "It's what they call a hunting knife, made by the Oregon firm of Forstmann, with their name on it. It has a broad blade about six inches long, is very sharp and pointed, has a striped rubber handle, black and white, with finger mouldings on it. Practically brand new. Is that an accurate description?"

"I only saw the striped rubber handle. The fact that the blade is quite broad, sharp, and pointed suggests that it's the same knife that stabbed Carol."

"So I told L. A. They're going to send me the knife for identification work."

"That's what I was going to suggest."

Bastian leaned forward, bringing his arms down heavily among the papers on his desk top. "You think somebody in town here stabbed him?"

"It's an idea worth considering."

"Why? For his share of the money?"

"It couldn't have been that. Harley had nothing left by the time he left Las Vegas. I talked to the high-roller who cleaned him out."

"I'm surprised Harley didn't shoot him."

"I gather there were professional guns around. Harley was never more than a semi-pro."

"Why then?" Bastian said, his eyebrows arched. "Why was Harley killed if it wasn't for money?"

"I don't think we'll know until we put our finger on the killer."

"Do you have any nominations?" he said.

"No. Do you?"

"I have some thoughts on the subject, but I'd better not think them out loud."

"Because I'm working for Hillman?"

"I didn't say that." His dark eyes veiled themselves, and he changed the subject. "A man named Robert Brown, the victim's father, was here asking for you. He's at the City Hotel."

"I'll look him up tomorrow. Treat him gently, eh?"

"I treat 'em all gently. Harold Harley called me a few minutes ago. He's taking his brother's death hard."

"He would. When did you let him go?"

"Yesterday. We had no good reason to hold him in custody. There's no law that says you have to inform on your own brother."

"Is he back home in Long Beach?"

"Yes. He'll be available for the trial, if there's anybody left to prosecute."

He was needling me about the death of Otto Sipe. On that note I left.

I made a detour up the coast highway on the way to my appointment with Dr. Weintraub, and stopped at Ben Daly's service station. Ben was there by the pump, with a bandage around his head. When he saw me he went into the office and didn't come out. A boy who looked like a teen-aged version of Ben emerged after a while. He asked in an unfriendly way if there was anything he could do for me.

"I'd like to talk to Mr. Daly for a minute."

"I'm sorry, Dad doesn't want to talk to you. He's very upset, about this morning."

"So am I. Tell him that. And ask him if he'll look at a picture for identification purposes."

The boy went into the office, closing the door behind him. Across the roaring highway, the Barcelona Hotel asserted itself in the sunlight like a monument of a dead civilization. In the driveway I could see a number of county cars, and a man in deputy's uniform keeping back a crowd of onlookers.

Daly's boy came back with a grim look on his face. "Dad

says he doesn't want to look at any more of your pictures. He says you and your pictures brought him bad luck.''

"Tell him I'm sorry."

The boy retreated formally, like an emissary. He didn't show himself again, and neither did his father. I gave up on Daly for the present.

Dr. Weintraub's office was in one of the new medical buildings on Wilshire, near Cedars of Lebanon Hospital. I went up in a self-service elevator to a waiting room on the fifth floor. This was handsomely furnished in California Danish and had soothing music piped in, which got on my nerves before I had time to sit down. Two pregnant women on opposite sides of the room caught me, a mere man, in a crossfire of pitying glances.

The highly made-up girl behind the counter in one corner said:

"Mr. Archer?"

"Yes."

"Dr. Weintraub will see you in a few minutes. You're not a patient, are you? So we needn't bother taking your history, need we?"

"It would give you the horrors, honey."

She moved her eyelashes up and down a few times, to indicate shocked surprise. Her eyelashes were long and thick and phony, and they waved clumsily in the air like tarantula legs.

Dr. Weintraub opened a door and beckoned me into his consulting room. He was a man about my age, perhaps a few years older. Like a lot of other doctors, he hadn't looked after himself. His shoulders were stooped under his white smock, and he was putting on weight. The curly black hair was retreating from his forehead.

But the dark eyes behind his glasses were extraordinarily alive. I could practically feel their impact as we shook hands. I recognized his face, but I couldn't place it.

"You look as though you could use a rest," he said. "That's free advice."

"Thanks. It will have to come later." I didn't tell him he needed exercise.

He sat down rather heavily at his desk, and I took the patient's chair facing him. One whole wall of the room was occupied by bookshelves. The books seemed to cover several branches of medicine, with special emphasis on psychiatry and gynecology.

"Are you a psychiatrist, doctor?"

"No, I am not." His eyes were melancholy. "I studied for the Boards at one time but then the war came along. Afterwards I chose another specialty, delivering babies." He smiled, and his eyes lit up. "It's so very satisfying, and the incidence of success if so very much higher. I mean, I seldom lose a baby."

"You delivered Thomas Hillman."

"Yes. I told you so on the telephone."

"Have you refreshed your memory about the date?"

"I had my secretary look it up. Thomas was born on December 12, 1945. A week later, on December 20 to be exact, I arranged for the baby's adoption by Captain and Mrs. Ralph Hillman. He made a wonderful Christmas present for them," he said warmly.

"How did his real mother feel about it?"

"She didn't want him," he said.

"Wasn't she married?"

"As a matter of fact, she was a young married woman. Neither she nor her husband wanted a child at that time."

"Are you willing to tell me their name?"

"It wouldn't be professional, Mr. Archer."

"Not even to help solve a crime, or find a missing boy?"

"I'd have to know all the facts, and then have time to consider them. I don't have time. I'm stealing time from my other—from my patients now."

"You haven't heard from Thomas Hillman this week?"

"Neither this week nor any other time." He got up bulkily and moved past me to the door, where he waited with courteous impatience till I went out past him.

23 _____

With its portico supported by fluted columns, the front of Susanna's apartment house was a cross between a Greek temple and a Southern plantation mansion. It was painted blue instead of white. Diminished by the columns, I went into the cold marble lobby. Miss Drew was out. She had been out all day.

I looked at my watch. It was nearly five. The chances were she had gone to work after her breakfast with Hillman. I went out and sat in my car at the curb and watched the rush-hour traffic crawling by.

Shortly after five a yellow cab veered out of the traffic stream and pulled up behind my car. Susanna got out. I went up to her as she was paying the driver. She dropped a five-dollar bill when she saw me. The driver scooped it up.

"I've been hoping you'd come to see me, Lew," she said without much conviction. "Do come in."

She had trouble fitting her key into the lock. I helped her. Her handsome central room appeared a little shabby to my eyes, like a stage set where too many scenes had been enacted. Even the natural light at the windows, the fading afternoon light, seemed stale and secondhand.

She flung herself down on a sofa, her fine long legs sprawling. "I'm bushed. Make yourself a drink."

"I couldn't use one. There's a long night ahead."

"That sounds ominous. Make me one then. Make me a Journey to the End of the Night cocktail, with a dash of henbane. Or just dip me a cup of Lethe, that will do."

"You're tired."

"I've been working all day. For men must weep and women must work, though the harbor bar be moaning."

"If you'll be quiet for a bit, I want to talk to you seriously."

"What fun."

"Shut up."

I made her a drink and brought it to her. She sipped it. "Thank you, Lew. You're really a dear man."

"Stop talking like a phony."

She looked up at me with hurt dark eyes. "Nothing I say is right. You're mad at me. Maybe I shouldn't have left Stella by

176

herself, but she was still sleeping and I had to go to work. Anyway, she got home all right. Her father called, to thank me, just before I left the office.''

"To thank you?''

"And to cross-examine me about you and a few other things. Stella seems to have left home again. Mr. Carlson asked me to get in touch with him if she comes here. Should I?''

"I don't care. Stella isn't the problem.''

"And I am?''

"You're part of it. You didn't leave Stella this morning because you had to go to work. You had breakfast with Ralph Hillman, and you ought to know that I know it.''

"It was in a public place," she said irrelevantly.

"That's not the point. I wouldn't care if it was breakfast in bed. The point is you tried to slur over the fact, and it's a damned important fact.''

The hurt in her eyes tried to erupt into anger, but didn't quite succeed. Anger was just another evasion, and she probably knew that she was coming to the end of her evasions. She finished her drink and said in a very poignant female voice:

"Do you mean important to you personally, or for other reasons?''

"Both. I talked to Mrs. Hillman today. Actually she did most of the talking.''

"About Ralph and me?''

"Yes. It wasn't a very pleasant conversation, for either of us. I'd rather have heard it from you.''

She averted her face. Her black head absorbed the light almost completely. It was like looking into a small head-shaped area of almost total darkness.

"It's a passage in my life that I'm not proud of.''

"Because he was so much older?''

"That's one reason. Also, now that I'm older myself, I know how wretchedly mean it is to try and steal another woman's husband.''

"Then why go on doing it?''

"I'm not!" she cried in resentment. "It was over almost as soon as it started. If Mrs. Hillman thinks otherwise, she's imagining things.''

"I'm the one who thinks otherwise," I said. "You had breakfast with him this morning. You had a phone call from him the other day, which you refused to discuss.''

Slowly she turned and looked up at my face. "But it doesn't *mean* anything. I didn't *ask* him to phone me. I only went out with him this morning because he was desperate to talk to someone and I didn't want to disturb Stella. Also, if you want the truth, so he couldn't make a pass at me."

"Does he go in rather heavily for that?"

"I don't know. I hadn't seen him in about eighteen years. Honestly. I was appalled by the change in him. He was in a bad way this morning. He'd been drinking, and he said he'd been up all night, wandering around Los Angeles, searching for his son."

"I've been doing a little searching myself, but nobody goes out to breakfast with me and holds my hand."

"Are you really jealous of him, Lew? You can't be. He's *old*. He's a broken-down old man."

"You're protesting too much."

"I mean it, though. I had an enormous sense of revulsion this morning. Not just against Ralph Hillman. Against my whole misguided little life." She looked around the room as if she perceived the shabbiness I had seen. "I'm liable to spill over into my autobiography at any moment."

"That's what I've been waiting for, Susanna. How did you meet him?"

"Make me another drink."

I made it and brought it to her. "When and how did you meet him?"

"It was in March of 1945, when I was working at Warner's. A group of Navy officers came out to the studio to see a preview of a war movie. They were planning a party afterwards, and I went along. Ralph got me drunk and took me to the Barcelona Hotel, where he introduced me to the stolen delights of illicit romance. It was my first time on both counts. First time drunk, first time bedded." Her voice was harsh. "If you wouldn't stand over me, Lew, it would be easier."

I pulled up a hassock to her feet. "But it didn't go on, you say?"

"It went on for a few weeks. I'll be honest with you. I was in love with Ralph. He was handsome and brave and all the other things."

"And married."

"That's why I quit him," she said, "essentially. Mrs. Hillman—Elaine Hillman got wind of the affair and came to my apartment in Burbank. We had quite a scene. I don't know what would have happened if Carol hadn't been there. But she got the two of us quieted down, and even talking sensibly to each other.'' She paused, and added elegiacally: ''Carol had troubles of her own, but she was always good at easing situations.''

''What was Carol doing in that situation?''

''She was living with me, didn't I tell you that? I took her into my home. Anyway, Carol sat there like a little doll while Elaine Hillman laid out for me in detail just what I was doing to her and her marriage. The ugliness of it. I saw I couldn't go on doing it to her. I told her so, and she was satisfied. She's quite an impressive woman, you know, at least she was then.''

''She still is, when you get under the surface. And Ralph Hillman is an impressive man.''

''He was in those days, anyway.''

I said to test her honesty: ''Didn't you have any other reason for dropping him, besides Elaine Hillman's visit?''

''I don't know what you mean,'' she said, failing the honesty test, or perhaps the memory test.

''How did Elaine Hillman find out about you?''

''Oh. That.'' The shame that lay beneath her knowledge of herself came up into her face and took possession of it. She whispered: ''Mrs. Hillman told you, I suppose?''

''She mentioned a picture.''

''Did she show it to you?''

''She's too much of a lady.''

''That was a nasty crack!''

''It wasn't intended to be. You're getting paranoid.''

''Yes, Doctor. Shall I stretch out on this convenient couch and tell you a dream?''

''I can think of better uses for a couch.''

''Not now,'' she said quickly.

''No. Not now.'' But in the darkest part of our transaction we had reached a point of intimacy, understanding at least. ''I'm sorry I have to drag all of this stuff out.''

''I know. I know that much about you. I also know you haven't finished.''

''Who took the picture? Otto Sipe?''

''He was there. I heard his voice.''

''You didn't see him?''

''I hid my face,'' she said. ''A flashbulb popped. It was like reality exploding." She passed her hand over her eyes. "I think it was another man in the doorway who took the picture."

"Harold Harley?"

"It must have been. I didn't see him."

"What was the date?"

"It's in my memory book. April 14, 1945. Why does it matter?"

"Because you can't explode reality. Life hangs together in one piece. Everything is connected with everything else. The problem is to find the connections."

She said with some irony: "That's your mission in life, isn't it? You're not interested in people, you're only interested in the connections between them. Like a—" she searched for an insulting word—"a plumber."

I laughed at her. She smiled a little. Her eyes remained somber.

"There's another connection we have to go into," I said. "This one involves the telephone, not the plumbing."

"You mean Ralph's call the other day."

"Yes. He wanted you to keep quiet about something. What was it?"

She squirmed a little, and gathered her feet under her. "I don't want to get him into trouble. I owe him that much."

"Spare me the warmed-over sentiment. This is for real."

"You needn't sound so insulting."

"I apologize. Now let's have it."

"Well, he knew you had seen me, and he said we had to keep our stories straight. It seems there was a discrepancy in the story he told you. He told you he hadn't met Carol, but actually he had. After Mike Harley was arrested, she made an appeal to him and he did what he could. I wasn't to tell you about his interest in Carol."

"He was interested in Carol?"

"Not in the way you mean," she said with a lift of her head. "I was his girl. He simply didn't like the idea of leaving a child bride like Carol alone in the Barcelona Hotel. He asked me to take her under my wing. My slightly broken wing. Which I did, as you know."

"It all sounds very innocent."

"It was. I swear it. Besides, I liked Carol. I loved her, that summer in Burbank. I felt as if the baby in her womb belonged to both of us."

"Have you ever had a child?"

She shook her head rather sadly. "I never will have now. I was sure I was pregnant once, that very spring we've been talking about, but the doctor said it was false, caused by wistful thinking."

"Was Carol seeing a doctor when she lived with you?"

"Yes, I made her go. She went to the same doctor, actually. Weintraub, his name was."

"Did he deliver her baby?"

"I wouldn't know. She'd already left me, remember, and gone off with Mike Harley. And I didn't go back to Dr. Weintraub on account of the unpleasant associations."

"Was he unpleasant to you?"

"I mean the association with Ralph Hillman. Ralph sent me to Dr. Weintraub. I think they were buddies in the Navy."

Dr. Weintraub's plump face came into my mind. At the same time I remembered where I had seen a younger version of it, stripped of excess flesh, that very day. Weintraub was a member of the group on the flight deck, in the picture hanging on Hillman's library wall.

"It's funny," Susanna was saying, "how a name you haven't heard for seventeen or eighteen years will crop up, and then a couple of hours or a couple of days later, it will crop up again. Like Weintraub."

"Has the name been cropping up in other contexts?"

"Just this afternoon at the office. I had a rather peculiar caller whom I meant to tell you about, but all these other matters pushed him out of my mind. He was interested in Dr. Weintraub, too."

"Who was he?"

"He didn't want to say. When I pressed him, he said his name was Jackman."

"Sam Jackman?"

"He didn't mention his first name."

"Sam Jackman is a middle-aged Negro with very light skin who looks and talks like a jazz musician on his uppers, which he is."

"This boy seemed to be on his uppers, all right, but he certainly isn't Sam. Maybe he's Sam's son. He can't be more than eighteen or nineteen."

"Describe him."

"Thin-faced, very good features, very intense dark eyes, so

intense he scared me a little. He seemed intelligent, but he was too excited to make much sense.''

"What was he excited about?" I said with a mounting excitement of my own.

"Carol's death, I think. He didn't refer to it directly, but he asked me if I had known Carol in 1945. Apparently he'd been all the way out to Burbank trying to find me. He came across an old secretary at Warner's whom I still keep in touch with, and used her name to get past my secretary. He wanted to know what I could tell him about the Harley baby, and when I couldn't tell him anything he asked me what doctor Carol had gone to. I dredged up Weintraub's name—Elijah Weintraub isn't exactly a forgettable name—and it satisfied him. I was quite relieved to get rid of him.''

"I'm sorry you did.''

She looked at me curiously. "Do you suppose he could be the Harley baby himself?''

I didn't answer her. I got out my collection of photographs and shuffled them. There was an electric tremor in my hands, as if time was short-circuiting through me.

Susanna whispered fearfully: "He isn't dead, is he, Lew? I couldn't bear to look at another dead picture.''

"He's alive. At least, I hope he is.''

I showed her Tom Hillman's face. She said: "That's the boy I talked to. But he's very much the worse for wear now. *Is* he the Harley baby?''

"I think so. He's also the baby that Ralph and Elaine Hillman adopted through Dr. Weintraub. Did you get the impression that he was on his way to see Weintraub?''

"Yes. I did." She was getting excited, too. "It's like an ancient identity myth. He's searching for his lost parentage.''

"The hell of it is, both of his parents are dead. What time did you see him?''

"Around four o'clock.''

It was nearly six now. I went to the phone and called Weintraub's office. His answering service said it was closed for the night. The switchboard girl wouldn't give me Weintraub's home address or his unlisted number, and neither would the manager of the answering service. I had to settle for leaving my name and Susanna's number and waiting for Weintraub to call me, if he was willing.

An hour went by. Susanna broiled me a steak, and chewed

unhungrily on a piece of it. We sat at a marble table in the patio and she told me all about identity myths and how they grew. Oedipus. Hamlet. Stephen Dedalus. Her father had taught courses in such subjects. It passed the time, but it didn't relieve my anxiety for the boy. Hamlet came to a bloody end. Oedipus killed his father and married his mother, and then blinded himself.

"Thomas Harley," I said aloud. "Thomas Harley Hillman Jackman. He knew he wasn't the Hillmans' son. He thought he was a changeling."

"You get that in the myths, too."

"I'm talking about real life. He turned on his foster parents and went for his real parents. It's too bloody bad they had to be the Harleys."

"You're very certain that he is the Harley child."

"It fits in with everything I know about him. Incidentally, it explains why Ralph Hillman tried to hush up the fact that he'd taken an interest in Carol. He didn't want the facts of the adoption to come out."

"Why, though?"

"He's kept it a secret all these years, even from Tom. He seems to be a little crazy on the subject."

"I got that impression this morning." She leaned across the corner of the table and touched my fingers. "Lew? You don't think he went off his rocker and murdered Carol himself?"

"It's a possibility, but a remote one. What was on his mind at breakfast?"

"Him, mostly. He felt his life was collapsing around his ears. He thought I might be interested in helping him to pick up the pieces. After eighteen years he was offering me my second big break." Her scorn touched herself as well as Hillman.

"I don't quite understand."

"He asked me to marry him, Lew. I suppose that's in line with contemporary *mores*. You get your future set up ahead of time, before you terminate your present marriage."

"I don't like that word 'terminate.' Did he say what he intended to do with Elaine?"

"No." She looked quite pale and haunted.

"I hope divorce was all he had in mind. What was your answer?"

"My answer?"

"Your response to his proposal."

"Oh. I told him I was waiting for a better offer."

Her dark meaningful eyes were on my face. I sat there trying to frame a balanced answer. The telephone rang inside before I had a chance to deliver it.

I went in through the door we had left open and picked up the receiver. "Archer speaking."

"This is Dr. Weintraub." His voice had lost its calmness. "I've just had a thoroughly upsetting experience—"

"Have you seen the Hillman boy?"

"Yes. He came to me just as I was leaving. He asked me essentially the same question you did."

"What did you tell him, Doctor?"

"I told him the truth. He already knew it, anyway. He wanted to know if Mike and Carol Harley were his parents. They were."

"How did he react to the information?"

"Violently, I'm afraid. He hit me and broke my glasses. I'm practically blind without them. He got away from me."

"Have you told the police?"

"No."

"Tell them, now. And tell them who he is."

"But his father—his adoptive father wouldn't want me—"

"I know how it is when you're dealing with an old commander, Doctor. He was your commander at one time, wasn't he?"

"Yes. I was his flight surgeon."

"You aren't any more, and you can't let Hillman do your thinking for you. Do you tell the police, or do I?"

"I will. I realize we can't let the boy run loose in his condition."

"Just what is his condition?"

"He's very upset and, as I said, violently acting out."

With his heredity, I thought, that was hardly surprising.

24

I kissed Susanna goodbye and drove down Wilshire through Westwood. I wanted to be at the Santa Monica bus station at nine, just in case Tom showed up, but there was still time for another crack at Ben Daly. I turned down San Vicente toward the coastal highway.

The sun was half down on the horizon, bleeding color into the sea and sky. Even the front of the Barcelona Hotel was touched with factitious Mediterranean pink. The crowd of onlookers in the driveway had changed and dwindled. There were still a few waiting for something more interesting than their lives to happen.

It was a warm night, and most of them were in beach costume. One man was dressed formally in a dark gray business suit and dark gray felt hat. He looked familiar.

I pulled up the drive on impulse and got out. The man in the dark gray suit was Harold Harley. He was wearing a black tie, which Lila had doubtless chosen for him, and a woebegone expression.

It deepened when he saw me. "Mr. Archer?"

"You can't have forgotten me, Harold."

"No. It's just that everything looks different, even people's faces. Or that hotel there. It's just a caved-in old dump, and I used to think it was a pretty ritzy place. Even the sky looks different." He raised his eyes to the red-streaked sky. "It looks hand-tinted, phony, like there was nothing behind it."

The little man talked like an artist. He might have become one, I thought, with a different childhood.

"I didn't realize you were so fond of your brother."

"Neither did I. But it isn't just that. I hate California. Nothing really good ever happened to me in California. Or Mike either." He gestured vaguely toward the cluster of official cars. "I wisht I was back in Idaho."

I drew him away from the little group of onlookers, from the women in slacks and halters which their flesh overflowed, the younger girls with haystacks of hair slipping down their foreheads into their blue-shadowed eyes, the tanned alert-looking boys with bleached heads and bleached futures. We stood under a magnolia tree that needed water.

185

"What happened to your brother started in Idaho, Harold."
And also what happened to you, or failed to happen.

"You think I don't know that? The old man always said
Mike would die on the gallows. Anyway, he cheated the
gallows."

"I talked to your father yesterday."

Harold started violently, and glanced behind him. "Is he in
town?"

"I was in Pocatello yesterday."

He looked both relieved and anxious. "How is he?"

"Much the same, I gather. You didn't tell me he was one
step ahead of the butterfly nets."

"You didn't ask me. Anyway, he isn't like that all the time."

"But he had to be committed more than once."

"Yeah." He hung his head. In the final glare of day I could
see the old closet dust in the groove of his hat, and the new
sweat staining the hatband.

"It's nothing to blame yourself for," I said. "It explains a
lot about Mike."

"I know. The old man was a terror when Mike was a kid.
Maw finally had him committed for what he did to Mike and
her. Mike left home and never came back, and who could
blame him?"

"But you stayed."

"For a while. I had a trick of pretending I was some place
else, like here in California. I finally came out here and went to
photography school."

I returned to the question that interested me. It was really a
series of questions about the interlinked lives that brought Mike
Harley and Carol Brown from their beginnings in Idaho to their
ends in California. Their beginnings and ends had become clear
enough. The middle still puzzled me, as well as the ultimate
end that lay ahead in darkness.

"I talked to Carol's parents, too," I said. "Carol was there
earlier in the summer, and she left a suitcase in her room. A
letter in it explained to me why you blamed yourself for the
Hillman extortion."

"You saw my letter, eh? I should never have written a letter
like that to Mike. I should have known better." He was
hanging his head again.

"It's hard to see ahead and figure what the little things we do will lead to. And you weren't intending to suggest anything wrong."

"Gosh, no."

"Anyway, your letter helped me. It led me back here to Otto Sipe, and I hope eventually to the Hillman boy. The boy was holed up here with Sipe from Monday morning till Wednesday night, last night."

"No kidding."

"How well did you know Otto Sipe?"

Harold winced away from the question. If he could, he would have disappeared entirely, leaving his dark business suit and black tie and dusty hat suspended between the crisp brown grass and the dry leaves of the magnolia. He said in a voice that didn't want to be heard:

"He was Mike's friend. I got to know him that way. He trained Mike for a boxing career."

"What kind of a career did he train you for, Harold?"

"Me?"

"You. Didn't Sipe get you the job as hotel photographer here?"

"On account of—I was Mike's brother."

"I'm sure that had something to do with it. But didn't Sipe want you to help him with his sideline?"

"What sideline was that?"

"Blackmail."

He shook his head so vehemently that his hat almost fell off. "I never had any part of the rake-off, honest. He paid me standard rates to take those pictures, a measly buck a throw, and if I didn't do it I'd lose my job. I quit anyway, as soon as I had the chance. It was a dirty business." He peered up the driveway at the bland decaying face of the hotel. It was stark white now in the twilight. "I never took any benefit from it. I never even knew who the people were."

"Not even once?"

"I don't know what you mean."

"Didn't you take a picture of Captain Hillman and his girl?"

His face was pale and wet. "I don't know. I never knew their names."

"Last spring at Newport you recognized Hillman."

"Sure, he was the exec of Mike's ship. I met him when I went aboard that time."

"And no other time?"

"No sir."

"When were you and Mike arrested? In the spring of 1945?"

He nodded. "The fifth of March. I'm not likely to forget it. It was the only time I ever got arrested. After they let me go I never came back here. Until now." He looked around at the place as if it had betrayed him a second time.

"If you're telling the truth about the date, you didn't take the picture I'm interested in. It was taken in April."

"I'm not lying. By that time Otto Sipe had another boy."

"What gave him so much power around the hotel?"

"I think he had something on the management. He hushed up something for them, long ago, something about a movie star who stayed here."

"Was Mike staying here at the time he was picked up?"

"Yeah. I let him and Carol use my room, the one that went with the job. I slept in the employees' dormitory. I think Otto Sipe let Carol stay on in the room for a while after me and Mike were arrested."

"Was it the room next door to his, at the end of the corridor?"

"Yeah."

"Did it have a brass bed in it?"

"Yeah. Why?"

"I was just wondering. They haven't changed the furnishings since the war. That interconnecting bathroom would have been handy for Sipe, if he liked Carol."

He shook his head. "Not him. He had no use for women. And Carol had no use for him. She got out of there as soon as she could make other arrangements. She went to live with a woman friend in Burbank."

"Susanna."

Harold blinked. "Yeah. That was her name, Susanna. I never met her, but she must have been a nice person."

"What kind of a girl was Carol?"

"Carol? She was a beauty. When a girl has her looks, you don't think much about going deeper. I mean, there she *was*. I always thought she was an innocent young girl. But Lila says you could fill a book with what I don't know about women."

I looked at my watch. It was past eight, and Harold had probably taken me as far as he could. Partly to make sure of this, I asked him to come across the highway and see his old acquaintance, Ben Daly. He didn't hang back.

Daly scowled at us from the doorway of his lighted office. Then he recognized Harold, and his brow cleared. He came out and shook hands with him, disregarding me.

"Long time no see, Har."

"You can say that again."

They talked to each other across a distance of years, with some warmth and without embarrassment. There was no sign of guilty involvement between them. It didn't follow necessarily, but I pretty well gave up on the idea that either of them was involved in any way with the recent crimes.

I broke in on their conversation: "Will you give me one minute, Ben? You may be able to help me solve that murder."

"How? By killing somebody else?"

"By making another identification, if you can." I brought out Dick Leandro's picture and forced it into his hand. "Have you ever seen this man?"

He studied the picture for a minute. His hand was unsteady. "I may have. I'm not sure."

"When?"

"Last night. He may be the one who came to the hotel last night."

"The one with the girl, in the new blue Chevvy?"

"Yeah. He could be the one. But I wouldn't want to swear to it in court."

25

The Santa Monica bus station is on a side street off lower Wilshire. At a quarter to nine I left my car at the curb and went in. Stella, that incredible child, was there. She was sitting at the lunch counter at the rear in a position from which she could watch all the doors.

She saw me, of course, and swung around to hide her face in a cup of coffee. I sat beside her. She put down her cup with an impatient rap. The coffee in it looked cold, and had a grayish film on it.

She spoke without looking directly at me, like somebody in a spy movie. "Go away. You'll frighten Tommy off."

"He doesn't know me."

"But I'm supposed to be alone. Besides, you look like a policeman or something."

"Why is Tommy allergic to policemen?"

"You would be, too, if they locked you up the way they locked him up."

"If you keep running away, they'll be locking you up, Stella."

"They're not going to get the chance," she said, with a sharp sideways glance at me. "My father took me to a psychiatrist today, to see if I needed to be sent to Laguna Perdida. I told her everything, just as I've told you. She said there was nothing the matter with me at all. So when my father went in to talk to her I walked out the front door and took a taxi to the bus station, and there was a bus just leaving."

"I'm going to have to drive you home again."

She said in a very young voice: "Don't teen-agers have any rights?"

"Yes, including the right to adult protection."

"I won't go without Tommy!"

Her voice rose and broke on his name. Half the people in the small station were looking at us. The woman behind the lunch counter came over to Stella.

"Is he bothering you, miss?"

She shook her head. "He's a very good friend."

This only deepened the woman's suspicions, but it silenced her. I ordered a cup of coffee. When she went to draw it, I said to Stella:

"I won't go without Tommy, either. What did your psychiatrist friend think about him, by the way?"

"She didn't tell me. Why?"

"I was just wondering."

The waitress brought my coffee. I carried it to the far end of the counter and drank it slowly. It was eight minutes to nine. People were lining up at the loading door, which meant that a bus was expected.

I went out the front, and almost walked into Tommy. He had on slacks and a dirty white shirt. His face was a dirty white, except where a fuzz of beard showed.

"Excuse me, sir," he said, and stepped around me.

I didn't want to let him get inside, where taking him would create a public scene that would bring in the police. I needed a chance to talk to him before anyone else did. There wasn't much use in trying to persuade him to come with me. He was lean and quick and could certainly outrun me.

These thoughts went through my head in the second before he reached the door of the station. I put both arms around his waist from behind, lifted him off his feet, and carried him wildly struggling to my car. I pushed him into the front seat and got in beside him. Other cars were going by in the road, but nobody stopped to ask me any questions. They never do any more.

Tom let out a single dry sob or whimper, high in his nose. He must have known that this was the end of running.

"My name is Lew Archer," I said. "I'm a private detective employed by your father."

"He isn't my father."

"An adoptive father is a father, too."

"Not to me he isn't. I don't want any part of Captain Hillman," he said with the cold distance of injured youth. "Or you either."

I noticed a cut on the knuckle of his right hand. It had been bleeding. He put the knuckle in his mouth and sucked it, looking at me over it. It was hard to take him seriously at that moment. But he was a very serious young man.

"I'm not going back to my cruddy so-called parents."

"You have nobody else."

"I have myself."

"You haven't been handling yourself too well."

"Another lecture."

"I'm pointing out a fact. If you could look after yourself decently, you might make out a case for independence. But you've been rampaging around clobbering middle-aged doctors—"

"He tried to make me go home."

"You're going home. The alternative seems to be a life with bums and criminals."

"You're talking about my parents, my real parents." He spoke with conscious drama, but there was also a kind of bitter awe in his voice. "My mother wasn't a bum and she wasn't a criminal. She was—nice."

"I didn't mean her."

"And my father wasn't so bad, either," he said without conviction.

"Who killed them, Tom?"

His face became blank and tight. It looked like a wooden mask used to fend off suffering.

"I don't know anything about it," he said in a monotone. "I didn't know Carol was dead, even, till I saw the papers last night. I didn't know Mike was dead till I saw the papers today. Next question."

"Don't be like that, Tom. I'm not a cop, and I'm not your enemy."

"With the so-called parents I've got, who needs enemies? All my—all Captain Hillman ever wanted was a pet boy around the house, somebody to do tricks. I'm tired of doing tricks for him."

"You *should* be tired, after this last trick. It was a honey of a trick."

He gave me his first direct look, half in anger and half in fear. "I had a right to go with my real parents."

"Maybe. We won't argue about that. But you certainly had no right to help them extort money from your father."

"He's not my father."

"I know that. Do you have to keep saying it?"

"Do you have to keep calling him my father?"

He was a difficult boy. I felt good, anyway. I had him.

"Okay," I said. "We'll call him Mr. X and we'll call your mother Madam X and we'll call you the Lost Dauphin of France."

"That isn't so funny."

He was right. It wasn't.

"Getting back to the twenty-five thousand dollars you helped to take them for, I suppose you know you're an accomplice in a major felony."

"I didn't know about the money. They didn't tell me. I don't think Carol knew about it, either."

"That's hard to believe, Tom."

"It's true. Mike didn't tell us. He just said he had a deal cooking."

"If you didn't know about the extortion, why did you ride away in the trunk of his car?"

"So I wouldn't be seen. Mike said my dad—" he swallowed the word, with disgust—"he said that Captain Hillman had all the police looking for me, to put me back in Laguna—"

He became aware of his present situation. He peered around furtively, scrambled under the wheel to the far door. I pulled him back into the middle of the seat and put an armlock on him.

"You're staying with me, Tom, if I have to use handcuffs."

"Fuzz!"

The jeering word came strangely from him, like a foreign word he was trying to make his own. It bothered me. Boys, like men, have to belong to something. Tom had felt betrayed by one world, the plush deceptive world of Ralph Hillman, with schools like Laguna Perdida on the underside of the weave. He had plunged blindly into another world, and now he had lost that. His mind must be desperate for a place to rest, I thought, and I wasn't doing much of a job of providing one.

A bus came down the street. As it turned into the loading area, I caught a glimpse of passengers at the windows, travel-drugged and blasé. California here we come, right back where we started from.

I relaxed my grip on Tom. "I couldn't let you go," I said, "even if I wanted to. You're not stupid. Try for once to figure out how this looks to other people."

"This?"

"The whole charade. Your running away from school—for which I certainly don't blame you—"

"Thanks a lot."

I disregarded his irony. "And the phony kidnapping and all the rest of it. An adopted son is just as important as a real one to his parents. Yours have been worried sick about you."

"I bet."

"Neither one of them gave a damn about the money, incidentally. It's you they cared about, and care about."

"There's something missing," he said.

"What?"

"The violin accompaniment."

"You're a hard boy to talk to, Tom."

"My *friends* don't think so."

"What's a friend? Somebody who lets you run wild?"

"Somebody who doesn't want to throw me into the Black Hole of Calcutta, otherwise known as Laguna Perdida School."

"I don't."

"You say you don't. But you're working for Captain Hillman, and he does."

"Not any more."

The boy shook his head. "I don't believe you, and I don't believe him. After a few things *happen* to you, you start to believe what people do, not what they say. People like the Hillmans would think that a person like Carol was a nothing, a nothing woman. But she wasn't to me. She liked me. She treated me well. Even my real father never raised his hand to me. The only trouble we had was about the way he treated Carol."

He had dropped his brittle sardonic front and was talking to me in a human voice. Stella chose this moment to come out of the loading area onto the sidewalk. Her face was pinched with disappointment.

Tom caught sight of her almost as soon as I did. His eyes lit up as if she was an angel from some lost paradise. He leaned across me.

"Hey! Stell!"

She came running. I got out of the car and let her take my place beside the boy. They didn't embrace or kiss. Perhaps their hands met briefly. I got in behind the wheel.

Stella was saying: "It *feels* as though you've been gone for ages."

"It does to me, too."

"You should have called me sooner."

"I did."

"I mean, right away."

"I was afraid you'd—do what you did." He jerked his chin in my direction.

"I didn't, though. Not really. It was his idea. Anyway, you have to go home. We both do."

"I have no home."

"Neither have I, then. Mine's just as bad as yours."

"No, it isn't."

"Yes, it is. Anyway," she said to clinch the argument, "you need a bath. I can smell you. And a shave."

I glanced at his face. It had a pleased silly embarrassed expression.

The street was empty of traffic at the moment. I started the car and made a U-turn toward the south. Tom offered no objection.

Once on the freeway, in that anonymous world of rushing lights and darkness, he began to talk in his human voice to Stella. Carol had phoned him, using his personal number, several weeks before. She wanted to arrange a meeting with him. That night, driving Ralph Hillman's Cadillac, he picked her up at the view-point overlooking the sea near Dack's Auto Court.

He parked in an orange grove that smelled of weddings and listened to the story of her life. Even though he'd often doubted that he belonged to the Hillmans, it was hard for him to believe that he was Carol's son. But he was strongly drawn to her. The relationship was like an escape hatch in Captain Hillman's tight little ship. He kept going back to Carol, and eventually he believed her. He even began to love her in a way.

"Why didn't you tell me about her?" Stella said. "I would have liked to know her."

"No, you wouldn't." His voice was rough. "Anyway, I had to get to know her myself first. I had to get adjusted to the whole idea of my mother. And then I had to decide what to do. You see, she wanted to leave my father. He gave her a hard time, he always had. She said if she didn't get away from him soon, she'd never be able to. She wasn't good at standing up for herself, and she wanted my help. Besides, I think she knew he was up to something."

"You mean the kidnapping and all?" she said.

"I think she knew it and she didn't know it. You know how women are."

"I know my mother," she answered sagely.

They had forgotten me. I was the friendly chauffeur, good old graying Lew Archer, and we would go on driving like this forever through a night so dangerous that it had to feel secure. I remembered a kind of poem or parable that Susanna had quoted to me years before. A bird came in through a window at one end of a lighted hall, flew the length of the hall, and out through another window into darkness; that was the span of a human life. The headlights that rose in the distance and swooped by and fell away behind us reminded me of Susanna's briefly lighted bird. I wished that she was with me.

Tom was telling Stella how he first met his father. Mike had been kept in the background the first week; he was supposed to be in Los Angeles looking for work. Finally, on the Saturday night, Tom met him at the auto court.

"That was the night you borrowed our car, wasn't it?"

"Yeah. My fa—Ralph had me grounded, you know. Carol spilled some wine on the front seat of the car and he smelled it. He thought I was driving and drinking."

"Did Carol drink much?"

"Quite a bit. She drank a lot that Saturday night. So did he. I had some wine, too."

"You're not old enough."

"It was with dinner," he said. "Carol cooked spaghetti. Spaghetti à la Pocatello, she called it. She sang some of the old songs for me, like 'Sentimental Journey.' It was kind of fun," he said doubtfully.

"Is that why you didn't come home?"

"No. I—" The word caught in his throat. "I—" His face, which I could see in the rear-view mirror, became contorted with effort. He couldn't finish the sentence.

"Did you want to stay with them?" Stella said after a while.

"No. I don't know."

"How did you like your father?"

"He was all right, I guess, until he got drunk. We played some gin rummy and he didn't win, so he broke up the game. He started to take it out on Carol. I almost had a fight with him. He said he used to be a boxer and I'd be crazy to try it, that his fists could kill."

"It sounds like a terrible evening."

"That part of it wasn't so good."

"What part of it was?"

"When she sang the old songs. And she told me about my grandfather in Pocatello."

"Did that take all night?" she said a little tartly.

"I didn't *stay* with them all night. I left around ten o'clock, when we almost had the fight. I—" The same word stuck in his throat again, as if it was involved with secret meanings that wouldn't let it be spoken.

"What did you do?"

"I went and parked on the view-point where I picked her up the first time. I sat there until nearly two o'clock, watching the stars and listening, you know, to the sea. The sea and the highway. I was trying to figure out what I should do, where I belonged. I still haven't got it figured out." He added, in a voice that was conscious of me: "Now I guess I don't have any choice. They'll put me back in the Black Hole of Calcutta."

"Me too," she said with a nervous giggle. "We can send each other secret notes. Tap out messages on the bars and stuff."

"It isn't funny, Stell. Everybody out there is crazy, even some of the staff. They get that way."

"You're changing the subject," she said. "What did you do at two a.m.?"

"I went to see Sam Jackman when he got off work. I thought I could ask him what to do, but I found out that I couldn't. I just couldn't tell him that they were my parents. So I went out in the country and drove around for a few hours. I didn't want to go home, and I didn't want to go back to the auto court."

"So you turned the car over and tried to kill yourself."

"I—" Silence set in again, and this time it lasted. He sat bolt upright, staring ahead, watching the headlights rise out of the darkness. After a time I noticed that Stella's arm was across his shoulders. His face was streaked with tears.

26

I dropped Stella off first. She refused to get out of the car until Tom promised that he wouldn't go away again, ever, without telling her.

Her father came out of the house, walking on his heels. He put his arms around her. With a kind of resigned affection, she laid her head neatly against his shoulder. Maybe they had learned something, or were learning. People sometimes do.

They went inside, and I turned down the driveway.

"He's just a fake," Tom said. "Stella lent me the car, and then he turned around and told the police I stole it."

"I believe he thought so at the time."

"But he found out the truth later, from Stella, and went right on claiming I stole it."

"Dishonesty keeps creeping in," I said. "We all have to watch it."

He thought this over, and decided that I had insulted him. "Is that supposed to be a crack at me?"

"No. I think you're honest, so far as you understand what you're talking about. But you only see one side, your own, and it seems to consist mainly of grievances."

"I have a lot of them," he admitted. After a moment he said: "You're wrong about me only seeing one side, though. I know how my—my adoptive parents are supposed to feel, but I know how I feel, too. I can't go on being split down the middle. That's how I felt, you know, these last few nights, like somebody took a cleaver and split me down the middle. I lay awake on that old brass bed, where Mike and Carol, you know, conceived me—with old Sipe snoring in the other room, and I was there and I wasn't there. You know? I mean I couldn't believe that I was me and this was my life and those people were my parents. I never believed the Hillmans were, either. They always seemed to be putting on an act. Maybe," he said half-seriously, "I was dropped from another planet."

"You've been reading too much science fiction."

"I don't *really* believe that. I *know* who my parents were. Carol told me. Mike told me. The doctor told me, and that made it official. But I still have a hard time telling *myself*."

"Stop trying to force it. It doesn't matter so much who your parents were."

"It does to me," he said earnestly. "It's the most important thing in my life."

We were approaching the Hillmans' mailbox. I had been driving slowly, immersed in the conversation, and now I pulled into the driveway and stopped entirely.

"I sometimes think children should be anonymous."

"How do you mean, Mr. Archer?" It was the first time he had called me by my name.

"I have no plan. I'd just like to change the emphasis slightly. People are trying so hard to live through their children. And the children keep trying so hard to live up to their parents, or live them down. Everybody's living through or for or against somebody else. It doesn't make too much sense, and it isn't working too well."

I was trying to free his mind a little, before he had to face the next big change. I didn't succeed. "It doesn't work when they lie to you," he said. "They lied to me. They pretended I was their own flesh and blood. I thought there was something missing in me when I couldn't feel like their son."

"I've talked to your mother about this—Elaine—and she bitterly regrets it."

"I bet."

"Let's not get off on that routine, Tom."

He was silent for a while. "I suppose I have to go and talk to them, but I don't want to live with them, and I'm not going to put on any phony feelings."

No phoniness, I thought, was the code of the new generation, at least the ones who were worth anything. It was a fairly decent ideal, but it sometimes worked out cruelly in practice.

"You can't forgive them for Laguna Perdida."

"Could you?"

I had to think about my answer. "It would depend on their reasons. I imagine some pretty desperate parents end up there as a last resort with some pretty wild sons and daughters."

"They're desperate, all right," he said. "Ralph and Elaine get desperate very easily. They can't stand trouble. Sweep it under the rug. All they wanted to do was get me out of sight, when I stopped being their performing boy. And I had all these terrible things on my mind." He put his hands to his head, to calm the terrible things. He was close to breaking down.

"I'm sorry, Tom. But didn't something crucial happen that Sunday morning?"

He peered at me under his raised arm. "They told you, eh?"

"No. I'm asking you to tell me."

"Ask them."

It was all he would say.

I drove up the winding blacktop lane to the top of the knoll. Lights were blazing outside and inside the house. The harsh white floods made the stucco walls look ugly and unreal. Black shadows lurked under the melodramatic Moorish arches.

There was something a little melodramatic in the way Ralph Hillman stepped out from one of the arches into the light. He wasn't the wreck Susanna had described, at least not superficially. His handsome silver head was sleekly brushed. His face was tightly composed. He held himself erect, and even trotted a few steps as he came toward my side of the car. He was wearing a wine-colored jacket with a rolled collar.

"Prodigal son returneth," Tom was saying beside me in scared bravado. "But they didn't kill the fatted calf, they killed the prodigal son."

Hillman said: "I thought you were Lieutenant Bastian."

"Are you expecting him?"

"Yes. He says he has something to show me."

He stooped to look in the window and saw Tom. His eyes dilated.

"My boy!" His hoarse, whisky-laden voice hardly dared to believe what it was saying. "You've come back."

"Yeah. I'm here."

Hillman trotted around to the other side of the car and opened the door. "Come out and let me look at you."

With a brief, noncommittal glance in my direction, Tom climbed out. His movements were stiff and tentative, like a much older man's. Hillman put his hands on the boy's shoulders and held him at arm's length, turning him so that his face was in the light.

"How *are* you, Tom?"

"I'm okay. How are you?"

"Wonderful, now that you're here." I didn't doubt that Hillman's feeling was sincere, but his expression of it was somehow wrong. Phony. And I could see Tom wince under his hands.

Elaine Hillman came out of the house. I went to meet her. The floodlights multiplied the lines in her face and bleached it of any color it might have had. She was pared so thin that she reminded me vaguely of concentration camps. Her eyes were brilliantly alive.

"You've brought him back, Mr. Archer. Bless you."

She slipped her hand through my arm and let me take her to him. He stood like a dutiful son while she stood on her toes and kissed him on his grimy tear-runneled cheek.

Then he backed away from both of them. He stood leaning against the side of my car with his thumbs in the waistband of his slacks. I'd seen a hundred boys standing as he was standing against cars both hot and cold, on the curb of a street or the shoulder of a highway, while men in uniform questioned them. The sound of the distant highway faintly disturbed the edges of the silence I was listening to now.

Tom said: "I don't want to hurt anybody. I never did. Or maybe I did, I don't know. Anyway, there's no use going on pretending. You see, I know who I am. Mike and Carol Harley were my father and mother. You knew it, too, didn't you?"

"I didn't," Elaine said quickly.

"But you knew *you* weren't my mother."

"Yes. Of course I knew that."

She glanced down at her body and then, almost wistfully, at her husband. He turned away from both of them. His face had momentarily come apart. He seemed to be in pain, which he wanted to hide.

"One of you must have known who I really was." Tom said to Hillman: "You knew, didn't you?"

Hillman didn't answer. Tom said in a high desperate voice: "I can't stay here. You're both a couple of phonies. You put on a big act for all these years, and as soon as I step out of line you give me the shaft."

Hillman found his voice. "I should think it was the other way around."

"Okay, so I did wrong. Stand me up against a wall and shoot me."

The boy's voice was slightly hysterical, but it wasn't that that bothered me so much. He seemed to be shifting from attitude to attitude, even from class to class, trying to find a place where he could stand. I went and stood beside him.

"Nobody's talking about punishing you," Hillman said. "But a homicidal attack is something that can't be laughed off."

"You're talking crap," the boy said.

Hillman's chin came up. "Don't *speak* to me like that!"

"Or what will you do? Lock me up with a bunch of psychos and throw away the key?"

"I didn't *say* that."

"No. You just went ahead and did it."

"Perhaps I acted hastily."

"Yes," Elaine put in. "Your father acted hastily. Now let's forget the whole thing and go inside and be friends."

"He isn't my father," Tom said stubbornly.

"But we can all be friends, anyway. Can't we, Tom?" Her voice and look were imploring. "Can't we forget the bad things and simply be glad they're over and that we're all together?"

"I don't know. I'd like to go away for a while and live by myself and think things through. What would be wrong with it? I'm old enough."

"That's nonsense." Hillman shouldn't have said it. A second later his eyes showed that he knew he shouldn't have. He stepped forward and put his hand on the boy's shoulder. "Maybe that isn't such a bad idea, after all. We're intelligent people, we ought to be able to work something out between us. There's the lodge in Oregon, for example, where you and I were planning to go next month. We could step up our schedule and synch our watches, eh?"

The performance was forced. Tom listened to it without interest or hope. After a bit Elaine put her hand inside her husband's arm and drew him toward the house. Tom and I followed along.

Mrs. Perez was waiting at the door. There was warmth in her greeting, and even some in Tom's response. They had a discussion about food. Tom said he would like a hamburger sandwich with pea soup. Mrs. Perez darted jouncily away.

Hillman surveyed the boy in the light of the chandelier. "You'd better go up and bathe and change your clothes."

"Now?"

"It's just a suggestion," Hillman said placatingly. "Lieutenant Bastian of the sheriff's department is on his way over. I'd like you—you should be looking more like yourself."

"Is he going to take me away? Is that the idea?"

"Not if I can help it," Hillman said. "Look, I'll come up with you."

"I can dress myself, Dad!" The word slipped out, irretrievable and undeniable.

"But we ought to go over what you're going to say to him. There's no use putting your neck in a noose—I mean—"

"I'll just tell him the truth."

The boy walked away from him toward the stairs. Ralph and Elaine Hillman followed him with their eyes until he was out of sight, and then they followed his footsteps with their ears. The difficult god of the household had returned and the household was functioning again, in its difficult way.

We went into the sitting room. Hillman continued across it into the bar alcove. He made himself a drink, absently, as if he was simply trying to find something to do with his hands and then with his mouth.

When he came out with the drink in his hand, he reminded me of an actor stepping out through a proscenium arch to join the audience.

"Ungrateful sons are like a serpent's tooth," he said, not very conversationally.

Elaine spoke up distinctly from the chesterfield: "If you're attempting to quote from *King Lear*, the correct quotation is: 'How sharper than a serpent's tooth it is to have a thankless child!' But it isn't terribly appropriate, since Tom is not your child. A more apt quotation from the same work would be Edmund's line, 'Now, gods, stand up for bastards!' "

He knocked back his drink and moved toward her, lurching just a little. "I resent your saying that."

"That's your privilege, and your habit."

"Tom is not a bastard. His parents were legally married."

"It hardly matters, considering their background. Did you and your precious Dr. Weintraub have to choose the offspring of criminals?"

Her voice was cold and bitter. She seemed, after years of silence, to be speaking out and striking back at him.

"Look," he said, "he's back. I'm glad he's back. You are, too. And we want him to stay with us, don't we?"

"I want what's best for him."

"I *know* what's best for him." He spread his arms, swinging them a little from side to side, as if he was making Tom a gift of the house and the life that went on inside it.

"You don't know what's best for anybody, Ralph. Having men under you, you got into the habit of thinking you knew. But you really don't. I'm interested in Mr. Archer's opinion. Come and sit here beside me," she said to me, "and tell me what you think."

"What exactly is the subject?" I said as I sat down.

"Tom. What kind of future should we plan for him?"

"I don't think you can do it for him. Let him do his own planning."

Hillman said across the room: "But all he wants to do is go away by himself."

"I admit that isn't such a good idea. We should be able to persuade him to tone it down. Let him live with another family for a year. Or send him to prep school. After that, he'll be going away to college, anyway."

"Good Lord, do you think he'll make it in college?"

"Of course he will, Ralph." She turned to me. "But is he ready now for an ordinary prep school? Could he survive it?"

"He survived the last two weeks."

"Yes. We have to thank God for that. And you."

Hillman came and stood over me, shaking the ice in his glass. "Just what was the situation with those people? Was Tom in league with them against us? Understand me, I don't intend to punish him or do anything at all about it. I just want to know."

I answered him slowly and carefully. "You can hardly talk about a boy being in league with his mother and father. He was confused. He still is. He believed you had turned against him when you put him in Laguna Perdida School. You don't have to be a psychiatrist to know that that isn't the kind of school he needs."

"I'm afraid you aren't conversant with all the facts."

"What are they?"

He shook his head. "Go on with what you were saying. Was he in cahoots with those people?"

"Not in the way you mean. But they offered him an out, physically and emotionally, and he took it. Apparently his mother was kind to him."

"*I* was always kind to him," Elaine said. She shot a fierce upward glance at her husband. "But there was falsity in the house, undermining everything."

I said: "There was falseness in the other house, too, at Dack's Auto Court. There's no doubt that Mike Harley was conning him, setting him up for the phony kidnapping. He didn't let his paternal feelings interfere. Carol was another matter. If she was conning Tom, she was conning herself, too. Tom put it something like this: she knew Harley was up to something, but she didn't let herself know. You get that way after twenty years of living with a man like Harley."

Elaine nodded slightly. I think it was a comment on her own marriage. She said, "I'm worried about Tom's heredity, with such parents."

The blood rushed into Hillman's face. "For God's sake, that's really reaching for trouble."

"I hardly need to reach for it," she said quietly. "It's in my lap." She looked at him as if he had placed it there.

He turned and walked the length of the room, returned part way, and went into the bar. He poured more whisky over the ice in his glass, and drank it down. Elaine watched him with critical eyes, which he was aware of.

"It settles my nerves," he said.

"I hadn't noticed."

He looked at his watch and paced up and down the room. He lost his balance once and had to make a side step.

"Why doesn't Bastian come and get it over with?" he said. "It's getting late. I was expecting Dick tonight, but I guess he found something more interesting to do." He burst out at his wife: "This is a dismal household, you know that?"

"I've been aware of it for many years. I tried to keep it together for Tom's sake. That's rather funny, isn't it?"

"I don't see anything funny about it."

I didn't, either. The broken edges of their marriage were rubbing together like the unset ends of a bone that had been fractured but was still living.

Bastian arrived at last. He came into the reception hall carrying a black metal evidence case, and he was dark-faced and grim. Even the news that Tom was safe at home failed to cheer him much.

"Where is he?"

"Taking a bath," Hillman said.

"I've got to talk to him. I want a full statement."

"Not tonight, Lieutenant. The boy's been through the wringer."

"But he's the most important witness we have."

"I know that. He'll give you his full story tomorrow."

Bastian glanced from him to me. We were just inside the front door, and Hillman seemed unwilling to let him come in any farther.

"I expected better cooperation, Mr. Hillman. You've had cooperation from us. But come to think of it, we haven't had it from you at any time."

"Don't give me any lectures, Lieutenant. My son is home, and it wasn't thanks to you that we got him back."

"A lot of police work went into it," I said. "Lieutenant Bastian and I have been working closely together. We still are, I hope."

Hillman transferred his glare to me. He looked ready to order us both out. I said to Bastian:

"You've got something to show us, Lieutenant, is that right?"

"Yes." He held up his evidence case. "You've already seen it, Archer. I'm not sure if Mr. Hillman has or not."

"What is it?"

"I'll show you. I prefer not to describe it beforehand. Could we sit down at a table?"

Hillman led us to the library and seated us at a table with a green-shaded reading lamp in the middle, which he switched on. It lit up the tabletop brilliantly and cast the rest of the room, including our faces, into greenish shadow. Bastian opened the evidence box. It contained the hunting knife with the striped handle which I had found stuck in Mike Harley's ribs.

Hillman drew in his break sharply.

"You recognize it, do you?" Bastian said.

"No. I do not."

"Pick it up and examine it more closely. It's quite all right to handle it. It's already been processed for fingerprints and blood."

Hillman didn't move. "Blood?"

"This is the knife that was used to kill Mike Harley. We're almost certain that it was also used to kill the other decedent, Carol Harley. Blood of her type was found on it, as well as her husband's type. Also it fits her wound, the autopsist tells me. Pick it up, Mr. Hillman."

In a gingerly movement Hillman reached out and took it from the box. He turned it over and read the maker's name on the broad shining blade.

"It looks like a good knife," he said. "But I'm afraid I don't recognize it."

"Would you say that under oath?"

"I'd have to. I never saw it before."

Bastian, with the air of a parent removing a dangerous toy, lifted the knife from his hands. "I don't want to say you're lying, Mr. Hillman. I do have a witness who contradicts you on this. Mr. Botkin, who owns the surplus goods store on lower Main, says that he sold you this knife." He shook the knife, point foremost, at Hillman's face.

Hillman looked scared and sick and obstinate. "It must have been somebody else. He must be mistaken."

"No. He knows you personally."

"I don't know him."

"You're a very well known man, sir, and Mr. Botkin is certain that you were in his store early this month. Perhaps I can refresh your recollection. You mentioned to Mr. Botkin, in connection with the purchase of this knife, that you were planning a little trip to Oregon with your son. You also complained to Botkin, as a lower Main Street businessman, about an alleged laxness at The Barroom Floor. It had to do with selling liquor to minors, I believe. Do you remember the conversation now?''

"No," Hillman said. "I do not. The man is lying."

"Why would he be lying?"

"I have no idea. Go and find out. It's not my job to do your police work for you."

He stood up, dismissing Bastian. Bastian was unwilling to be dismissed. "I don't think you're well advised to take this attitude, Mr. Hillman. If you purchased this knife from Mr. Botkin, now is the time to say so. Your previous denial need never go out of this room."

Bastian looked to me for support. I remembered what Botkin had said to me about The Barroom Floor. It was practically certain that his conversation with Hillman had taken place. It didn't follow necessarily that Hillman had bought the knife, but he probably had.

I said: "It's time all the facts were laid out on the table, Mr. Hillman."

"I can't tell him what isn't so, can I?"

"No. I wouldn't advise that. Have you thought of talking this over with your attorney?"

"I'm thinking about it now." Hillman had sobered. Droplets of clear liquid stood on his forehead as if the press of the situation had squeezed the alcohol out of him. He said to Bastian: "I gather you're more or less accusing me of murder."

"No, I am not." Bastian added in a formal tone: "You can, of course, stand on your constititutional rights."

Hillman shook his head angrily. Some of his fine light hair fell over his forehead. Under it his eyes glittered like metal triangles. He was an extraordinarily handsome man. His unremitting knowledge of this showed in the caressive movement of the hand with which he pushed his hair back into place.

"Look," he said, "could we continue this séance in the morning? I've had a hard week, and I'd like a chance to sleep on this business. I've had no real sleep since Monday."

"Neither have I," Bastian said.

"Maybe you need some sleep, too. This harassing approach isn't really such a good idea."

"There was no harassment."

"I'll be the judge of that." Hillman's voice rose. "You brought that knife into my home and shook it in my face. I have a witness to that," he added, meaning me.

I said: "Let's not get bogged down in petty arguments. Lieutenant Bastian and I have some business to discuss."

"Anything you say to him you'll have to say in front of me."

"All right."

"After I talk to the boy," Bastian said.

Hillman made a curt gesture with his hand. "You're not talking to him. I don't believe I'll let you talk to him tomorrow, either. There are, after all, medical considerations."

"Are you a medical man?"

"I have medical men at my disposal."

"I'm sure you do. So do we."

The two men faced each other in quiet fury. They were opposites in many ways. Bastian was a saturnine Puritan, absolutely honest, a stickler for detail, a policeman before he was a man. Hillman's personality was less clear. It had romantic and actorish elements, which often mask deep evasions. His career had been meteoric, but it was the kind of career that sometimes left a man empty-handed in middle life.

"Do you have something to say to the lieutenant?" Hillman asked me. "Before he leaves?"

"Yes. You may not like this, Mr. Hillman. I don't. Last night a young man driving a late-model blue Chevrolet was seen in the driveway of the Barcelona Hotel. It's where Mike Harley was found stabbed, with that knife." I pointed to the evidence box on the table. "The young man has been tentatively identified as Dick Leandro."

"Who made the identification?" Bastian said.

"Ben Daly, the service-station operator."

"The man who killed Sipe."

"Yes."

"He's either mistaken or lying," Hillman said. "Dick drives a blue car, but it's a small sports car, a Triumph."

"Does he have access to a blue Chevrolet?"

"Not to my knowledge. You're surely not trying to involve Dick in this mess."

"If he's involved, we have to know about it." I said to

Bastian: "Maybe you can determine whether he borrowed or rented a blue Chevrolet last night. Or it's barely possible that he stole one."

"Will do," Bastian said.

Hillman said nothing.

27

Bastian picked up his evidence case and shut it with a click. He walked out without a sign to either of us. He was treating Hillman as if he no longer existed. He was treating me in such a way that I could stay with Hillman.

Hillman watched him from the entrance to the library until he was safely across the reception hall and out the front door. Then he came back into the room. Instead of returning to the table where I was, he went to the wall of photographs where the squadron on the flight deck hung in green deep-sea light.

"What goes on around here?" he said. "Somebody took down Dick's picture."

"I did, for identification purposes."

I got it out of my pocket. Hillman came and took it away from me. The glass was smudged by fingers, and he rubbed it with the sleeve of his jacket.

"You had no right to take it. What are you trying to do to Dick, anyway?"

"Get at the truth about him."

"There *is* no mysterious truth about him. He's a perfectly nice ordinary kid."

"I hope so."

"Look here," he said, "you've accomplished what I hired you to do. Don't think I'm ungrateful—I'm planning to give you a substantial bonus. But I didn't hire you to investigate those murders."

"And I don't get the bonus unless I stop?"

"I didn't say that."

"You didn't have to."

He spread his hands on the table and leaned above me, heavy-faced and powerful. "Just how do you get to talk to your betters the way you've been talking to me?"

"By my betters you mean people with more money?"

"Roughly, yes."

"I'll tell you, Mr. Hillman. I rather like you. I'm trying to talk straight to you because somebody has to. You're headed on a collision course with the law. If you stay on it, you're going to get hurt."

His face stiffened and his eyes narrowed. He didn't like to be told anything. He liked to do the telling.

"I could buy and sell Bastian."

"You can't if he's not for sale. You know damn well he isn't."

He straightened, raising his head out of the light into the greenish shadow. His face resembled old bronze, except that it was working. After a time he said:

"What do you think I ought to do?"

"Start telling the truth."

"Dammit, you imply I haven't been."

"I'm doing more than imply it, Mr. Hillman."

He turned on me with his fists clenched, ready to hit me. I remained sitting. He walked away and came back. Without whisky, he was getting very jumpy.

"I suppose you think I killed them."

"I'm not doing any speculating. I am morally certain you bought that knife from Botkin."

"How can you be certain?"

"I've talked to the man."

"Who authorized you to? I'm not paying you to gather evidence against me."

I said, rather wearily: "Couldn't we forget about your wonderful money for a while, and just sit here and talk like a couple of human beings? A couple of human beings in a bind?"

He considered this. Eventually he said: "You're not in a bind. I am."

"Tell me about it. Unless you actually did commit those murders. In which case you should tell your lawyer and nobody else."

"I didn't. I almost wish I had." He sat down across from me, slumping forward a little, with his arms resting on the tabletop. "I admit I bought the knife. I don't intend to admit it to anyone else. Botkin will have to be persuaded to change his story."

"How?"

"He can't make anything out of that store of his. I ought to know, my father owned one like it in South Boston. I can give Botkin enough money to retire to Mexico."

I was a bit appalled, not so much by the suggestion of crude subornation—I'd often heard it before—as by the fact that Hillman was making it. In the decades since he commanded a squadron at Midway, he must have bumped down quite a few moral steps.

I said: "You better forget about that approach, Mr. Hillman. It's part of the collision course with the law I was talking about. And you'll end up sunk."

"I'm sunk now," he said in an even voice.

He laid his head down on his arms. His hair spilled forward like a broken white sheaf. I could see the naked pink circle on the crown which was ordinarily hidden. It was like a tonsure of mortality.

"What did you do with the knife?" I said to him. "Did you give it to Dick Leandro?"

"No." Spreading his hands on the tabletop, he pushed himself upright. His moist palms slipped and squeaked on the polished surface. "I wish I had."

"Was Tom the one you gave it to?"

He groaned. "I not only gave it to him. I told Botkin I was buying the bloody thing as a gift for him. Bastian must be aware of that, but he's holding it back."

"Bastian would," I said. "It still doesn't follow that Tom used it on his father and mother. He certainly had no reason to kill his mother."

"He doesn't need a rational motive. You don't know Tom."

"You keep telling me that. At the same time you keep refusing to fill in the picture."

"It's a fairly ugly picture."

"Something was said tonight about a homicidal attack."

"I didn't mean to let that slip out."

"Who attacked whom and why?"

"Tom threatened Elaine with a loaded gun. He wasn't kidding, either."

"Was this the Sunday-morning episode you've been suppressing?"

He nodded. "I think the accident must have affected his mind. When I got home from the judge's house, he had her in his room. He was holding my revolver with the muzzle against her head"—Hillman pressed his fingertip into his temple—"and he had her down on her knees, begging for mercy. Literally begging. I didn't know whether he was going to give me the gun, either. For a minute he held it on me. I half expected him to shoot me."

I could feel the hairs prickling at the nape of my neck. It was an ugly picture, all right. What was worse, it was a classic one: the schizophrenic execution killer.

"Did he say anything when you took the gun?"

"Not a word. He handed it over in a rather formal way. He acted like a kind of automaton. He didn't seem to realize what he'd done, or tried to do."

"Had he said anything to your wife?"

"Yes. He said he would kill her if she didn't leave him alone. She'd simply gone to his room to offer him some food, and he went into this silent white rage of his."

"He had a lot of things on his mind," I said, "and he'd been up all night. He told me something about it. You might say it was the crucial night of his young life. He met his real father for the first time"—Hillman grimaced—"which must have been a fairly shattering experience. You might say he was lost between two worlds, and blaming you and your wife for not preparing him. You should have, you know. You had no right to cheat him of the facts, whether you liked them or not. When the facts finally hit him, it was more than he could handle. He deliberately turned the car over that morning."

"You mean he attempted suicide?" Hillman said.

"He made a stab at it. I think it was more a signal that his life was out of control. He didn't let go of the steering wheel, and he wasn't badly hurt. Nobody got hurt in the gun incident, either."

"You've got to take it seriously, though. He was in dead earnest."

"Maybe. I'm not trying to brush it off. Have you talked it over with a psychiatrist?"

"I have not. There are certain things you don't let out of the family."

"That depends on the family."

"Look," he said, "I was afraid they wouldn't admit him to the school if they knew he was that violent."

"Would that have been such a tragedy?"

"I had to do something with him. I don't know what I'm going to do with him now." He bowed his disheveled head.

"You need better advice than I can give you, legal and psychiatric."

"You're assuming he killed those two people."

"Not necessarily. Why don't you ask Dr. Weintraub to recommend somebody?"

Hillman jerked himself upright. "That old woman?"

"I understood he was an old friend of yours, and he knows something about psychiatry."

"Weinie has a worm's-eye knowledge, I suppose." His voice rasped with contempt. "He had a nervous breakdown after Midway. We had to send him stateside to recuperate, while men were dying. While men were dying," Hillman repeated. Then he seemed to surround himself with silence.

He sat in a listening attitude. I waited. His angry face became smooth and his voice changed with it. "Jesus, that was a day. We lost more than half of our T.B.D.'s. The Zekes took them like sitting ducks. I couldn't bring them back. I don't blame Weinie for breaking down, so many men died on him."

His voice was hushed. His eyes were distant. He didn't even seem aware of my presence. His mind was over the edge of the world where his men had died, and he had died more than a little.

"The hell of it is," he was saying, "I love Tom. We haven't been close for years, and he's been hard to handle. But he's my son, and I love him."

"I'm sure you do. But maybe you want more than Tom can give you. He can't give you back your dead pilots."

Hillman didn't understand me. He seemed bewildered. His gray eyes were clouded.

"What did you say?"

"Perhaps you were expecting too much from the boy."

"In what way?"

"Forget it," I said.

Hillman was hurt. "You think I expect too much? I've been

getting damn little. And look what I'm willing to give him.''
He spread his arms again, to embrace the house and everything
he owned. "Why, he can have every nickel I possess for his
defense. We'll get him off and go to another country to live."

"You're away ahead of yourself, Mr. Hillman. He hasn't
been charged with anything yet."

"He will be." His voice sounded both fatalistic and defiant.

"Maybe. Let's consider the possibilities. The only evidence
against him is the knife, and that's pretty dubious if you think
about it. He didn't take it with him, surely, when you put him
in Laguna Perdida."

"He may have. I didn't search him."

"I'm willing to bet they did."

Hillman narrowed his eyes until they were just a glitter
between the folded lids. "You're right, Archer. He didn't have
the knife when he left the house. I remember seeing it afterwards, that same day."

"Where was it?"

"In his room, in one of the chests of drawers."

"And you left it in the drawer?"

"There was no reason not to."

"Then anybody with access to the house could have got hold
of it?"

"Yes. Unfortunately that includes Tom. He could have
sneaked in after he escaped from the school."

"It also includes Dick Leandro, who wouldn't have had to
sneak in. He's in and out of the house all the time, isn't he?"

"I suppose he is. That doesn't prove anything."

"No, but when you put it together with the fact that Dick
was probably seen at the Barcelona Hotel last night, it starts
you thinking about him. There's still something missing in this
case, you know. The equations don't balance."

"Dick isn't your missing quantity," he said hastily.

"You're quite protective about Dick."

"I'm fond of him. Why shouldn't I be? He's a nice boy, and
I've been able to help him. Dammit, Archer." His voice
deepened. "When a fellow reaches a certain age, he needs to
pass on what he knows, or part of it, to a younger fellow."

"Are you thinking of passing on some money, too?"

"We may eventually. It will depend on Elaine. She controls
the main money. But I can assure you it couldn't matter to
Dick."

"It matters to everybody. I think it matters very much to Dick. He's a pleaser."

"What is that supposed to mean?"

"You know what it means. He lives by pleasing people, mainly you. Tell me this. Does Dick know about the gun incident in Tom's room?"

"Yes. He was with me that Sunday morning. He drove me to the judge's house and home again."

"He gets in on a lot of things," I said.

"That's natural. He's virtually a member of the family. As a matter of fact, I expected him tonight. He said he had something he wanted to talk over with me." He looked at his watch. "But it's too late now. It's past eleven o'clock."

"Get him out here anyway, will you?"

"Not tonight. I've had it. I don't want to have to pull my face together and put on a front for Dick now."

He looked at me a little sheepishly. He had revealed himself to me, a vain man who couldn't forget his face, a secret man who lived behind a front. He pushed his silver mane back and patted it in place.

"Tonight is all the time we have," I said. "In the morning you can expect Bastian and the sheriff and probably the D.A. pounding on your door. You won't be able to put them off by simply denying that you bought that knife. You're going to have to explain it."

"Do you really think Dick took it?"

"He's a better suspect than Tom, in my opinion."

"Very well, I'll call him." He rose and went to the telephone on the desk.

"Don't tell him what you want him for. He might break and run."

"Naturally I won't." He dialed a number from memory, and waited. When he spoke, his voice had changed again. It was lighter and younger. "Dick? You said something to Elaine about dropping by tonight. I was wondering if I was to expect you . . . I know it's late. I'm sorry you're not too well. What's the trouble? . . . I'm sorry. Look, why don't you come out anyway, just for a minute? Tom came home tonight, isn't that great? He'll want to see you. And I particularly want to see you . . . Yep, it's an order. . . . Fine, I'll look for you then." He hung up.

"What's the matter with him?" I asked.

"He says he doesn't feel well."

"Sick?"

"Depressed. But he cheered up when I told him Tom was home. He'll be out shortly."

"Good. In the meantime I want to talk to Tom."

Hillman came and stood over me. His face was rather obscure in the green penumbra. "Before you talk to him again, there's something you ought to know."

I waited for him to go on. Finally I asked him: "Is it about Tom?"

"It has to do with both of us." He hesitated, his eyes intent on my face. "On second thought, I don't think I'll let my back hair down any further tonight."

"You may never have another chance," I said, "before it gets let down for you, the hard way."

"That's where you're wrong. Nobody knows this particular thing but me."

"And it has to do with you and Tom?"

"That's right. Now let's forget it."

He didn't want to forget it, though. He wanted to share his secret, without taking the responsibility of speaking out. He lingered by the table, looking down at my face with his stainless-steel eyes.

I thought of the feeling in Hillman's voice when he spoke of his love for Tom. Perhaps that feeling was the element which would balance the equation.

"Is Tom your natural son?" I said.

He didn't hesitate in answering. "Yes. He's my own flesh and blood."

"And you're the only one who knows?"

"Carol knew, of course, and Mike Harley knew. He agreed to the arrangement in exchange for certain favors I was able to do him."

"You kept him out of Portsmouth."

"I helped to. You mustn't imagine I was trying to mastermind some kind of plot. It all happened quite naturally. Carol came to me after Mike and his brother were arrested. She begged me to intervene on their behalf. I said I would. She was a lovely girl, and she expressed her gratitude in a natural way."

"By going to bed with you."

"Yes. She gave me one night. I went to her room in the Barcelona Hotel. You should have seen her, Archer, when she took off her clothes for me. She lit up that shabby room with the brass bed—''

I cut in on his excitement: ''The brass bed is still there, and so was Otto Sipe, until last night. Did Sipe know about your big night on the brass bed?''

''Sipe?''

''The hotel detective.''

''Carol said he was gone that night.''

''And you say you only went there once.''

''Only once with Carol. I spent some nights in the Barcelona later with another girl. I suppose I was trying to recapture the rapture or something. She was a willing girl, but she was no substitute for Carol.''

I got up. He saw the look on my face and backed away. ''What's the matter with you, is something wrong?''

''Susanna Drew is a friend of mine. A good friend.''

''How could I know that?'' he said with his mouth lifted on one side.

''You don't know much,'' I said. ''You don't know how sick it makes me to sit here and listen to you while you dabble around in your dirty little warmed-over affairs.''

He was astonished. I was astonished myself. Angry shouting at witnesses is something reserved for second-rate prosecutors in courtrooms.

''Nobody talks to me like that,'' Hillman said in a shaking voice. ''Get out of my house and stay out.''

''I'll be delighted to.''

I got as far as the front door. It was like walking through deep, clinging mud. Then Hillman spoke behind me from the far side of the reception hall.

''Look here.'' It was his favorite phrase.

I looked there. He walked toward me under the perilous chandelier. He said with his hands slightly lifted and turned outward:

''I can't go on by myself, Archer. I'm sorry if I stepped on your personal toes.''

''It's all right.''

''No, it isn't. Are you in love with Susanna?''

I didn't answer him.

''In case you're wondering,'' he said, ''I haven't touched her since 1945. I ran into some trouble with that house detective, Sipe—''

I said impatiently: "I know. You knocked him down."

"I gave him the beating of his life," he said with a kind of naive pride. "It was the last time he tried to pry any money out of me."

"Until this week."

He was jolted into temporary silence. "Anyway, Susanna lost interest—"

"I don't want to talk about Susanna."

"That suits me."

We had moved back into the corridor that led to the library, out of hearing of the room where Elaine was. Hillman leaned on the wall like a bystander in an alley. His posture made me realize how transient and insecure he felt in his own house.

"There are one or two things I don't understand," I said. "You tell me you spent one night with Carol, and yet you're certain that you fathered her son."

"He was born just nine months later, December the twelfth."

"That doesn't prove you're his father. Pregnancies often last longer, especially first ones. Mike Harley could have fathered him before the Shore Patrol took him. Or any other man."

"There was no other man. She was a virgin."

"You're kidding."

"I am not. Her marriage to Mike Harley was never consummated. Mike was impotent, which was one reason he was willing to have the boy pass as his."

"Why was that so necessary, Hillman? Why didn't you take the boy and raise him yourself?"

"I did that."

"I mean, raise him openly as your own son."

"I couldn't. I had other commitments. I was already married to Elaine. She's a New Englander, a Puritan of the first water."

"With a fortune of the first water."

"I admit I needed her help to start my business. A man has to make choices."

He looked up at the chandelier. Its light fell starkly on his hollow bronze face. He turned his face away from the light.

"Who told you Mike Harley was impotent?"

"Carol did, and she wasn't lying. She was a virgin, I tell you. She did a lot of talking in the course of the night. Her whole life. She told me Mike got what sex he got by being spanked, or beaten with a strap."

"By her?"

"Yes. She didn't enjoy it, of course, but she did it for him willingly enough. She seemed to feel that it was less dangerous than sex, than normal sex."

A wave of sickness went through me. It wasn't physical. But I could smell the old man's cow barn and hear the whining of his one-eyed dog.

"I thought you were the one who was supposed to be impotent," I said, "or sterile."

He glanced at me sharply. "Who have you been talking to?"

"Your wife. She did the talking."

"And she still thinks I'm sterile?"

"Yes."

"Good." He turned his face away from the light again and let out a little chuckle of relief. "Maybe we can pull this out yet. I told Elaine at the time we adopted Tom that Weintraub gave me a test and found that I was sterile. I was afraid she'd catch on to the fact of my paternity."

"You may be sterile at that."

He didn't know what I meant. "No. It's Elaine who is. I didn't need to take any test. I have Tom to prove I'm a man."

He didn't have Tom.

28

We went into the sitting room, the waiting room. Though Tom was in the house the waiting seemed to go on, as if it had somehow coalesced with time. Elaine was in her place on the chesterfield. She had taken up her knitting, and her stainless-steel needles glinted along the edge of the red wool. She looked up brightly at her husband.

"Where's Tom?" he said. "Is he still upstairs?"

"I heard him go down the back stairs. I imagine Mrs. Perez if feeding him in the kitchen. He seems to prefer the kitchen to the sitting room. I suppose that's natural, considering his heredity.''

"We won't go into the subject of that, eh?''

Hillman went to the bar alcove and made himself a very dark-looking highball. He remembered to offer me one, which I declined.

"What did that policeman want?'' Elaine asked him.

"He had some stupid questions on his mind. I prefer not to go into them.''

"So you've been telling me for the past twenty-five years. You prefer not to go into things. Save the surface. Never mind the dry rot at the heart.''

"Could we dispense with the melodrama?''

"The word is tragedy, not melodrama. A tragedy has gone through this house and you don't have the mind to grasp it. You live in a world of appearances, like a fool.''

"I know. I know.'' His voice was light, but he looked ready to throw his drink in her face. "I'm an ignorant engineer, and I never studied philosophy.''

Her needles went on clicking. "I could stand your ignorance, but I can't stand your evasions any longer.''

He drank part of his drink, and waved his free hand loosely over his head. "Good heavens, Elaine, how much do I have to take from you? This isn't the time or place for one of those.''

"There never is a time or place,'' she said. "If there's time, you change the clocks—this is known as crossing the International Ralph Line—and suddenly it's six o'clock in the morning, in Tokyo. If there's a place, you find an escape hatch. I see your wriggling legs and then you're off and away, into the wild Ralph yonder. You never faced up to anything in your life.''

He winced under her bitter broken eloquence. "That isn't true,'' he said uneasily. "Archer and I have been really dredging tonight.''

"Dredging in the warm shallows of your nature? I thought you reserved that pastime for your women. Like Susanna Drew.''

Her name sent a pang through me. It was a nice name, innocent and bold and slightly absurd, and it didn't deserve to be bandied about by these people. If the Hillmans had ever been innocent, their innocence had been frittered away in a marriage of pretenses. It struck me suddenly that Hillman's affair with Susanna had also been one of pretenses. He had persuaded her to take care of Carol without any hint that he was the father of the child she was carrying.

"Good Lord," he was saying now, "are we back on the Drew girl again after all these years?"

"Well, are we?" Elaine said.

Fortunately the telephone rang. Hillman went into the alcove to answer it, and turned to me with his hand clapped over the mouthpiece.

"It's Bastian, for you. You can take the call in the pantry. I'm going to listen on this line."

There wasn't much use arguing. I crossed the music room and the dining room to the butler's pantry and fumbled around in the dark for the telephone. I could hear Mrs. Perez in the kitchen, talking to Tom in musical sentences about her native province of Sinaloa. Bastian's voice in the receiver sounded harsh and inhuman by comparison:

"Archer?"

"I'm here."

"Good. I checked the matter of Dick Leandro's transportation, in fact I've just been talking to a girl friend of his. She's a senior at the college, named Katie Ogilvie, and she owns a Chevrolet sedan, this year's model, blue in color. She finally admitted she lent it to him last night. He put over a hundred miles on the odometer."

"Are you sure she wasn't with him? He had a girl with him, or another boy, Daly wasn't quite sure."

"It wasn't Miss Ogilvie," Bastian said. "She was peeved about the fact that he used her car to take another girl for a long ride."

"How does she know it was a girl?"

"The lady dropped a lipstick in the front seat. A very nice white gold lipstick, fourteen carat. I don't think," he added dryly, "that Miss Ogilvie would have testified so readily if it wasn't for that lipstick. Apparently Leandro impressed the need for secrecy on her."

"Did he say why?"

"It had something to do with the Hillman kidnapping. That was all she knew. Well, do we pick up Leandro? You seem to be calling the shots."

"He's on his way out here. Maybe you better follow along."

"You sound as if things are building up to a climax."

"Yeah."

I could see its outlines. They burned on my eyeballs like the lights of Dack's Auto Court, I sat in the dark after Bastian hung up, and tried to blink them away. But they spread out into the darkness around me and became integrated with the actual world.

Sinaloa, Mrs. Perez was saying or kind of singing to Tom in the kitchen, Sinaloa was a land of many rivers. There were eleven rivers in all, and she and her family lived so close to one of them that her brothers would put on their bathing suits and run down for a swim every day. Her father used to go down to the river on Sunday and catch fish with a net and distribute them to the neighbors. All the neighbors had fish for Sunday lunch.

Tom said it sounded like fun.

Ah yes, it was like Paradise, she said, and her father was a highly regarded man in their *barrio*. Of course it was hot in summer, that was the chief drawback, a hundred and twenty degrees in the shade sometimes. Then big black clouds would pile up along the Sierra Madre Occidental, and it would rain so hard, inches in just two hours. Then it would be sunny again. Sunny, sunny, sunny! That was how life went in Sinaloa.

Tom wanted to know if her father was still alive. She replied with joy that her father lived on, past eighty now, in good health. Perez was visiting him on his present trip to Mexico.

"I'd like to visit your father."

"Maybe you will some day."

I opened the door. Tom was at the kitchen table, eating the last of his soup. Mrs. Perez was leaning over him with a smiling maternal mouth and faraway eyes. She looked distrustfully at me. I was an alien in their land of Sinaloa.

"What do you want?"

"A word with Tom. I'll have to ask you to leave for a bit." She stiffened.

"On second thought, there won't be any more secrets in this house. You might as well stay, Mrs. Perez."

"*Thank* you."

She picked up the soup bowl and walked switching to the sink, where she turned the hot water full on. Tom regarded me across the table with the infinite boredom of the young. He was very clean and pale.

"I hate to drag you back over the details," I said, "but you're the only one who can answer some of these questions."

"It's okay."

"I'm not clear about yesterday, especially last night. Were you still at the Barcelona Hotel when Mike Harley got back from Vegas?"

"Yes. He was in a very mean mood. He told me to beat it before he killed me. I was intending to leave, anyway."

"And nobody stopped you?"

"He wanted to get rid of me."

"What about Sipe?"

"He was so drunk he hardly knew what he was doing. He passed out before I left."

"What time did you leave?"

"A little after eight. It wasn't dark yet. I caught a bus at the corner."

"You weren't there when Dick Leandro arrived?"

"No sir." His eyes widened. "Was he at the hotel?"

"Evidently he was. Did Sipe or Harley ever mention him?"

"No sir."

"Do you know what he might have been doing there?"

"No sir. I don't know much about him. He's *their* friend." He shrugged one shoulder and arm toward the front of the house.

"Whose friend in particular? His or hers?"

"His. But she uses him, too."

"To drive her places?"

"For anything she wants." He spoke with the hurt ineffectual anger of a displaced son. "When he does something she wants, she says she'll leave him money in her will. If he doesn't, like when he has a date, she says she'll cut him out. So usually he breaks the date."

"Would he kill someone for her?"

Mrs. Perez had turned off the hot water. In the steamy silence at her end of the kitchen, she made an explosive noise that sounded like "Chuh!"

"I don't know what he'd do," Tom said deliberately. "He's a yacht bum and they're all the same, but they're all different, too. It would depend on how much risk there was in it. And how much money."

"Harley," I said, "was stabbed with the knife your father gave you, the hunting knife with the striped handle."

"I didn't stab him."

"Where did you last see the knife?"

He considered the question. "It was in my room, in the top drawer with the handkerchiefs and stuff."

"Did Dick Leandro know where it was?"

"I never showed him. He never came to my room."

"Did your mother—did Elaine Hillman know where it was?"

"I guess so. She's always—she was always coming into my room, and checking on my things."

"That's true," Mrs. Perez said.

I acknowledged her comment with a look which discouraged further comment.

"I understand on a certain Sunday morning she came into your room once too often. You threatened to shoot her with your father's gun."

Mrs. Perez made her explosive noise. Tom bit hard on the tip of his right thumb. His look was slanting, over my head and to one side, as if there was someone behind me.

"Is that the story they're telling?" he said.

Mrs. Perez burst out: "It isn't true. I heard her yelling up there. She came downstairs and got the gun out of the library desk and went upstairs with it."

"Why didn't you stop her?"

"I was afraid," she said. "Anyway, Mr. Hillman was coming—I heard his car—and I went outside and told him there was trouble upstairs. What else could I do, with Perez away in Mexico?"

"It doesn't matter," Tom said. "Nothing happened. I took the gun away from her."

"Did she try to shoot you?"

"She said she would if I didn't take back what I said."

"And what did you say?"

"That I'd rather live in an auto court with my real mother than in this house with her. She blew her top and ran downstairs for the gun."

"Why didn't you tell your father about this?"

"He isn't my father."

I didn't argue. It took more than genes to establish fatherhood. "Why didn't you tell him, Tom?"

He made an impatient gesture with his hand. "What was the use? He wouldn't have believed me. Anyway, I *was* mad at her, for lying to me about who I was. I did take the gun and point it at her head.''

"And want to kill her?''

He nodded. His head seemed very heavy on his neck. Mrs. Perez invented a sudden errand and bustled past him, pressing his shoulder with her hand as she went. As if to signalize this gesture, an electric bell rang over the pantry door.

"That's the front door,'' she said to nobody in particular.

I got there in a dead heat with Ralph Hillman. He let Dick Leandro in. The week's accelerated aging process was working in Leandro now. Only his dark hair seemed lively. His face was drawn and slightly yellowish. He gave me a lackluster glance, and appealed to Hillman:

"Could I talk to you alone, Skipper? It's important.'' he was almost chattering.

Elaine spoke from the doorway of the sitting room. "It can't be so important that you'd forget your manners. Come in and be sociable, Dick. I've been alone all evening, or so it seems.''

"We'll join you later,'' Hillman said.

"It's very late already.'' Her voice was edgy.

Leandro's dim brown glance moved back and forth between them like a spectator's at a tennis game on which he had bet everything he owned.

"If you're not nice to me,'' she said lightly, "I won't be nice to you, Dick.''

"I do-don't care about that.'' There was strained defiance in his voice.

"You will.'' Stiff-backed, she retreated into the sitting room.

I said to Leandro: "We won't waste any more time. Did you do some driving for Mrs. Hillman last night?''

He turned away from me and almost leaned on Hillman, speaking in a hushed rapid voice. "I've *got* to talk to you alone. Something's come up that you don't know about.''

"We'll go into the library,'' Hillman said.

"If you do, I go along,'' I said. "But we might as well talk here. I don't want to be too far from Mrs. Hillman.''

The young man turned and looked at me in a different way, both lost and relieved. He knew I knew.

Hillman also knew, I thought. His proposal to Susanna tended to prove it; his confession that Tom was his natural son had provided me with evidence of motive. He leaned now on the wall beside the door, heavy and mysterious as a statue, with half-closed eyes.

I said to the younger man: "Did you drive her to the Barcelona Hotel, Dick?"

"Yessir." With one shoulder high and his head on one side, he held himself in an awkward pose which gave the effect of writhing. "I had no w-way of knowing what was on her mind. I *still* don't know."

"But you have a pretty good idea. Why all the secrecy?"

"She said I should borrow a car, that they had phoned for more money and Skipper wasn't here so we would have to deliver it. Or else they'd kill him. We were to keep it secret from the police, and afterwards she said I must never tell anyone."

"And you believed her story?"

"I c-certainly did."

"When did you start to doubt it?"

"Well, I couldn't figure out how she could get hold of all that c-cash."

"How much?"

"Another twenty-five thousand, she said. She said it was in her bag—she was carrying her big knitting bag—but I didn't actually see the money."

"What did you see?"

"I didn't actually *see* anything." Like a stealthy animal that would eventually take over his entire forehead, his hair was creeping down toward his eyes. "I mean, I saw this character, the one she—I saw this character come out of the hotel and they went around the back and I heard this scream." He scratched the front of his throat.

"What did you do?"

"I stayed in the car. She told me to stay in the car. When she came back, she said it was an owl."

"And you believed her?"

"I don't know much about birds. Do I, Skipper?"

Elaine cried out very brightly from her doorway: "What under heaven are you men talking about?"

I walked toward her. "You. The owl you heard last night in the hotel garden. What kind of an owl was it?"

"A screech—" Her hand flew up and pressed against her lips.

"He looked human to me. He wasn't a very good specimen, but he was human."

She stopped breathing, and then gasped for breath. "He was a devil," she said, "the scum of the earth."

"Because he wanted more money?"

"It would have gone on and on. I had to stop him." She stood shuddering in the doorway. With a fierce effort of will, she brought her emotions under control. "Speaking of money, I can take care of you. I'm sure the police would understand my position, but there's no need to connect me with this—this—" She couldn't think of a noun. "I can take care of you and I can take care of Dick."

"How much are you offering?"

She looked at me imperiously, from the moral stilts of inherited wealth.

"Come into the sitting room," she said, "and we'll talk about it."

The three of us followed her into the room and took up positions around her chesterfield. Hillman looked at me curiously. He was very silent and subdued, but the calculator behind his eyes was still working. Dick Leandro was coming back to life. His eyes had brightened. Perhaps he still imagined that somehow, somewhere, sometime, there would be Hillman money coming to him.

"How much?" I said to her.

"Twenty-five thousand."

"That's better than a knife between the ribs. Does that mean twenty-five thousand overall or twenty-five thousand for each murder?"

"Each murder?"

"There were two, done with the same knife, almost certainly by the same person. You."

She moved her head away from my pointing finger, like a stage-shy girl. A stage-shy girl playing the role of an aging woman with monkey wrinkles and fading fine blonde hair.

"Fifty thousand then," she said.

"He's playing with you," Hillman said. "You can't buy him."

She turned toward him. "My late father once said that you can buy anyone, anyone at all. I proved that when I bought you." She made a gesture of repugnance. "I wish I hadn't. You turned out to be a bad bargain."

"You didn't buy me. You merely leased my services."

They faced each other as implacably as two skulls. She said: "Did you have to palm her bastard off on me?"

"I wanted a son. I didn't plan it. It happened."

"You made it happen. You connived to bring her baby into my house. You let me feed and nurture him and call him mine. How could you be such a living falsity?"

"Don't talk to me about falsity, Elaine. It seemed the best way to handle the problem."

"Stallion," she said. "Filth."

I heard a faint movement in the adjoining room. Straining my eyes into the darkness, I could see Tom sitting on the bench in front of the grand piano. I was tempted to shut the door, but it was too late, really. He might as well hear it all.

Hillman said in a surprisingly calm voice: "I never could understand the Puritan mind, Ellie. You think a little fun in bed is the ultimate sin, worse than murder. Christ, I remember our wedding night. You'd have thought I was murdering you."

"I wish you had."

"I almost wish I had. You murdered Carol, didn't you, Ellie?"

"Of course I did. She phoned here Monday morning, after you left. Tom had given her his telephone number. I took the call in his room, and she spilled everything. She *said* she had just caught on to her husband's plans, and she was afraid he would harm Tom, who wasn't really his son. I'm sure it was just an excuse she used to get her knife into me."

"Her knife?" I said.

"That was a badly chosen image, wasn't it? I mean that she was glorying over me, annulling the whole meaning of my existence."

"I think she was simply trying to save her son."

"*Her* son, not mine. Her son and Ralph's. That was the point, don't you see? I felt as if she had killed me. I was just a fading ghost in the world, with only enough life left to strike back. Walking from where I left the Cadillac, I could feel the rain fall through me. I was no solider than the rain.

"Apparently her husband had caught her phoning me. He took her back to the cottage and beat her and left her unconscious on the floor. She was easy for me to kill. The knife slipped in and out. I hadn't realized how easy it would be.

"But the second time wasn't easy," she said. "The knife caught in his ribs. I couldn't pull it out of him."

Her voice was high and childish in complaint. The little girl behind her wrinkles had been caught in a malign world where even things no longer cooperated and even men could not be bought.

"Why did you have to stick it into him?" I said.

"He suspected that I killed Carol. He used Tom's number to call me and accuse me. Of course he wanted *money*." She spoke as if her possession of money had given her a special contemptuous insight into other people's hunger for it. "It would have gone on and on."

It was going on and on. Tom came blinking out of the darkness. He looked around in pity and confusion. Elaine turned her face away from him, as if she had an unprepossessing disease.

The boy said to Hillman: "Why didn't you tell me? It could have made a difference."

"It still can," Hillman said with a hopefulness more grinding than despair. "Son?"

He moved toward Tom, who evaded his outstretched hands and left the room. Walking rather unsteadily, Hillman followed him. I could hear them mounting the stairs, on different levels, out of step.

Dick Leandro got up from his place, rather tentatively, as if he had been liberated from an obscure bondage. He went into the alcove, where I heard him making himself a drink.

Elaine Hillman was still thinking about money. "What about it, Mr. Archer? Can you be bought?" Her voice was quite calm. The engines of her anger had run down.

"I can't be bought with anything you've offered."

"Will you have mercy on me, then?"

"I don't have that much mercy."

"I'm not asking for a great deal. Just let me sleep one more night in my own house."

"What good would that do you?"

"This good. I'll be frank with you. I've been saving sleeping pills for a considerable time—"

"How long?"

"Nearly a year, actually. I've been in despair for at least that long—"

"You should have taken your pills sooner."

"Before all this, you mean?" She waved her hand at the empty room as if it was a tragic stage littered with corpses.

"Before all this," I said.

"But I couldn't die without knowing. I knew my life was empty and meaningless. I had to find out why."

"And now it's full and meaningful?"

"It's over," she said. "Look, Mr. Archer, I was frank with you today. Give me a *quid pro quo*. All I'm asking for is time to use my pills."

"No."

"You owe me something. I helped you as much as I dared this afternoon."

"You weren't trying to help me, Mrs. Hillman. You only told me what I already knew, or what I was about to find out. You gave me the fact that Tom was adopted in such a way that it would conceal the more important fact that he was your husband's natural son. You kept alive the lie that your husband was sterile because it hid your motive for murdering Carol Harley."

"I'm afraid your reasoning is much too subtle for me."

"I hardly think so. You're a subtle woman."

"I? Subtle? I'm a ninny, a poor booby. The people in the streets, the scum of the earth knew more about my life than I—" She broke off. "So you won't help me."

"I can't. I'm sorry. The police are on their way now."

She regarded me thoughtfully. "There would still be time for me to use the gun."

"No."

"You're very hard."

"It isn't me, really, Mrs. Hillman. It's just reality catching up."

The sheriff's car was in the driveway now. I rose and went as far as the sitting-room door and called out to Bastian to come in. Elaine sighed behind me like a woman in passion.

Her passion was a solitary one. She had picked up her knitting in both hands and pressed both steel needles into her breast. She struck them into herself again before I reached her. By the middle of the following day she had succeeded in dying.

ABOUT THE AUTHOR

"ROSS MACDONALD" was the pseudonym of Kenneth Millar. Born outside San Francisco in 1915, he grew up in Vancouver, British Columbia. He returned to the U.S. in 1938, earned a Ph.D. at the University of Michigan, served in the Navy during World War II and published his first novel in 1944. He served as president of the Mystery Writers of America and was awarded both the Silver Dagger award by the Crime Writers' Association of Great Britain and the Grand Master Award by the Mystery Writers of America. He was married to the novelist Margaret Millar. He died in 1983.